GRAVE DEBT

ALSO BY T. G. AYER

Young Adult Paranormal

THE VALKYRIE SERIES

Dead Radiance

Dead Embers

Dead Chaos

Dead Wrath

Dead Silence

Joshua - Dead Radiance

Joshua II - Dead Embers

Joshua III - Dead Chaos

Joshua IV - Dead Wrath

Joshua V - Dead Silence

THE HAND OF KALI SERIES

Fire & Shadow

Blood & Gold

Time & Fate

Fury & Virtue

Spirit & Soul

Adult Urban Fantasy

THE DARKWORLD SKINWALKER SERIES

Skin Deep

Lost Soul

Last Chance

Blood Promise

Scorched Fury

Fate's Edge

Grave Debt

Oath Bound

Rebel Heart

THE DARKWORLD SOULTRACKER SERIES

Blood Magic

Demon Kin

Blood Curse

Demon Soul

Blood Moon

Demon Bones

Blood Born

Demon Scourge

Blood Veil

THE DARKWORLD ORIGINS

Pyros (Logan)

Ailuros (Kailin)

THE DARKWORLD IRIN CHRONICLES SERIES

Retribution

Requiem

Resonance

Revelation

Reckoning

Restitution

THE DARK SIGHT SERIES

Dark Sight

Cursed Sight

Vissarion

Shadow Sight

Dark Prophecy

Cursed Prophecy

Shadow Prophecy

THE APSARA CHRONICLES

Immortal Bound

Gods Ascendent

Dominion Falling

Vengeance Born

Last Legion

Realms Asunder

Adult Sci-Fi

HAND'S ASSASSIN

Death Dealer

Death Mark

Death Strike

NEW ADULT CONTEMPORARY THRILLER W/A TONI VALLAN

Beautiful Collision

Beautiful Conviction

PSYCHOLOGICAL HORROR W/A TONI VALLAN

Dark Shadows

Splinter

GRAVE DEBT

A SKIN WALKER NOVEL BOOK 7

Cover art by Eduardo Priego

ISBN-13: 978-0-9951125-8-2

INFINITE INK BOOKS

GRAVE DEBT

USA TODAY BESTSELLING AUTHOR

T.G. AYER

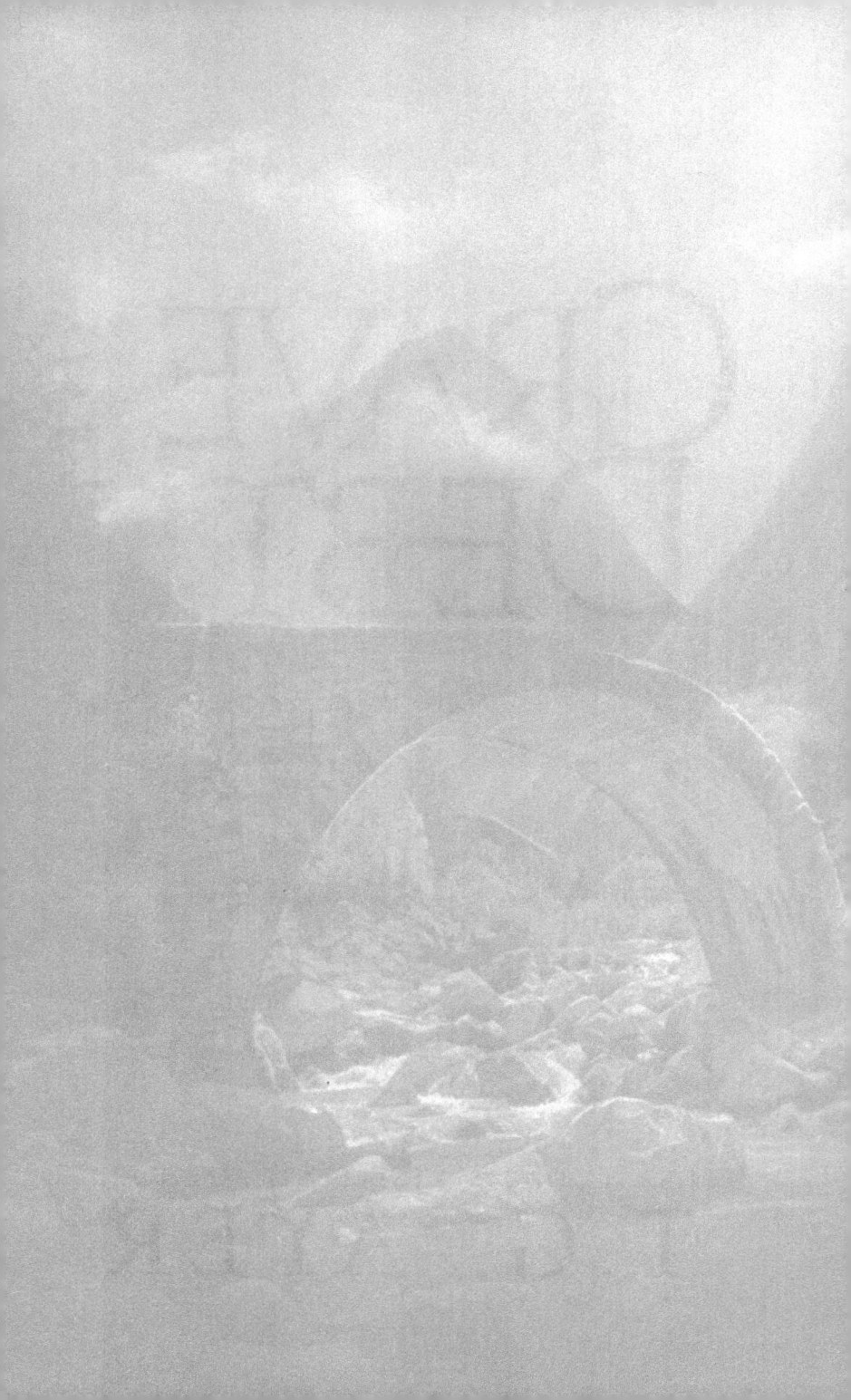

CHAPTER 1

LOGAN

It was a dick move.

It was a dick move, and Logan knew it. He'd taken the coward's way out, but he hoped he'd worded his letter in such a way that Kai would know he hadn't meant it was over between them—because it wasn't.

Not by a long shot.

How could it possibly be over when the woman meant more to him than life itself? Though the irony wasn't lost on him that he was, for all intents and purposes, fleeing from her in the dark of night—well, not really since the new day was in full force.

What would Kai think when she finally did read the letter?

Logan wasn't all that sure he wanted to know. He had no idea how long it would take before Kai returned home with Celeste, but Logan knew that though his gut churned with worry about both mother and daughter, he couldn't wait any longer.

He had to leave.

Leave when she needs you the most?

"You are such an asshole," muttered Sienna, her dark tone slicing deep into his heart as her eyes and her body—and now too, her voice—displayed their utter disgust, disapproval, and disappointment in his actions.

Sienna's arms were folded as she paced the carpet in what had been Logan's room for the duration of his recuperation. Her narrow naked feet made no sound on the carpet as she strode back and forth, blue-painted toes sinking deep into the thick pile. Her bearing and her expression though screeched her fury, louder than any dragon-call.

Sienna's golden eyes were cast down upon the wool fibers in a dark glare, as though the red and green interweaving patterns were somehow responsible for the status of the asshole in question.

Logan—who stood leaning against the wall beside the window, and somewhat safely out of the way of his fuming twin —didn't answer. His thoughts focused on Ivy whom he'd crossed paths with only minutes ago; a crossroads at the coffee machine, where he'd asked her a question he was pretty certain should have ended with Grams' double espresso all over his head.

That Logan had had the gall to rope Ivy into his subterfuge, and as a result, would soon abandon her to face her granddaughter's ire alone, still surprised him.

Though at first reluctant, Ivy had eventually conceded, thankfully without drenching him with her morning caffeine, and was oddly enough in lukewarm agreement with Logan's need for a quick departure—an agreement that had somehow escaped Sienna's awareness as she now broadcasted her fury at him.

With his mind on Grams, Logan missed a timeous response to his sister's question, his silence now drawing a disgusted snort from Sienna. He glanced up just as she snapped, "Well, I suppose the fact that you've admitted what you are—and that you're not denying your status—should count for something."

She huffed and paced some more, arms now unfolded, fingers flexing restlessly at her sides. As she walked, she waggled her hands near her thighs, and every so often a brilliant gold-orange flame or two would spark at the tips of her long elegant fingers, followed by a cloud of tiny embers which spun around and around, then floated to the dark carpet.

"You'd better be careful, Sienna." Logan gave a soft chuckle, losing control of the urge to smile. "Keep doing that, and we'll be repairing carpets before we leave. Or worse yet, watching as the Odel home burns to the ground."

Sienna stopped pacing and spun around to face Logan, her eyes flickering with undulating fire. "I'm not stupid, Logan. If anything, *that's* a label best kept for you," she said tipping her head in the direction of the blackened wall on the other side of the bed. Sienna smirked, eyes—despite her anger—sparkling in amusement as Logan's cool narrowed gaze settled on the round scorch-mark emblazoned on the wall of Kai's bedroom.

Though Logan cast about for a suitable snarky response, his guilt made it somewhat difficult to absolve himself, even if it meant his defense against his smartass sibling.

At last, he shook his head. "That's what you would call being overwhelmed with emotion and lacking full control." It was a weak argument, but Logan wasn't lying.

On hearing of Kai's injuries and admission to hospital, and then of the deliberate attempt to frame her for the murder of Anjelo's mother, Logan had been filled with emotion, with such fear and rage that he hadn't been able to control his DragonFyr. As a result, said fire had exploded from his hands, a flaming ball of near-destruction.

Thankfully, he'd managed to grasp hold of the energy and rein in the full force of the power just in time. But, he'd had only a split second to decide where to redirect the fire, and had made a mess of the wall, with its tiny red-flowered wallpaper, and seared the top half of the white-painted wainscoting. He'd been grateful the damage hadn't been any worse.

Sienna twisted her lips. "Pfft. Excuses. And don't think I didn't notice that neatly done change of subject." She shook her head, then blew a lock of her coppery hair away from her eyes. "Can't you just face her like a man? Talk to her, explain what you need to do." Sienna let out a disgusted breath—she'd stopped talking so suddenly that Logan stiffened with concern before eyeing her suspiciously from beneath his eyelashes.

Then, after having confirmed Sienna wasn't about to lose her shit, Logan inhaled slowly. "I know her way better than you, Sienna," he said softly. "She won't just let me go. She'd want to help me. She'd insist on coming with, to support me. That's just who Kai is."

"And what's so bad about that?" Sienna folded her arms again, her chin jutting out as she spoke. She lifted an eyebrow. "I have it on good authority that the walker in question is pretty reasonable and understanding. It's what I like most about her—straight-talker, no beating around the bush and no hiding away truths." The words were accusation enough, each dagger-sharp and impaling him mercilessly.

Logan shook his head. "Firstly, Kai has enough on her mind. The Walker High Council nonsense is enough to twist anyone up with all their rules. And now this frame-up?"

Sienna snorted again. "So, you're running away because some stupid council said you and Kai can't be together?"

Overwhelmed by the urge to snap at her, to tell her to leave him alone, Logan had to take a second to still himself. He forced the urge away, knowing that his sister's first concern was for Kai.

The two had grown close, with Sienna having the utmost respect for Kai. The fact that Kai had been instrumental in helping Sienna accept and use her ability to shift only added to the strength of that bond.

Logan smiled, hiding the ripple of sadness filtering through him behind a weak attempt at cheer. "It's not a matter of running away. Kai has her responsibilities, and right now, *I'm* the distraction. I've been that for her ever since I went into that coma. And Kai gives her all when it comes to people she cares about. With me out of her hair, Kai may be able to see things a little clearer. Without her emotions—and mine too—clouding her decisions."

"And you? Are you leaving her because you need a clear head, too?" Sienna asked, her tone part curious, part critical as she turned to face him, body and eyes tense in anticipation of his reply.

Logan nodded. "Partly. I'm not sure what we're going to be facing when we get to Drakys...get home."

"So what exactly are you expecting?" asked Sienna after a brief pause, one eyebrow raised. A myriad emotions flickered in her fiery eyes, all of which Logan knew arose from her unequivocal love for him. Something even time and distance had been unable to shatter.

Logan blinked away the sentimentality. "I'm not entirely certain what to expect," he said, at first playing it safe with a neutral reply. When Sienna's eyes flickered again, and he recognized a hint of disappointment in them, he sighed and relented. "What if they don't accept me? *You,* they know already—you've had the way paved albeit in a strange way. But *me*? I'm still not even sure I understand why I'm needed."

Sienna took the three steps over to Logan and put her hand on his arm. "I've told you as much as I already know, but there is a crapload of knowledge that's retained exclusively for the ears of the pair of rulers on the throne. They'll tell us a whole bunch before the ceremony and everything else after we're initiated. Of that, I'm pretty sure."

His sister's eyes held a confidence that seemed to rub off on him, and he prayed that she wasn't just spouting embellished truths in order to make things easier for him to handle.

Logan put his arm around Sienna's shoulders and gave her a squeeze. He was sometimes surprised at how much he cared for her—this tiny slip of a thing—and, given that he'd spent the majority of his life entirely ignorant that she existed, it surprised him too to understand the depths of his love for her.

He'd also spent half his life believing he'd been the one who'd murdered his parents—or rather, the man and woman he'd believed were his parents—not to mention all the other lives he'd taken on that fateful day.

Logan had struggled for almost a decade, shouldering the burden of being a mass-murderer who also bore a notch in his belt held the name Sonia—Sonia Odel who had been Kai's sister-in-law. Iain's wife.

Only, that burden hadn't been Logan's to bear, a truth he was now well aware of. A truth he had no intention of revealing to Sienna anytime soon.

Or ever, if he could help it.

More secrets.

Logan had to wonder at the wisdom of keeping the truth from Sienna, but her recollections of her childhood were filled with pleasant, happy memories. Could he willingly destroy that by handing the soul-crushing weight of *his* guilt over to her?

The door opened, and Darcy entered, swiping her long blonde hair out of her face. She'd taken to wearing it open in the last few weeks, and Logan had to wonder how much of the new style had to do with Kai's brother. It seemed likely that Iain had at last found in the MindMelder, a woman capable of grounding him.

"Hey, you two," Darcy said as she walked over to them, fingers gripping the strap of her handbag as she stared from one face to the other.

"I'm assuming you want Logan?" asked Sienna softly.

Logan suppressed a ripple of concern. Sienna's interactions with Darcy had remained polite, perching on the fence between neutrality and mild affection, as though she constantly hesitated to move, preferring the freedom of not committing to something as tangible as a friendship. Logan had promised himself that he'd uncover the reason for Sienna's distance from Darcy, no matter what stood in his way.

"Unfortunately, I have to do one final check on Logan before you two leave," said Darcy, her expression serene, no hint at all that she was aware of Sienna's almost-indifference. "Your brother thought he'd be able to leave without my final assessment just because he was literally disappearing from the face of the Earth at the ungodly hour of nine in the morning. And I wasn't going to let that happen," the MindMelder said, throwing an arch look at Logan.

Sienna nodded in reply though Logan didn't miss the smirk she tried and failed to hide as she took a handful of steps backward, then spun on her heel, heading for the door. "I'll go finish packing," she said to nobody in particular as she left the room. She closed the door gently behind her, leaving Darcy and Logan with full privacy.

Darcy sighed, the sound a low rush of air tapering off into a soft growl that broadcasted her weariness and the status of her almost non-existent patience. "Does my professional opinion not matter at all to you?" An eyebrow quirked, eyes darkening for lack of humor.

Logan snorted. "Are we going to do this again?" She was right; he had wanted to sneak off without an examination, but, despite his guilt, he didn't want to waste time rehashing his reasons.

A sharp roll of Darcy's eyes followed his words. "If I thought it would make any difference, I would," she snapped. "But I think I know you well enough by now, so I won't bother."

A wave of ragged laughter bubbled free from Logan, though the sound grated even on his own ears. "Aren't you the one who said you know me better than I'll ever know myself what with getting all up close and personal with my mind?"

Her eyes narrowed, lips pursing as though she was considering some form of suitable punishment. "And that won't change until you're fully healed, and all your memories return. Also, I have to reiterate that leaving now may be detrimental to your progress."

Darcy's eyes darkened, now with worry, as she studied Logan's face, her head tilted upward, neck exposed, the action trusting in that it made her so very vulnerable to him.

Sighing, Logan ran a hand over his face and felt the fatigue simmer within his limbs. "I wish I could do as you want, Darcy, but it really is time to leave." His words rang in his ears, a loud accusation that they were just an excuse to get away.

He ignored them.

"What?" asked Darcy, her expression clouding with concern. "Did you get some sort of summons to return home?"

"Something like that."

At his clipped response, Darcy let out a huff, shook her head and grabbed hold of Logan's arm. She led him to the bed and pointed for him to sit, her expression stony as she dropped her bag on the floor and seated herself primly, then waited in taut silence.

Logan blinked, well aware he had little choice but to obey. So he did, seating himself as he mentally threw his hands up in the air. It seemed, no matter how hard he tried, he couldn't get rid of the people who cared about his well-being.

And was that really such a bad thing?

CHAPTER 2

LOGAN

Logan had decided to obey as resistance was futile when Darcy meant business.

Which she did.

The stiff finger pointing like a dagger had been more than a hint, and the cold, stony expression had sealed the deal. Logan convinced himself that having the MindMelder give him the all-clear before he left for Drakys would only be an advantage to him—never mind that such an all-clear would be one of the temporary variety.

He submitted as Darcy held her fingers to his temples and joined her mind with his. He used to marvel at her ability, but that was back when it had been new. Now he was so used to it that he barely even thought about the fact that it was unusual to have another person rooting around inside his mind.

After a few long and silent moments, Logan said, "So? Am I cleared, or am I still a basket-case?"

Darcy smirked, fingers still in contact with his skin. "Unfortunately, I never did guarantee I could cure your crazy." Then she sighed and let his temples go, dropping her hands to her sides.

"When do you plan on telling her?" she asked, voice low and almost conspiratorial.

Logan stiffened and glanced at the closed door, the movement instinctive—and all too revealing as Darcy's raised eyebrow revealed she hadn't missed his guilt in action. "I'm not sure what you mean," he said, his smile the picture of innocence.

She clicked her tongue. "Logan. I've been inside your mind, dude. You really think you can pull off lying to me?" She raised an eyebrow, well aware that her invasion of his mind was a sensitive topic which used to have Logan all resistant and behaving as though she was standing in his room, watching him dance around naked.

He wasn't far wrong about the vulnerability he felt, especially since he was of the opinion that a naked body revealed infinitely less than one's naked thoughts. Now, he met her eyes, hesitating for a moment.

Darcy shook her head and said, "Fart bombs."

Logan groaned. "Fine. You win. Nobody wants to be reminded of that."

She chuckled. "Only a boy would think it's a good idea to try to light your farts on fire." She shook her head and gave a giggle-snort.

"Ugh." Logan rolled his eyes. "Don't remind me, okay. I couldn't sit for a week after that."

Darcy's eyes widened. "Did the flames get a little too close to your butt?" she asked, smirking, eyes sparkling.

"If only. No, my dad nearly flayed me alive. Whipped my ass well and good." The mention of Karl Westin—who was most emphatically not his dad—erased Logan's mirth.

He'd fallen silent, but Darcy shook him by the arm. "Hey. Stop it. You'd think by now you'd be able to forgive yourself, especially with what you know."

Logan shifted his head, lifting his chin to meet Darcy's eyes. "All those years carrying that knowledge was painful enough. But knowing the truth? It makes the burden all the harder," Logan shook his head, saying no to the thought that one day Sienna would have to learn the truth.

Darcy was waving a finger at him now. "Which brings me back to my original question. When will you tell her?"

Logan let out a silent growl and got to his feet. "When she's stronger, and when we're both settled into our duties, know the lay of the land better. She's still fragile. I want her to be stronger before she has to face this. I know the weight of this burden, Darcy. It's a weight I'd rather she didn't have to carry."

Exhaling slowly, the MindMelder asked, "Have you considered that Sienna may not suffer beneath that burden as much as you did?"

Logan stiffened at the question, understanding that it held more than one implication. "What do you mean by that?"

"Settle down," Darcy said softly, waving her hand at him. "All I meant is she's served within the court of the Queen of all Drakys these past years. She's been labeled a brilliant diplomat and political strategist. Maybe Sienna, with her strength and experience, will be capable of handling now what you were unable to deal with because of your youth and innocence. You were so very young, Logan. And the scars of that day...they never healed, not entirely. And Sienna bore no scars from that event. Her memories of that night are gone. And with it, her guilt and self-recrimination."

"So is that a confirmation?" Logan asked, his tone hard, though only because he was steeling himself against Darcy's inevitable 'No.'

Which he didn't get. Instead, Darcy's gaze flickered away as she replied, "Ward did a deeper removal than I ever did with you. I left crumbs for you, stored memories elsewhere for you to find. Ward did his job as instructed. He removed those memories forever."

Logan shook his head. "I thought you said there was a way to give her back her memories?"

"There would have been if Ward was still alive. He would have had to join with Sienna's mind and repair what he'd done."

"And if he refused?"

Darcy shrugged. "A different method but the same result. A second MindMelder could theoretically bridge the gap between Ward and Darcy, and retrieve what he took. It would be a risky procedure, and MindMelders have been known to go insane if things went wrong, but I've heard of many more successes than failures. Which is moot anyway...because Ward is dead."

The sigh Darcy emitted held a note of agony and Logan didn't miss the glitter of fury and pain in her eyes.

"What did he do to you?" he whispered, unable to stomach the thought of what a man as powerful as Ward was capable of.

"What?" Darcy's tone was light, her laughter tinkling as she attempted to shift the mood of the conversation. "You think you can shrink me now?" she asked, smiling.

Logan wasn't about to let it go so easily. "Darcy, this Mind-Melding thing...you told me in the beginning that the connection was even deeper than sex. I can vouch for that. But what I can also vouch for is the fact that I've had you poking around inside here," Logan tapped a finger to his temple, "for so long that I'm pretty sure I'm somewhat familiar with your mind as well."

Darcy opened her mouth to reply, then let out a soft sigh. "It's complicated. And a long story." She glanced over at Logan's duffel on the floor beside the bed. "And...I don't believe you want me to delay your departure."

Shaking his head, Logan smirked. "I see what you're doing. And fine. We're at an impasse then."

"How about we take a rain-check? Let's discuss when you get back." Darcy's sad smile made it clear to Logan that she suspected they'd never get to have that conversation.

He didn't dispel her of the notion.

And then Darcy got to her feet, giving him a sad smile. "Are you ready for this?" she asked softly.

Logan shook his head and stood. "No...yes? As ready as I'll ever be, I guess." He knew it was pointless to lie to her. Then he quirked his lips. "Good thing I can make fire. That glacier's gonna be cold."

Darcy retrieved her bag and had begun to walk slowly toward the door, but at his words, she paused and turned to look over her shoulder at him. "You do know that you and Sienna don't need to go to the Mendenhall Glacier, right?"

Logan frowned. "What do you mean? I thought the glacier was the only portal available for access to Drakys from this realm. Kai said the one in Sand Beach was out of commission."

Darcy shook her head, frowning as she replied, "Not for you and Sienna. You're the rulers of the realm. And, for what it's worth, I'm pretty sure that's how Sienna's been going back and forth these last few weeks."

"She's what?" asked Logan, scowling as he stepped toward Darcy. "What do you mean?"

"Oh," Darcy said softly, tapping her finger to her lips. "I suppose you didn't know. I'm sorry..." She hesitated for a second then threw her hands in the air. "I give up. You two and your secrets," she said, shaking her head, frustration rolling off her.

"Are you going to tell me or do I have to wring it out of my sister's neck," Logan asked, the threat in his voice clear.

The MindMelder merely arched an eyebrow. "Let's just keep death and violence to a minimum, okay? As far as my knowledge goes, Sienna has been returning to Drakys over the last few weeks in order to assure the council and the regent of your health and your progress toward recovery. There was some pressure from them for your healing process to speed up, but I'm pretty sure your sister would have told them where to shove their demands."

"And how do you know she's been going home? I'm not sure she'd have told anyone if she was keeping it a secret from me."

Darcy tapped her temple. "I've been treating her as well, Logan. Helping to heal some of the scars that Ward left behind. She's got a long road ahead, but she's been recovering slowly."

"And I guess you bumped into a few secrets inside that stubborn skull of hers. Did you question her?"

"No. I just assumed you'd have known about it, hence my slip in revealing it to you."

Logan nodded. "I see. So you wouldn't have mentioned it had my departure not come up?"

"Not sure either way," Darcy said with a shrug. "I'm not here to keep secrets for you and your sister. You both have enough of those already, and in my opinion, it's time for the two of you to break down those barriers instead of continuing to build them up some more. She's keeping secrets from you. You're keeping truths from her. And the dumb thing is both of you will claim to be protecting the other by lying. Go figure." Darcy shook her head, her expression revealing how tired, and fed up she was.

And Logan understood—Darcy cared—but he wasn't about to agree with her. She was right though, and he'd have to question Sienna before they left. He let out a sigh. "Well, she's definitely going to have to tell me before we leave. Don't believe she'll risk a trip to the glacier before revealing the truth."

"If she doesn't?" Darcy smirked. "What if she does take you to Mendenhall to keep up the ruse?"

Logan gave a dark snort. "Let her try. I'll gladly wring her neck."

Darcy shook her head, smiling as she walked over to Logan and raised her arms. "C'mere, you big lunk."

Logan reached out and hugged the MindMelder back, then straightened and patted her on the top of her head, his expression sober and serious.

"Hey," she squawked, slapping his hand away. "I'm older than you, kid."

He snorted. "I'm bigger." Logan fell silent, smiling sadly as he looked down at her. "Thank you, Darcy. For being brave and for telling me the truth, even though it must have been so hard. And for staying with me to help get me—and Sienna—better. That was going above and beyond."

"It's the least I could do," Darcy said, her nonchalant shrug not reflecting the pain that shadowed her eyes.

"You didn't need to, Darcy. You only did what Omega instructed you to do. You weren't personally responsible. But even then, you laid the groundwork so I could get my memories back. That in itself is enough."

"You didn't think so at first." Darcy tilted her head, her smile sad.

Logan's skin warmed with shame. "I know. I was an asshole. I shouldn't have said those things."

Darcy shook her head, though he was sure he saw the intensity of her pain fade. "You were in a dark place, Logan. I understood."

"But my words hurt you, and that was the last thing I meant to do. Everything's so fucked up...so much hurt in our lives. You didn't deserve more."

Darcy reached up and patted his cheek. "Logan, you were only a small part of the hurt I caused. And even if that was done in the course of my job, as a means to help my family, it still doesn't absolve me of those actions. I'll have to live with what I've done."

"And carry that pain around with you everywhere?" Logan asked curtly.

"If I have to," Darcy said with a nod. "It's *my* burden to bear. But at least one part of that burden has been laid to rest."

"You mean this Ward guy?" Logan asked softly. He'd accidentally bumped into a memory of Darcy's, and he suspected, from the fragments he'd seen, that she and this MindMelder called Ward, had had a showdown of sorts.

Darcy nodded. "He's out of my life now. I just need to focus on picking up the pieces and putting my life back together."

"Darcy, you know I'm here for you, right?" Logan said softly, meaning every word with all his heart.

She nodded, tears glinting in her eyes. "I do. And thank you. I'll consider us even."

Logan chuckled as he shook his head. "Not sure if we're ever going to be even." He smirked.

Darcy patted his arm and walked off toward the door. She opened it and stood on the threshold, looking back at him over her shoulder.

"You take care of yourself, Lyandr, Son of the House of Yl. And watch out for that sister of yours too, okay?" Darcy said, her eyes now shining with tears.

Logan grinned. "Yes, ma'am."

"Oh, and Logan?"

Logan looked up, an eyebrow curved in question.

Before she disappeared into the hallway, Darcy said, "Please try not to kill Sienna."

CHAPTER 3

LOGAN

Logan had just lifted his duffel onto his shoulder when a voice cut into his thoughts.

"Why are you being warned against killing me?" asked Sienna from the open doorway.

Logan glanced over at his sister who was standing, arms folded as she leaned against the doorframe. "Probably because you deserve it," he said, watching her expression closely.

Sienna's lips thinned, and she rolled her eyes, though he didn't miss the flare of guilt she failed to hide. "We should get moving. We need to get there bright and early so let's go. Time difference between EarthWorld and the city Dyr is four hours behind our time, and we don't want to arrive too late in the morning. Things get busy for Aunt Lyra and for Uncle Vyrian as the day progresses. And our ride will be here soon."

She tacked on the last sentence as she pushed off the doorframe and flitted away like a shadow, leaving her instructions echoing in her wake.

Logan lifted an eyebrow as he followed her out into the hall toward the stairs. What Sienna had failed to mention was Kai and Celeste's impending arrival.

One thing was certain, this trip to Drakys was a step that equated to the answering of an obligation. Still, he wasn't blind to the guilt that accompanied the decision like so much unwanted baggage.

Sienna was still furious with him, and he was all too aware that asking Ivy to give Kai his letter of farewell had been a cowardly move of epic proportions.

Logan was also aware, from his conversation with Ivy, that Kai and Celeste had both undergone a few tests at the Elite HQ and were expected to return to the Odel home before noon.

At which time Logan planned to be gone.

A dick move if ever there was one.

The house was quiet, with Corin attending to Lily's morning treatments, and Iain off at a council meeting. Baz was likely sleeping in—if vamplings slept?—having just returned from a visit to the mentor Logan had connected him with; Asher should look after the kid, give him the kind of guidance he needed but wasn't able to get from those who didn't understand the intricacies of the vampiric form.

Logan caught up with Sienna, and the siblings descended the stairs side by side, blanketed by a strange silence in which Logan waited, wondering what Sienna was going to come up with to explain their method of travel home, and in which Sienna remained as silent as the dead.

The guilty dead.

As they reached the bottom of the stairs, she stamped her foot and let out a disgusted groan. "Ugh, I can't keep up this stupid lie anymore."

Logan frowned. "What you talking about, kid?" he said, feigning innocence.

Sienna lifted an eyebrow, her eyes sparkling with annoyance.

"Well, spit it out. We do need to get moving," Logan said, careful not to mention glaciers and portals.

Sienna let out a huff and stepped closer to him. She peered up at him—boy was he ever glad he was taller than this spitfire of a sister of his—then raised a finger and pointed it, and its silver-tipped fingernail, at him. "You know?" she growled, her tone accusing.

He just shrugged.

"How?" She grunted the word out, frustration flaring in her golden eyes.

Logan smirked. "When were you planning on telling me? *After* we get to the glacier? Or were you going to keep up the whole charade until we got to Drakys?"

Sienna shook her head and growled again. "I was going to call off the jumper to take us to Alaska. And then I chickened out."

Logan shook his head, clicking his tongue like a disapproving wife. "You should know better. How about canceling the call now?"

"Too late," said a cheery voice from the kitchen. "Although, I'll consider this a free trip to say hi to a buddy." Larsson smiled as he left the kitchen, his palm cradling a blueberry-bran muffin as he spoke, mouth full with fresh-baked goodness.

Logan laughed. "Good to see you, Red."

Larsson gave a haughty glare. "Think that name's more appropriate for someone else?" He rolled his eyes suggestively in Sienna's direction.

Sienna glanced over at the jumper, her glare filled with fake-anger. "You watch it, or I'll be forced to incinerate you. Try jumping when you're just a pile of ash."

Larsson chortled, then began to choke as a stray crumb went down the wrong way. Sienna sighed and hurried over to him to thump him on the back. "There. Wouldn't want you to die on my watch."

"But you just threatened me with a fiery death. That also happens to be classified as dying, in case you didn't know."

"Watch it," Sienna snapped, though her eyes sparkled with laughter.

"Yes, your highness," Larsson said as he dropped into a low curtsey, his eyes shining with amusement as he straightened to flick crumbs from his face. After dragging a finger across the muffin cup, he scooped up a drop of cream cheese and stuck his finger in his mouth. "Divine. I'm going to miss being paid in muffins."

"I'm sure you will, Freckles," Sienna said, smiling broadly now.

Logan was both amused and surprised. He'd spent so much time inside his sister's head, that he'd almost forgotten she had a personality other than what she revealed to him. His connection with Sienna was a whole new level of whack.

I mean, who wanted your sister to know where you kept your trashy nudie mags, or about how badly your first kiss sucked, or even how you felt about the woman you loved?

It was a baring of souls that many would say was best left between a man and his god—or whatever entity or higher sentience he believed in.

And yet, Logan was meant to share this deeply invasive bond with his *sister*?

And now, as he watched her flirt with the red-headed jumper—however mildly—he realized that the usual brotherly protectiveness and jealousy when another man steps into his sister's life, was going to reach an epically fucked-up level of craziness.

Logan was going to have to prepare. What the hell was he going to do on her wedding night?

Something hard pummeled Logan's arm, and he blinked as his attention focused on his attacker who stood at his right shoulder.

"Are you deaf?" Sienna snapped. "Larsson was saying goodbye."

Logan blinked and shook his head.

"Where'd you go, bro?" Larsson asked, frowning.

"Trust me, Lars. You do not want to know."

CHAPTER 4

LOGAN

After Larsson disappeared, leaving the siblings standing in the front hall, Sienna turned to face Logan, her lips pursed in trite apology. "I'm sorry for not telling you," she said softly.

He shook his head as he looked down at Sienna's face. "I'm assuming you had a good reason for this omission?" he said sternly.

She rolled her eyes. "Geez. You already sound like old Vyrian. You'll be taking over from him easily enough." She made a face and folded her arms.

"You're stalling," Logan said as she'd remained silent for a few moments. Sienna huffed and sank onto the bottom step of the stairs. "Sienna? Why did you keep this from me? We could have gone back to Drakys days ago."

Her hand shot toward Logan, finger aimed straight at his nose, its silver point glittering like a blade. "And...that's the reason right there," Sienna said, springing to her feet again. "You would have wanted to go running off back to Drakys before you were healthy enough to travel, and before you and Kai reached an understanding. Although, from what I've seen, the latter is now moot."

"Sienna, you kno—"

Sienna held her hand up imperiously, palm an inch from Logan's nose. "I don't want to hear it. Anyway, back to your question: The transition isn't easy if you're compromised. I could have taken you, but I hadn't yet understood the technique well enough to transport two people, let alone one."

"You've been going back and forth all along?" he asked, not caring that the accusation was clear in his tone.

"Did you really think I'd want to leave things all to Aunt Lyra? She may be our mother's sister, but she's not as strong as she tries to make herself look."

Logan chuckled. "You think she'd bungle things in her final scene?"

"Who knows with her." Then Sienna chuckled. "Actually, not really. Aunt Lyra's got our best interests at heart, that much I know. But she's a little too kind, and easily taken advantage of. Great-Uncle Vyrian has to keep a solid eye on her sometimes. She's amazing with the political stuff, but matters of the heart...things can get a little muddy."

"She has kept the place afloat all these years, hasn't she?"

Sienna's eyebrows rose. "And she almost sold me off to that bastard of an elf king, too. All because she couldn't judge his true intentions because he'd used his thrall on her and she wasn't strong enough to fight against his hold."

"All the more reason for us to have gone back earlier."

Sienna let out a disgusted snort. "You'd have had to take Darcy with you. There was no way she was about to let you go anywhere until she was sure things were looking better under the hood," she said, folding her arms.

"Which I'm told is the case at this point. Is there any reason to continue delaying the inevitable?" asked Logan, his fingers tightening around the strap of his duffel.

Sienna cleared her throat. "Well. You've had zero training."

"Something you should have thought about before this, don't you think?" replied Logan, his tone cool.

Sienna glanced over at him, spine stiff as though ready for a fight. But as soon as she met Logan's eyes she deflated, shoulders drooping. "Fine. I get it. I should have told you earlier...given you a chance to build up your skill at it. Which also means I'll deserve it when we arrive and you want to rip my head off."

"And why would I want to do such a thing?" Logan asked, a little more worried now as he wondered what else she hadn't told him.

Sienna cleared her throat. "Well, the first time tends to have an overall effect on your body. Dizziness, disorientation, and nausea are the biggest concerns." Sienna paused and looked over at Logan. "And I know as the new ruler, the last thing you'd want is to spray your breakfast all over Aunt Lyra and old Vyrian the moment you arrive."

Logan gritted his teeth. "This is perfect," he said darkly.

Still, Logan wasn't so afraid of emasculation through vomit. Perhaps he'd have to ensure he kept close to the ground and maintain a low trajectory. Just in case, of course. And he was pretty certain he had a hardier gut than Sienna believed.

"Does our arrival have to be welcomed with pomp and ceremony?" he asked.

"The Queen Regent and the General are the least bit pomp and ceremony you'll get. Trust me, you'd prefer arriving to their presence than to a grand reception of the full council and all their entourages."

Logan took a deep, slow breath, forcing calm into his mind. "Sienna—"

Again, his sister cut him off with a slim finger near his nose. "Don't get your panties in a twist. I've got things under control. We'll arrive elsewhere within the castle and walk to the throne room instead. Lyra and Vyrian will be disappointed, but I'd rather you save face in front of them. You have enough obstacles to overcome when you take on your role. Can't have you starting off on the wrong foot."

"So where exactly are we going to arrive?" Logan asked, aware that he was a little nervous. The thought of the journey through the portal had somewhat extended the moment of arrival, giving him the idea that he'd have a slower progression to his arrival. Instantly appearing inside the palace hadn't even been a distant possibility.

Suck it up, Saleem's voice said in Logan's mind. The damn djinn was like a ghost in Logan's head, and he had to wonder why the voice of his conscience had taken on Saleem's rough baritone. It only made Logan focus harder on the fact that he hadn't heard from the djinn in a while.

Kai's last words regarding Saleem also weighed on his mind. She'd said they had a crazy important thing, which required Logan to rest up. Was Saleem in some sort of trouble?

But Logan couldn't concentrate on the djinn right now. If Saleem needed help, he'd find a way to let Logan know about it.

So, for now, he concentrated on Sienna who was saying something about a bedroom covered in dust.

"What bedroom?"

"Are you not listening to me?" she asked, narrowing her eyes at him.

She could have easily just slipped into his mind to find out what he was thinking, but she'd stopped doing that a few days ago.

It had taken Logan long enough to learn to raise his defenses in order to keep some parts of his mind private from his sister. Sienna, of course, had mastered that art well before Logan, but she still suffered from momentary lapses when she was too emotionally invested in something.

Now she poked him in his arm. "We'll be arriving in your bedroom. It's been prepared for you, and you're going to thank me. You should have seen what they did with the place the first time around. Who in the world would have thought my brother, the General of Drakys, would want to sleep in a powder-blue and gold bedroom? It looked like Caryssa's Bordello down in the Eastern Quarter."

Sienna stopped speaking abruptly as she registered her words, then quickly slipped her hand into the crook of Logan's arm.

"Come. We'd better be going. Hold tight to your duffel. There's a high chance it's going to get flung somewhere. Let's hope we don't break anything important."

Logan's last thoughts as his physical form fragmented into shards of shadows had nothing to do with how he'd feel on arrival in Drakys.

All he could think about was how Sienna had inside knowledge of what a bordello looked like.

CHAPTER 5

LOGAN

The arrival of His Majesty, Lyandr, General of the Realm of Drakys within his royal suites was *the* most unceremonious of landings he'd ever experienced. And he was infinitely glad that Sienna had had the forethought to ensure their appearance in Drakys was a private, unwitnessed event.

The duffel bag had gone flying—as his sister had predicted—and had engaged in a vigorous altercation with a six-foot-high wrought-iron column that had supported a gigantic bouquet of burnt orange flowers.

Said flowers—with their ragged-edged petals and blood-red hearts, were now strewn across the carpet, a sight to behold considering that each splash of brightness was larger than a dinner plate. The woven-metal column had survived the attack, now leaning precariously against the wall, a single spoke of iron the only thing keeping disaster at bay.

His Majesty, though, was a little uncertain of the prospect of his own survival.

Logan's stomach muscles spasmed, his gut churning, his throat closing and opening of its own volition as he bent over and threw up. The destination of the contents of his stomach had turned out to be a gleaming golden bowl large enough for a small child to bathe within.

It appeared Sienna had been well prepared.

Logan raised his head a quarter inch to ask her if she was okay, but had barely moved when another wave of nausea flooded his senses. His eyes widened, and for the tiniest moment, he considered fighting the urge. Then he dropped down toward the bowl and retched again, the sound loud as the vomit slapped the sides of the golden basin and echoed back at him.

Logan had not felt this miserable in a long, long time.

Well, no. That is a bald-faced lie.

He had felt this way only a few days ago when Kai had ended up in the hospital. Now, feeling as though hours had passed since he and Sienna had materialized in his blue-and-gold royal suites, he hung his head over the golden bowl and retched some more, even though he was pretty certain there was nothing left.

At last, Sienna handed him a wet, soapy towel, and then a dry one after he'd cleaned his face up with the former. Logan dabbed his face dry now and let out a groan as he struggled to his feet and studied the room—which wavered dangerously in his vision.

"Woah, not so fast. You'll need a minute." Sienna grabbed Logan's arm and guided him to a small seating-arrangement of two armchairs and matching footstools, separated by a low round coffee table. Logan didn't complain about being babied, just sank into the soft cushion of the armchair and allowed Sienna to prop his feet up on the footstool.

"Now, sit tight. I'll grab you something to drink." Sienna spun on her heel, reddish gold hair flying, and rushed to a sideboard to Logan's left. The long, dark-wood piece sat against a wall between two of six floor-to-ceiling windows that lead out onto a balcony large enough to fit a second bedroom.

Or maybe even an entire apartment.

Looking up though, turned out to be a bad idea, and Logan sucked in a harsh grunt and sank lower, hunching his shoulders as he took slow deep breaths while Sienna bustled around in a most motherly way. He'd dozed off a few times too, the jump itself having worn him out—never mind the killer upchuck attack.

Through lowered lids, Logan watched his sister, and caught glimpses of a memory from when they were younger—a more diminutive version of Sienna, holding a small pail filled with apples in one hand, the other grasping a too-full bucket of water. Great droplets sloshed against her skirt as she marched toward him, but she didn't care, her face scrunched up with determination as she hauled her two burdens to the veranda.

Logan straightened from chopping the wood and called out to her to take it easy, but his sister had climbed the stairs and yelled out that she wanted all the chores done before *he* came 'cos she was damned if she was going to see Mom get another blue eye.

Logan let out a grunt as the memory settled into his mind, as emotion filled him to overflowing just as much as his kid sister's bucket of water—this was a picture of his past that he'd not possessed until this very moment.

"You okay?" came Sienna's voice as she hurried over to him. "Here, drink some of this. It's like cranberry juice. Nice and tart and good for your stomach." Her tone was light, but he didn't miss the edge of concern.

Logan forced a smile, though he suspected it revealed itself merely as a thin grimace, took the proffered goblet and sipped slowly, taking notice of the gilded stem and the crystal bell of the wineglass.

So much luxury in the first moments of being back in Drakys. Logan wasn't sure he'd be able to take too much of it; luxury was something he was far from used to.

The drink was a deep blue and tart, and so very similar to the flavor of cranberry that he felt a little disoriented at the color. Logan shut his eyes firmly and sipped again, then sat back and let out a low sigh. "How long before this is over?" he asked, barely able to speak.

Sienna's brow furrowed, her honey eyes still reflecting concern. "Can take a few minutes. Or a few hours. You've passed out three times already, so I'm beginning to think a certain MindMelder knew what she was talking about." Her lip curled in a reluctant smile.

"I thought I'd already had a nap or two," Logan said with a soft chuckle.

"Not naps, you dolt. You were lights out for almost forty minutes. Three times." One eyebrow curved as she smirked.

"What's the time?" Logan asked, a flick of alarm momentarily clearing his mind-fog.

"Eight-thirty…ish." Sienna waved her hand. "Don't worry. You'll be fine. Just take it easy. I don't want to have Darcy on my ass in case you kick the bucket on my watch."

Logan chuckled.

And he may have passed out again because when he blinked, eyelids heavy, a low thud-thud drew his gaze to the pale carpet where Sienna was tapping her foot "—I'd prefer you on the bed but it's a little too far away from you right now, and I ain't carrying you." Her arms were folded as she glanced momentarily over her shoulder at the bed, then met his eyes, forehead rumpled, making it clear she was trying hard to come up with a plan.

He let out a snort-laugh, wondering how far away a bed could be from him considering he was sitting inside the bedroom of his suites—a word he imagined himself drawing air quotes around every time he thought of it.

Logan forced his lids open and peered over the top of his goblet, then blinked as the gigantic bed, with its gold-and-bronze carved headboard, seemed to swim in the distance like a mirage.

"What are you laughing at?" Sienna asked reaching out with a napkin to wipe Logan's cheek. He didn't protest.

"The bed is too far away," he said, chuckling again as he stared at the huge mattress.

Sienna clicked her tongue. "That's what I just said, you dolt." Then she let out a sigh. "Okay, I get it. Yeah, this place does tend to get a bit over the top. You get used to it." Her eyes took on a faraway look as she took a breath, as though memories—whether fond or not, he didn't know—had descended upon her.

Logan smiled, this time the expression more than a half-baked attempt as the churning in his stomach began to fade. "You're the queen, though. I imagine your bedroom looks a damn sight more flamboyant than mine."

Sienna blinked, her eyes clearing as she focused on Logan, her fingers twisted around the red napkin. She sighed and sank onto the footstool beside his boots—which he prayed he hadn't splattered with puke.

"I think I already explained some things to you…about the way the realm is ruled. Seems like you either didn't hear me or you think I'm saying it to soothe your stupid ego," she said, shaking her head.

Logan cleared his throat. "I've just never heard of a joint rule by a queen and a general. To me, a queen outranks a general like...a billion to one." She had explained, but not to his satisfaction.

"That's just it, Logan. The word for *general* in the Drakyr tongue doesn't translate so well. For all intents and purposes, it means the Leader of the Armies of Drakys. The queen is the diplomatic leader. And the siblings rule with one hand until death ends their reign."

Sienna's explanation sobered Logan, and he opened his eyes a fraction wider. "I don't remember you saying that...exactly."

She shrugged. "Remember that I'm still learning myself. What I'd been taught in the last few years appeared to have been a superficial edification. But Aunt Lyra has been guiding me a little more these past weeks, schooling on the history and the traditions in more detail."

"And when would *I* have received this education?" asked Logan, shimmying—very slowly—in his seat as he pulled his feet off the footstool.

"You wouldn't have." Sienna's answer had Logan's eyes snapping up to meet hers. But she didn't wait for his curt question. "There wouldn't be any need for education as such. Aunt Lyra was merely satisfying my curiosity. During the Ascension Ceremony, the incoming ruling pair receives the memories of all the previous rulers of the kingdom, going back as far as our people have had organized rule in this realm."

As she spoke, Sienna pointed at the bed, and Logan grunted in response, more in his surprise at the revelation, at how odd it sounded to his ears, than his disinclination to obey her instruction. He lifted an eyebrow. "And how exactly does this memory-transfer occur?" he asked as he wobbled over to the enormous bed, trying to quell the smile that had begun to curve his lips.

But Sienna wasn't paying his amusement any mind. Her brow was furrowed as she guided him onto the bed and fluffed his pillows. "That's the part that nobody has told me," she said at last as she straightened, her words sharply edged with frustration. "It's not recorded anywhere that I know of, and believe me, I've searched the libraries high and low."

"So what? We're expected to submit to this initiation with zero understanding as to the details of the ceremony, or preparation for how this knowledge is *given* to us?" asked Logan, well aware his skepticism was out in the open.

But again, his sister didn't care, instead rolling her eyes and smiling. "I guess you and I are a little different...in terms of our upbringing and...well...." Then she paused, a shadow smearing the hint of amusement from her eyes, "All the previous ruling pairs would have ascended after having known their whole lives what their destiny was. I guess we're EarthWorld people in a foreign realm when it comes to Drakys and its customs. But Logan," Sienna took a step closer and lowered her voice to a murmur, "that's one thing you cannot reveal."

Logan squinted at the seriousness in her face as she hovered before him. "That we're *Earth* people?"

"No...I mean that you doubt. There are members of the council who would look—hell who am I kidding?—that *are* looking right now for every reason to overturn the current laws. For generations, the Drakyr people have been ruled by a perceived matriarchy. But a small group of councilmen—many of whom have spent time in the EarthWorld—have come to believe that it's time for a king on the throne. A king and not a queen."

Logan nodded slowly. "Politics, huh?"

Sienna let out a soft huff. "Those old goats don't know anything about politics. All they can see is taking control. They have this weird idea that the rule of the queen has subjugated them for generations, emasculated them in a way."

"And that isn't the case?" asked Logan carefully, watching Sienna's face closely.

Her eyes were wide and flashed with annoyance. "What do you take me for? Of course, I did my research. I was approached by a number of councilmen and their women—"

"Women? Polygamy?" Logan smirked.

"No, silly. Some of the men are open about their mistresses. And a few mistresses are quite vocal about their relationships."

"Sounds like unofficial polygamy to me."

"Whatever it is, some of these women appear to have been converted to the type of male-centric rule, believing that women are not born to be rulers. Clearly, the whole concept of the powers of the Twin Rulers is lost on them."

"Great. A polygamous cult," was Logan's only response.

Sienna shook her head, let out an angry little huff then clapped her hands. Apparently, she'd given up. "You sleep now, and I'll be back to fetch you. I'll get us something to eat and let Aunt Lyra know we're both in one piece."

Logan smirked as she walked off to the door. "Geez. If this is what matriarchal rule looks like, I can understand why the men want to take back the power."

Halfway to the door, Sienna—spine now taut—spun on her heel and glared at him, her eyes wide with shock, mouth open to lash out at him. When she saw his smirk, she relaxed and grinned. "Logan, you're such an idiot. But you'd better get yourself ready. You're going to get lobbied up the wazoo the moment they know you're here."

Logan smirked and shook his head. "I'm a little concerned about what the lobbying entails. What are the chances of my wazoo withstanding such an onslaught?" Logan asked Sienna who had resumed her journey to the door.

She let out an annoyed grunt and was about to speak when Logan laughed, the sound rough and loud. "Wait, I got this," he said, receiving a grunt in response as she paused to frown over her shoulder at him, her hand still firmly gripping the door-handle. Said frown transformed into a burst of laughter as Logan replied, his voice thin and high to mimic hers, "Logan, you're such an idiot."

CHAPTER 6

KAI

When I opened my eyes, it felt like the very act of forcing my heavy lids apart was a crime. Just as much as it was a crime to have the afternoon sun stealing through the narrow slit between the heavy drapes in my bedroom.

At some point, some well-meaning soul has been thoughtful enough to shut out the sun, likely believing they would encourage a deeper more restful slumber—perhaps Lily, since she'd been overly attentive since my return, walking around on tiptoe as though every step would cause my numerous pains to multiply tenfold.

Or even my father, Corin, whose time was now divided unevenly between attending to wife and daughter, both whose bodies and minds had been ravaged by various levels of scientifically related tortures.

Or perhaps Grams—who'd lurked on the edges of the group-hugs and the hollow voices, pitched a note or two higher in fake non-concern—eyes large and filled with a faded sorrow for daughter and granddaughter, emotions in an upheaval not too dissimilar to what I was feeling.

But now, as I squinted and angled my head to avoid the golden brightness of the slicing sunbeam, I merely cursed the good Samaritan for not ensuring the drapes had been fully shut so I wouldn't have to deal with the pain now surging and simmering behind my eyes, the constant spiking in my head only been exacerbated by the invading sunlight.

I let out a soft sigh, careful to release the air slowly as the intensity of the pulsing agony within my skull never faded and instead graduated to unbearable while doing normal things like blinking. It had taken mere seconds after reaching freedom from the stabbing ray of sunlight for every limb, every muscle within my body, to remember that everything hurt. And to understand that *everything* made that hurt worse.

Even breathing.

And, as breathing was apparently a compulsory activity, I endured the task though I soon learned that rapid inhalation pushed that incessant throbbing to heights that teased my consciousness with a sensation of falling, an indescribable drunken weightlessness usually experienced just before one passed out.

If I had to think about it, I'd say it felt very much like that dizzy weakness I sometimes get when I sing—if for argument's sake my pathetic warbling were to be considered singing—and hit a note that's a fraction too high for my vocal cords. This strange vibration and lightheadedness was something akin to euphoria—which I had little doubt a mediocre voice such as mine certainly did not deserve.

I took a second long slow breath, glad to find the pulsing didn't worsen—nor did it alleviate, but I wasn't in the habit of having high expectations.

Life, lately, had told me I was shit out of luck if I thought every bad came with a bunch of good thrown in just because the universe loved Kai Odel.

I sniffed at the thought then adjusted my limbs, urging my

body to roll slowly onto my back. The low lines of the sun's rays spotlighted the dark variegated strokes of soot and burned wallpaper as they flared out from a dusky center, implied the time to be mid-afternoon, the added silence within the house only served as confirmation.

I needed to get up and check on Mom—we'd both been herded upstairs to bed by Dad and Grams, neither given time to speak, to properly confirm the other was truly well, that we had both really survived the strange horror of the Division 7 lab.

But my body refused to obey my mental instruction, insisting on staying put, muscles languid and thick as glue, joints afire with a strange, inexplicable heat. I shifted again and tilted my head to get a more expansive view of Logan's artistic rendition to my right, a better view than the peripheral vision a single eye had provided.

Another long slow breath and half a dozen weary heavy-lidded blinks later and I was studying the scorch-mark the way you would stare at a painting hanging on the wall of a museum or an art gallery, the way you'd scrunch up your face and nod to maintain the illusion of approval all the while wondering why in the world art connoisseurs believed ten splashes of red paint on a rusted piece of corrugated iron was considered a true example of modern art.

But today, my expression wasn't in confusion as to the classification of that art but rather the creation of it.

Logan's explanation the previous night of the creation of the scorch-mark had simmered in the back of my mind, the memory swathed in an entirely different scent of pain. I'd stopped by at the house before Mel was to jump me to the Chief's pre-arranged minivan for transport out of Chicago, and I'd hoped that Logan would have had some explanation for the glaring lack of any form of concern for my health and well-being on his part.

His absence at the hospital had wounded me deeper than I'd expected it to—and I'd always believed myself to be a very reasonable woman, even within a relationship. As such I would have thought Logan's non-reaction to my at-the-time dire medical state, would have had little to no consequence to me.

I knew well the depth and breadth of his love for me, knew the trust we'd grown and nurtured, and around which we'd built our love, our passions, and I knew that such an absence of action on Logan's part would have had a multitude of possible reasons.

And yet, his explanation of having been asleep for most of the time that I'd been in triage and surgery hadn't sat well at all; it niggled, like the feeling of having something stuck in your throat and no amount of swallowing would dislodge it, and every time you breathe you get the odd sensation that it's still there—not so much a physical feeling but rather a strange knowing, an awareness of its presence even when you have confirmed that nothing is there.

At least nothing that you can see with your own eyes.

And I'd accepted his words with an understanding I didn't feel, with an awareness that the balance of things had shifted slightly, not so much as to tip the pair of us into an ocean of turmoil, but just a fraction enough that the world beneath our feet now tilted at a strange and unnatural incline—a change of which neither of us could feign ignorance.

A change of which we'd both shared in making.

I blinked a few times, then scrunched my eyes tight, ignoring the spiking of pain in the dark recesses of my brain, the sharp snick that bore a strange malice, as though my pain was sentient and would inflict further agony if I gave it half a chance.

I raised my shoulders and torso, and let out a soft groan during the valiant battle to sit upright, one that proved a full skirmish with an army of agonizingly sharp lances striking deep within my brain.

My body screamed, muscles shrieking, joints grating as they fell beneath the onslaught of pain. But my mind—as my mother had happily noted not too long ago—was strong and determined and infallible.

So I made it all the way to a seated position, legs swung around with my feet now resting on the rug, left foot sinking into the thick cool pile, the right swallowed up by the warmth of the sun-soaked half. I smiled at the incongruity of the sensations, a foot immersed in cold while its partner was soaking in heat—definitely something that confused a person's brain, that much was sure.

I cleared my throat and reached for a glass of water from the nightstand. It was a little unsettling that Dad had put me back into my own bedroom—which had housed Logan until just this morning.

A part of me wanted to sink back into the bed, find the hollow in the mattress that Logan's body had created, where the heat from his fire-sweats had sunk into the foam layers, melting and reforming them to remember the shape of him. The heat of him. That same part of me wanted to spill the unspent tears I'd held back with every fiber of my being, wanted to breathe in what scent there was left of him within this room.

But even as I struggled with that temptation, I knew I didn't have the luxury of time. Mel's reminder that the djinn awaited our help in Mithras was the other thing I'd kept on that over-crowded backburner, a reminder too that I needed to check on the tracker.

From what I'd been told, in snippets of conversation with the Chief, Chloe, Grams, and Dad, Mel's exposure to the lightning had sent her on an uncontrolled astral journey. The details of that experience were sparse, as from what I'd also been told, the tracker had fallen unconscious and had been encouraged to sleep as much as possible.

Grams had assured me that Mel was fine, that her brain activity was still within the normal elevated range for a master teleporter and that—other than unrequested astral travel at the most inconvenient times—she had not appeared to have suffered any lasting physical damage.

Which was probably not the case when it came to me.

More sparks flared in my brain as I pushed to my feet, then reached for the robe at the foot of the bed. It was then that I registered that I'd been stripped of my outer clothing and was now wearing a pair of bright pink hot-pants and a neon green tank.

I grimaced. Whoever had dressed me needed a good talking to. The colors alone were enough to give me a headache, and I had to wonder if this was Lily's idea of a welcome-back-to-the-land-of-the-living prank.

With short jerky movements, I drew the silky knee-length robe over my gaudy underthings, glad that this particular garment had come in a more neutral shade of shimmering copper. The only reason I was not currently rolling my eyes was I knew all too well such a movement would have incurred the wrath of the pain-demon that had taken up residence inside my brain.

So instead, I tied the silken belt around my waist and knotted it hard before limping slowly toward the door. I found soon enough that activity became easier to endure the more I was in motion, and I was able to leave my room and cross the hall to Greer's old room where Dad had sequestered his second patient.

Mom.

CHAPTER 7

LOGAN

Logan had awakened refreshed and ready, and after a quick meal of a spiced-rice dish filled with raisins, nuts, and chicken, he felt ready to face his aunt and great uncle. Sienna now led Logan down the halls of the Grand Palace of Krytis, where the luxurious furnishings were only slightly less ostentatious than that of his royal *suites*.

"So what was the deal with Aunt Lyra's first choice of powder-blue decor?" he asked in a stage whisper as they strode across a long hall, its carpet patterned in deep burgundy and emerald green interlocking swirls reminiscent of EarthWorld's Persian and Moroccan handwoven tapestries.

Sienna glanced over at Logan. "It used to be your room when you were a baby. For some reason, Aunt Lyra thought that baby-blue was somehow appropriate for a grown-ass man."

"What color did she choose for you?" Logan lifted an eyebrow.

"She didn't get the chance," she replied, her haughty expression underlining how proud she was of her own lucky escape. "I was here when the decorators arrived. They'd swatched your bedroom first, thank goodness."

"Thank God for their man-comes-first way of thinking," Logan whispered again.

Sienna snickered. "Now, you just behave yourself," she snapped, throwing him a warning glare.

"Aren't we supposed to be the ones in charge?" teased Logan.

Sienna's face now took on an expression of such seriousness that he'd felt a sudden stab of pain in his heart. Was it possible that they'd lose each other to their royal duties even before they got a chance to enjoy having found each other?

Now, his sister rolled her eyes at him. "Let's just get through this without Lyra losing her shit. Smooth sailing will be a good sign."

"Is she that bad?"

"Not all that bad. She's just used to running things, and of course, now we're here, and we're taking over the reins, I think she might feel like she's no longer useful, no longer needed. I don't want to hurt her feelings." Sienna's voice had taken on a deep vibrancy that matched the shine in her eyes, revealing clearly the depth of her affection for their aunt.

"Which could also mean she'd feel as though she was never wanted in the first place," muttered Logan.

"Exactly."

Logan grunted. "Which would make her a desperate woman," he said dramatically. "And everyone knows, a desperate woman is a dangerous woman."

Sienna chuckled. "I think you have the wrong queen. Lyra's kind to the core. Her heart is in the right place. But there are people on the council, in the service of the queen, hell even across the damned realm, who have made it clear to her that she never deserved to rule. She's worked her frickin' butt off, making sure she looked after the realm, hoping all that time that the Grygyns, would find us."

"Grygyns?" Logan frowned. "Er...that like secret agent trackers or something?"

Logan's question faded away as they reached the large double-doors, also made of gold. The doors were carved to resemble the trunks of a tree, though within the knots glowed gemstones and lines of precious metals.

Logan grunted softly. "Never thought the tales of dragons being fond of gold were true."

Sienna didn't reply. Instead, she just glared a warning at Logan and paused as the doors were opened for them. An armored guard saluted, slapped his open hand onto his breastplate and remained unmoving as Sienna and Logan strode past him.

"Was I supposed to salute back?" Logan asked out the side of his mouth.

Sienna didn't reply. A man's loud baritone rang out across the large hall. "All hail Queen Synestra of the House of Yl." The guard paused, cleared his throat and said, "And her Majesty's most welcome guest."

Logan had almost forgotten Sienna's name. He'd been reminded of his own true name, his Royal designation as the son of a great ruling family in Drakys by Darcy last night. But even as he tried to think of himself as Lyandr, or Sienna as Synestra, his brain just refused to obey. And even now he had to force himself to refrain from wincing at the sound of it.

Good thing he managed to pull it off as on the dais ahead of Logan and Sienna, a man and woman rose from a pair of golden chairs as the Royal name had been called.

The woman was small and curvaceous, though her eyes held a weariness that Logan assumed could only be caused by the weight of an unwanted crown.

Unless she *had* wanted that crown after all.

Then Logan and Sienna had to watch their backs.

The pair drew to a stop before the dais, but the two occupants had already descended and were standing on floor-level, waiting to greet the arriving siblings.

Lyra held out her hands. "Ah, Lyandr, my boy. You're the very image of your dear father. I can't tell you how pleased I am to see you." Logan leaned in for the hug the woman appeared intent on giving. When she finally did release him, Logan was almost certain she was going to ignore Sienna. Or perhaps wave her away. Because, for the briefest moment, Lyra had given Sienna an odd glance.

Then Lyra turned red and cleared her throat. "I do apologize, Synestra. I fear I have become far too used to treating Your Majesty as someone in the service of the royal family." Lyra bowed and remained there as she said, "If you wish to serve a suitable punishment upon me, General Vyrian will advise what options you have to select from."

Sienna's mouth had dropped open, and she was shaking her head as she stared at her aunt. "I...punishment?"

"Yes, my dear. I have treated you to one of the highest insults. I will happily take the punishment. And in fact, I quite likely do deserve a lot more for the years during which I was rude to you."

Sienna finally found her breath and stepped toward their aunt, grabbing her hands and forcing the older woman to straighten. "Aunt Lyra, please. There's no need for punishment. This is nonsense."

Lyra shook her head and refused to look up. "There may well be. I was a real bitch toward you, Your Majesty."

Logan let out a choked laugh, though he managed to turn it into a strangled cough.

Sienna shook her head again. "Come now, Aunt Lyra. This is ridiculous. What's gotten into you? We do need to stop this. You can't keep apologizing for the past. You had no idea who I was."

Lyra hesitated for a moment, then nodded and straightened at last, though her cheeks were still pink. Logan cleared his throat. "I'm assuming such problems could be avoided in future merely by refraining from being a bitch to anyone at all, don't you think?" asked Logan softly. The general's head snapped up, the old man struggling to control the grin on his face as he met Logan's eyes.

Meanwhile, Lyra was nodding and smiling. "That is very true. I shall endeavor to adhere to those rules, Sire."

I'm not sure I like Aunt Lyra in this subservient from. She's making me uncomfortable with all this groveling. Especially when she's never really been unkind to me. Not in any way to justify her constant apologies.

Logan grunted, a little taken aback at the sound of Sienna's voice in his head. *A little warning would be good before you jump into my head.*

What? Did you expect me to knock?

Logan swallowed the urge to laugh again, glad when the old general stepped forward for his introduction. "I'm Vyrian, Sire. I have had the utmost pleasure in handling the reins for your armies. Though, I too am glad Your Majesty is now here to relieve me of these duties."

Logan raised a hand as he smiled at the older man. "I'm sure you've been doing a fine job, Great Uncle, and I don't think it's wise to rush into things. Especially not before you show me the ropes."

Vyrian nodded slowly, though his gray eyes turned a pale silver and his expression grew wearier—if that were possible. Logan cleared his throat. "Would you be so kind as to remain at my side in an advisory capacity until such time as I feel comfortable to handle things myself? I'm certain I will need the wealth of experience that you've amassed in the years in which you've looked after the armies in my stead."

Old Vyrian nodded, the skin beneath his neck wobbling as the man smiled weakly. "At the risk of appearing rude, would Your Majesty be kind enough to learn fast? I fear I am not long for this world."

Sienna's face darkened, and her amusement at the man's

request disappeared, to be replaced with fear. "Vyrian? That's not something to joke about?"

"Why not my dear? A Drakyr lives a long and happy life. I'm fast approaching my 350th year, and I can't lie that these last years have been good to me. The death of your dear mother had ramifications that were more than any of us had expected."

Sienna patted the man's arm, the gentle touch drawing a smile from the old general. "We'll learn fast, Uncle. I promise."

The old general smiled down at Sienna, his affection for Logan's sister obvious in the man's eyes. Then Vyrian straightened as he looked over at Logan. "Your Majesty, do you wish to tour the barracks and watch the men in training?"

Logan glanced at Sienna and then at Lyra. "Is this the process or is there something more formal that needs to take place?"

Lyra smiled and waved her hand. "There really isn't a process as something like your ascension to the throne has never happened before. There is no precedent so we'll have to play it by ear. There will be an ascension ceremony which will take place in the Stone Palace as soon as you're ready. It's a mere formality at any rate."

Logan glanced at Vyrian and then at Lyra. "Is there time for us to discuss a few concerns. I'd like to be briefed on the political atmosphere—from what Sienna has said, I believe there are elements of concern?"

Lyra blinked and then glanced over at Vyrian before letting out a slow sigh. "Uncle, I do believe you've been right all along." Then the short, elegant blonde let out a soft growl and stamped her foot. "Merlin's balls. The Azure Lakes!"

Logan and Sienna exchanged glances, first of concern and then of amusement as the pieces fell into place.

"Well, my dear. You've always been a little too confident. Let this be a lesson to you," Vyrian smirked and winked at Sienna before saying, "I'm assuming you'll arrange delivery of the painting by tonight?"

Lyra paled, then reddened in two spots on the crest of her cheeks. "Of course, I will, Uncle. I'm a woman of my word."

Vyrian inclined his head, though his smile still lingered. Then Lyra brightened as she strode over to the old man and tucked her hand into the crook of his elbow. "Now, dearest Uncle, might I inquire as to the distribution of your possessions when you do depart the mortal realm? Could I perhaps request to be named in your legacy as the recipient of The Azure Lakes?"

"And why would I do that, Lyra?" asked the old man as he led his niece toward a set of double doors along the back wall of the Throne Room.

Lyra glanced up at the old man, an eyebrow arching in shock. "You wish to leave the Lakes to Kylin?"

Vyrian harrumphed as the pair strode inside a small meeting room. "Point taken, girl. Perhaps we ought to cancel the delivery. Though it's still mine until I breathe my last."

Lyra narrowed her eyes at the old general, then let out a breath. "Agreed. You strike a hard bargain, you old badger."

"It's in the blood, child." The general smirked and led his niece to a chair at the head of the table. It appeared that even the old man was moving out of habit. But Lyra paused and patted the man's hand.

"General Vyrian, you may lead Lyandr of the House of Yl, Ruler of the Armies of Drakys, to his rightful seat at the head of the War Table."

Woah, now that's a bit of formality right there, said Sienna. *Lyra definitely has the art of regalspeak perfected.*

One would hope so considering she's had her butt on a throne for two decades, replied Logan.

Good point, brother.

CHAPTER 8

KAI

I knocked lightly on the door—and having received no response—I opened it and slipped inside the shadowed room. Here too the drapes had been drawn, but not enough that I was unable to see the proof of what my mother had gone through at the lab.

I stared at her naked back, her skin—what little I was able to still see—was a soft cream, not too different from my own. I kept staring, unable to look away, breath caught in my throat like a living thing, slick-feathered, sharp-clawed, and desperately struggling to escape.

I forced my limbs to move, still in a state of disbelief, as if I existed in an alternate reality, one in which every breath had been turned into something horrible, something so macabre that the malevolent stench of evil hung thick in the air, either feeding the thing that was lodged within my throat, or perhaps even being it.

Mom shifted as she positioned her arms beneath her head. Her breathing, though, remained long and even. I stiffened, thinking it was best not to disturb her, especially when she was actually sleeping—unlike me.

But, just as I took a step away, Mom lifted her head and twisted her neck to look over her shoulder at me.

Her smile was weak, and yet it was filled with a depth of strength that sent a bolt of relief straight to my heart. She was hurt, damaged, physically battered, and bruised, but whatever they'd done to Celeste Odel, they were not able to break her spirit.

Now, *this* was my mother, The Hunter.

I let out that trapped breath—the thing with its wings and claws and darkness evaporating into nothing more than a languid puff of warmth—and I walked over to the side of the bed, studying the destruction of her back with dead eyes.

The sight of her wounds fueled a simmering heat in my veins as I blinked away the sting of grief and swallowed against that stubborn fluttering darkness which had returned so swiftly.

Experiments.

Research.

In the name of their research, the scientists had used electric shock as either a form of torture or as part of tolerance tests. I was merely guessing though, but the layering of bruises told a tale of almost daily torture, the older ones scarred over and wrinkled and shiny in patches, the energy having destroyed the cells of Mom's skin.

Then there were the patches of missing skin, neat little quarter-sized circles where epidermis and a layer of flesh had been excised with precision from random areas of her back.

The room was thick with silence, thicker still as seconds passed and shadows crept deeper, as dark anger and black grief seeped from our spirits to join with the shredded darkness, enveloping us.

Suffocating us.

I took a shuddering breath, lungs clenching in admonition for having forgotten to inhale.

But what was breathing in the face of the agony Mom had endured?

I shook my head and climbed up on the bed, performing a careful balancing act as I snuck under the covers and slid down beside her. As I lowered my head, I found it almost magically cushioned by the softness of a pillow.

Mom shifted the down-filled pillow, so it fit snug against my shoulder, just the way I liked it, and then smiled as I sank against it and relaxed.

We lay there for a few moments, as the shadows crept further, as the darkness deepened around us, as the pain seemed to fade away, dark wings taking flight so gently that only the soft rush against your cheeks told you of its surreptitious departure.

Just being close to Mom brought a sense of peace to my soul and I took a slow breath—still careful to keep it even and controlled. Green eyes stared into a mirror, dark curls obscured foreheads and cheeks, full lips thinned, bitten between teeth to halt...what? Pulses of pain? I'm sorry's?

I blinked.

Mom blinked.

And then she said, "Thank you for saving me, honey." Her whispered words wafted over me, but the warmth of them faded as they struck my ears.

I shook my head and looked away. "We didn't come to save you, Mom. I got myself abducted, remember?" I said, my tone sharp with guilt, hollow with the mocking weight of failure.

Mom smiled, sadness and pride shimmering in her green eyes, echoing in the gentle curve of her lips. "You still did everything you could to get me out, Kai. For that, I am so thankful," she said, her words no more than a whisper as she reached out to tuck a lock of hair around my ear.

I pursed my lips. "And for that, you have to thank Mel. She's been through a fair bit in order to get you to safety."

Mom nodded. “I’m glad I was there to see that. That girl is an amazing asset.”

“Spoken like a true agent of espionage.”

“I’m afraid my days of agenting and hunting are probably over.”

“Why? You’re recovering. Dad said you just need time and you’ll be physically healthy soon enough.”

Mom grinned. “Physically healthy? Now, what is going on in that man’s mind?”

I forgot about the pain and rolled my eyes. “Mom! If anyone’s got a dirty mind, it’s you. Poor man speaking from the position of your doctor and all you can think of is hanky-panky.” Then I gave an exaggerated shudder. “Ugh, got any bleach around? I need to rinse my brain to get that thought out of my mind.”

Mom chuckled, the sound rumbling through the mattress and into my bones. I shifted and pulled the covers up over my shoulder, snuggling closer to Mom’s shoulder.

“Do you need to be exposed like this? Do the wounds hurt?” I asked, giving Mom’s bare back a quick glance.

Mom shook her head. “No. I had to wait ten minutes until the ointment dried. It’s just gone twenty...think I fell asleep.”

“Okay if I pull the covers up over you?”

Mom nodded and turned toward me as I pulled the soft duvet over her. As she moved, I caught a glimpse of more bare flesh and winced before tucking the covers tightly against her neck. “Geez, Mom. What’s with the boob-show? No wonder the man is thinking about physical well-being. You’re languishing around here all day with nothing but a sheet between the two of you.”

Mom laughed softly. “Yes, it’s actually a wonder that he hasn’t had his way with me already.”

“Mom?! Really?” I said, my voice cracking on an indignant shriek.

Sometimes I had to wonder if my parents were so openly affectionate around me more because they knew they’d get a horrified reaction than because they believed in the benefit of PDAs for raising a well-rounded child.

I snorted. "Why don't you try to get yourself healthy first, okay? Or do I have to go dig out my old chastity belt for you?"

Mom's eyes widened. "Chastity belt?" she asked in a low, horrified, and somewhat affronted tone.

I nodded soberly. "Yes. When I was fourteen, Dad thought it was well within his rights as a single father to broach the topic of a chastity belt."

Mom's eyes were still wide. "I can't believe he'd even do such a thing? What was Ivy doing while this nonsense was going on?"

"Oh, Ivy? Well, *she* was helping make it."

"What?" Mom yelped, lifting herself up on her elbow.

I choked, turned it into a cough then blocked my eyes with one hand. "Boobs," I said, waving my free hand at her bare torso where the covers had slipped from her body with her movements. "Ugh, seriously. Put those things away before you poke someone's eye out."

Mom burst into laughter then let out a soft moan. "Oh, Kai. Trust you to say the strangest things."

"Well...at least they're amusing, right?" Mom nodded and tried to dial down her grin. When she failed, I smirked and said, "Okay, let's make a deal. You keep the girls under control, and I'll tell you the rest of the chastity belt story."

Mom lifted an eyebrow. "Deal. And once we're done, that man's going to get a piece of my mind."

I hid a smile and said, "Well, Dad proposed the CB—as Greer and Iain began to call it—and I was all 'Categorically no.' I refused to discuss it even when he said I could go out as often as I wanted, go on as many dates as I wanted, just as long as I wore the thing."

The details of the incident returned full force, and I had to admit that though I'd believed all my memories of being raised by my father had lacked his emotional contribution, I hadn't been entirely correct.

I recalled the amusement and tender affection in his eyes as he'd teased me, the smile as he'd touched my shoulder when I'd simply stood there, still as a statue, his hand-drawn plans for the chastity belt hanging loosely from my fingertips.

I laughed. "So, Grams lent Dad a hand and they presented me with the finished product. They even used an old hatbox of Grams' as a gift box. When I took it out of the box, I was more than horrified. It looked like it was made of gold." I wrinkled up my nose.

Mom groaned. "Tell me you didn't complain about the color."

I nodded. "My exact words were 'I suppose I have no choice but to wear this thing, but did you have to choose gold? It's so...trashy.'"

CHAPTER 9

KAI

Mom choked on her laughter, one hand over her mouth as her eyes glistened with tears of amusement.

I shook my head, well aware that she'd predicted my reaction even when she hadn't even been there. I cleared my throat, and my expression sobered. "I was standing there, beside the table, CB hanging from my hand, all gold and shiny. I was staring at Dad when I said that, and his reaction was just epic...he burst out laughing and had to sit back down or I swear he would have fallen.

"Maybe it was the way I said the word 'Trashy'? I dunno. But he was shaking his head and laughing, Grams was laughing just as hard. I was only glad that Iain and Greer hadn't been there for the presentation. And then Dad straightened and eventually sobered. And he tilted his head and asked me if I was still going to wear it if it was gold, or did he have to order in a different color. And I hesitated. But seriously, I couldn't see a way out of it. And Dad didn't really know that I had no reason to be afraid for my virtue. Few boys ever showed interest in me. The boys like their girls compliant and submissive. That wasn't me. And I was Alpha, so there was that. I should have realized long before that Dad was playing a joke. But I fell for it. Why wouldn't I have?"

"And your answer?"

I shrugged. "I said the color really didn't matter because it wasn't as if any boy was going to look under my clothes."

"And Dad?"

"He asked why, and I said because if anyone tried, I'd break their hands, but also that nobody would because I was stronger than them and I was Alpha. And that nobody asked me out to parties or dates anyway because I don't get up to all the wrong stuff. And that being the Alpha's daughter meant that there was always the possibility that I'd tell on the kids if they did something wrong, so they were just protecting their turf."

"Bet your father was at a loss for words," said Mom as she positioned herself with her head on her own pillow.

"Nope. In fact, he was very serious when he sat on the edge of the table so we could look at each other eye to eye. And he said 'I have never been prouder of you, Kailin. Always remember that strength of body is an asset but strength of mind is its own virtue. Never compromise on that. Age takes away strength of body, and loss and grief and failure can eat away at strength of spirit, but nothing can affect the strength of your mind. Not unless you allow it. You are your mother's daughter. Never forget it.' And then he walked out and took the CB with him."

Mom was silent then, clearly more at a loss for words than she'd predicted her husband to be. Then she let out a breath. "I'm impressed. I knew he had it in him though...I quite like being right."

I made a face. "I never quite understood what he meant by me being your daughter. Not until now. All those years of being brittle, unbending stubborn Kai, and I never saw what he'd been hiding from me all that time."

"And what was he hiding, honey?"

"His love for me. He showed it, like in the CB disaster. But mostly he was aloof and stern. Grew worse the older I got."

"And the more you acted up?"

"No. The more I looked like you," I said with a wry apologetic smile. Mom's face lost the glow of pride for the rebel her daughter had been, and I felt the loss of that smile keenly. I shifted closer. "I'm sorry. I didn't mean to hurt you by saying that. Maybe I shouldn't have."

"No, honey," Mom whispered in the narrow space between our faces as we stared at each other. "It is the truth. You do not hide from the truth, nor should you hide the truth from those you love and who love you back."

"Even when the truth hurts? When the truth can destroy?" I asked, tucking my hand beneath the pillow and scooching forward, dimly aware as Mom wrapped her arm around my shoulders.

I'd meant to ask how she was feeling, if she was recovering. I'd meant to ask her what had happened on her trip to Galakris in search of the Krisl flower for Dad's work on the drug for Lily. How she'd ended up caught by the researchers. But I didn't ask those questions for fear of spoiling the moment.

How long had it been since we'd last cuddled, since my mother had last held me in her arms to give comfort, to envelop me within her care and her love? I couldn't recall.

Not so long ago, a life lived walking the path of a steely cold indifference to this woman, had been all I'd known. I'd lived and breathed, and hated her, the mother who had left me all those years ago, the mother who'd abandoned me, left me to defend myself, my heart, and my mother herself from the taunts of those who would call themselves my friends. Children were cruel in their innocence, their unknowing use of the swords of words that cut you to the quick, that wound deep and leave behind scars thick and wrinkled.

And even in the well of her abandonment, I'd bloodied noses, and snapped a bone or two in defense of the woman who had left me alone, who when she'd left had taken with her the love of my father.

But I'd learned mere months ago, that nothing in my past was as it seemed. The panther walker mother who'd abandoned her children had turned out to be a human mage hunter, a panther alpha teen had turned out to be a half-breed, that abandonment had been revealed as an act of protection and deep sacrifice. And that father who hadn't shown the love I'd craved had in fact loved deeper than I'd even thought was possible.

And the mother?

She'd shown herself for who she truly was—a strong independent woman, a woman who would sacrifice anything, her life, even her marriage, in order to protect her family, a dangerous, skilled demon hunter and supernatural operative.

That was my mother.

CHAPTER 10

LOGAN

Vyrian raised a hand and waggled it toward Logan—who now had little choice but to meet the old man at the large chair taking pride of place at the far end of the dark wood table.

Logan had paid little attention to the surface of the grandly named War Table until now, but as he stood in place—and before he moved to lower himself into the chair—he found himself transfixed, in awe as he studied the undulating curves of a landscape depicted in carved wood so well that harsh mountains and smooth planes and dangerous seas were all brought to life in the polished wood.

"This is?" Logan pointed at the mountains, rivers, and settlements, all depicting an area which appeared more vast than all the continents of the EarthWorld, oceans included.

Vyrian coughed, then cleared his throat as he waved a hand across the table. "This is the lands of Drakys. It's interpretive in some locations, where mortals have feared to explore, but ninety percent of the realm has been mapped. Which is what we see here." Vyrian aimed a gnarled forefinger at a range of dangerously sharp-peaked mountains. "That's the Black Mountains, and this is the river bend where the Black Lily flowers caused so much trouble. Within these mountains are the Stone Palace and the Hollow of the Life's Blood temple where our twin rulers undergo the Rite of Ascension."

Logan nodded as he studied the lands, his mind already turning over defense strategies. "I'm very interested in what systems and infrastructure we have to ensure security. In terms of enemies...do we have many within the realm?" Logan asked, bringing the conversation around to the question he'd wanted to pose to Vyrian and Lyra.

Sienna's almost imperceptible nod of approval eased Logan's tensions somewhat.

Then Lyra cleared her throat. "Currently two elements are of a concern, other than Andyr Dar-ys, who I don't for one second believe is done with us." Lyra paused and took a seat beside Sienna who'd claimed the spot on the other end of the large table. "First point of concern is the Venerable Fathers of Truth."

Sienna snickered, and Lyra nodded at the sound, though the regent's face still retained the hard, angry expression. "Yes, they are a rather presumptuous lot. Headed by Powys, the Don of the House of Krt, they have slowly been gaining strength by garnering support from men who feel threatened by the matriarchal rule of our realm. There is a strong argument for toppling the old laws and replacing them with either a Kingship held by the General, or eliminating Royal rule altogether and replacing it with a formal council rule with Powys at its helm. The latter is in a similar vein as what is being argued by our second faction, that of the Society for the Equal Governance of All Drakys. Were I to be given a choice, I'd choose the Egads as the more palatable of our two oppositions."

Logan suppressed the temptation to grin at his aunt's mocking title. He cleared his throat. "And the Fathers? What are they proposing that can be considered worse than equal government?" asked Logan. Having been raised in a realm which functioned mostly on a government rule, he could understand the attraction, but he was careful to ensure his thoughts remained unrevealed.

"The key tenets of the order question a woman's right and ability to rule," said Lyra, her tone strained. "Their claim is that the core duty of a woman is to bear her husband offspring. As such, she is not in any position to hold office, or to perform male-centric roles which include holding any type of job outside of that of a nurturing female. Roles available to women would be as teachers, cooks, and food-related jobs like preserving, canning, etc., dressmakers, cleaners, harvesters. And even then, they will not be allowed to own a business, and the roles must be overseen by a superior male."

"Wow," said Sienna as she scratched her head. "This is so much worse than I'd thought."

Lyra nodded, her complexion having taken on a gray tinge. "The irony is that the Fathers appear to have the intensely passionate support of the women of their households. Which in and of itself is rather strange. I can't quite understand how anyone in a position of respect and authority would forgo that for complete subjugation. Equality, I'd understand, but that in itself is ridiculous because we have always been an equal society."

"Is Drakys not a matriarchal-run realm?" Logan asked. Sienna had explained a little of the details to him, but he wanted to hear what Lyra had to say.

Lyra opened her mouth to reply, but Vyrian cut her off. "Ever since our people can remember, the realm has thrived under the guiding hand of the Rule of the Entwined Dragons. The title of Queen given to the female sibling has never detracted from the equality of that rule. I believe it harks back to a time when the husband of the queen would receive the title of King. Wars were fought over a mere right to title, and the laws were amended. A common enough question as to why the male is referred to as general instead of King, also draws on a time long past when the twin rulers were referred to as King and Queen, but the naming held distinct incestuous connotations—which the people were keen to dispel."

Logan made a face. "I take it there is some historical truth to that?"

"It's a little complicated, but to make it brief, Drakys is not the only Realm of Dragons. There are three other realms, of which one, Drogyr, has a history rife with incestuous pairings, and of course the desire for conquest. Ancient archives show a tyrannical rule over Drakys for two centuries, until the people of this realm rose up and took back what was theirs. A result of the uprising was the joint rule of the Royal twins during which both bear equal power in managing the realm and its people."

"And the Fathers?" asked Logan, scowling as he voiced his suspicion. "Can I ask if any of the families loyal to the Fathers originally rejected the new law?"

"Very astute. He has a very sharp mind, much like his sister," Vyrian said almost to himself.

Lyra glanced over at the old man, hesitated, then dragged her attention back to Logan. "Two of the leading proponents of the Fathers belong to families originally from Drogyr. Granted it's a history that goes back more than two centuries, but one has to wonder if their old ways have been perpetuated behind closed doors all these centuries."

Logan nodded slowly. "And you expect some opposition before our ascension? Would it not benefit the Fathers and even the Equals, to thwart the proceedings? Attempt a coup perhaps?"

Vyrian nodded. "There has been talk, which is why we wanted to suggest a private ascension ceremony as soon as possible. Then we notify the realm and proceed with the celebrations after the rites are completed. Overthrowing an already ascended ruler isn't an easy sell, even to the most rebellious of our people."

"Consequences?" asked Logan.

Lyra shrugged, and Vyrian merely pursed his lips in reply.

"Other than infuriating anyone who had planned on crashing the party and performing a more dramatic takeover?" the regent said. "We at least thwart any attempts to sabotage the ascension ceremony. And should anyone wish to object, you and the queen can address those objections as you see fit, and in a manner less inclined to spill blood."

Logan paused, the urgency of the state of affairs within the Drakys realm had become startlingly clear during Lyra's monologue. "What's been happening over the last few weeks while I've been recovering? Why has no one attempted a coup in our absence?"

"You haven't been absent." Lyra shook her head and gave a sneaky smile. "Synestra has been here regularly, which has given the council and the citizens the impression that your arrival is imminent."

Logan glanced over at his sister, unsure if he ought to be annoyed that she'd delayed his arrival or glad that she'd covered for him.

Before he could question Sienna, his aunt cut him off. "There is one thing of utmost importance."

Both Logan and Sienna focused on their aunt. Her profile was sharp, her cheeks hollow, almost gaunt.

Lyra cleared her throat. "It's about your Drakyrin. After the Rite of Ascension—and during the Grand Procession—the new rulers must bless the realm with their winged flight. You will travel together to visit the noble houses across the realm. And you do need to be ready, and be strong enough to handle such a long journey."

Logan had been expecting this, but having heard the words, his gut twisted. Though he was tempted to look at Sienna, he was afraid the consternation he felt would be revealed in his face, so he merely nodded.

But Lyra appeared oblivious to Logan's discomfort. "You shouldn't worry too much," she said with an airy wave of her gold-tipped fingers. "I just wanted to warn you so you can practice and build up your stamina as soon as possible."

Logan scratched his chin and then nodded. "So what's our agenda? Secret ascension, informal introductions to the realm, learning the ropes and then formal announcement and realm blessing."

"In a nutshell, yes." Lyra tapped one of her fingernails on the dark wood, an inch away from a carving of a volcano spewing red lava. "Vyrian and I will prepare for the ascension. We can fly out at daybreak, if that's suitable?"

Logan shared a glance with Sienna before nodding, ensuring his expression remained sober as Sienna replied, "Daybreak is fine. Since the ceremony is private, do we care about the regalia and the Royal armor?"

Lyra pursed her lips. "I suppose it really doesn't matter. Dress appropriately. Just none of those hideous EarthWorld blue jeans atrocities. I'll bring along a trunk of the more adjustable armor items in case you do want it to feel a little special." Lyra smiled at Sienna and then at Logan before getting to her feet. "Come, Synestra. We have a meeting with the northern ambassadors about an adjustment in trade goods. Something about low crop-yield due to flooding and they have something else to offer as a substitute."

Logan glanced up at the two women as they rose from their chairs. At that moment, Lyra looked over at him. "After the introduction, you will be included in these meetings when you're available. But as for now, let's keep up the pretense that you haven't yet arrived. I'm sure the two of you can discuss things," she smirked as she tapped a finger to her temple, "before Synestra makes any big decisions."

Then Logan's aunt was striding out of the room, his sister in tow.

I'd sure hate to be on her bad side, he said to Sienna.

Yeah. Trust me, it's not at all pleasant.

CHAPTER 11

KAI

"It was a setup," came Mom's voice, drifting toward me on a haze of slumber.

I'd fallen asleep—if but for an instant—and perhaps Mom had too. From the pull on my limbs and my lids, I suspected we'd slept for at least a few minutes.

I cleared my throat and burrowed deeper under the covers, aware that the robe had twisted almost halfway around my body, the knot of the belt currently digging into my hip.

Beside me, Mom was probably still seriously lacking clothes, unless she'd snuck out of the bed during my short nap and found herself something to wear. I wasn't planning to check.

I swallowed before saying, "What was a setup?" The question scraped across a parched throat, and I blinked and looked at Mom, aware my eyes felt just as dry and gritty.

She gave a soft cough, cupping her hand over her mouth in one of her reflexive proper-behavior-for-classy-women actions. Shifting her head, to look at me, she said, "My appointment in Galakris with the herb merchant for the Krisl stamens. I walked right into a trap, clueless and unsuspecting." Mom's eyes hardened to icy emerald chips, and her jaw tightened as she looked away, focusing on the corner of the room. "I dropped my guard. I was distracted. And when you don't keep your head in the game, you open yourself up to potential problems."

"You can't be so hard on yourself, Mom. You've been running and hiding for so long. You weren't even able to be with us for Greer's funeral. And then you come home to discover your family in danger and Lily needing a deeper strength of the Synthe?"

As I spoke, it struck me that for the first time, it was me that was justifying her actions, or perhaps—in the lingo of my abandonment-anger phase—making excuses for her.

Mom shook her head and turned her head to face me. "I should have been careful. I didn't follow protocol. I didn't do the recon. I walked into a trap, blind and clueless. And I got myself caught." The rock-hard edge in her voice spoke volumes.

I exhaled slowly. "You're forgetting something that's a little more important than you being distracted."

"Which is?"

"The fact that it was a trap," I said, lifting one eyebrow. Mom's quizzical look made me roll my eyes. "They went to all that trouble to set up an ambush and abduct you—from a demon realm of all places. How many questions does that raise? How did they know you were going to Galakris? Who is feeding Division 7 information on your movements?"

Mom was silent for a moment, and then she blinked. "I've known Ryzva for more than a decade. He was the last person I'd have expected to turn on me. We've traded a number of favors over the years, probably owe each other our lives. I just never expected to have to be suspicious of a friend."

"Well, in reference to my most recent experiences with ShapeChangers, I have it on good authority that it's entirely possible for anyone to plant one of them within your environment and be able to pull the wool over your eyes without much trouble. These ShapeChangers...they're way too good. It's just uncanny how accurate they are." I shuddered, and there was nothing mocking about the movement.

After seeing Mom—or rather the person I'd believed was Mom—in the lab, and having been convinced it was her, the horror I'd experienced at my discovery that I'd been duped by a ShapeChanger hadn't lessened with time even one iota. And had I not stumbled on a clue from the more intricate details of Mom's past, and our family history, I'd never have been the wiser.

And then, Cassandra's shifting into my face and form, had been a second reminder. I knew well enough how easy it was to be fooled. I snorted. "If I hadn't known I was me, *I* would have been fooled. That's how good Cassie was. And you know, I'm pretty sure she'd have fooled you and Dad as well. So, I think it's time for you to add a ShapeChanger as a possibility. Your friend Ryzva may well still be loyal to you."

"Or he may well be dead." Mom's expression was devoid of amusement as she considered—seemingly for the first time—that her friend may have been compromised and could have been murdered in order to gain access to her.

I let out a soft sigh. "So, any thoughts on who could have snitched? Who knew you were going to Galakris?"

Mom shook her head. "We'd have to perform a proper investigation. A lot of people were aware. Everyone under this roof, for starters. Then the circle widens with everyone they would have come into contact with, who we all trusted enough to confide in. And the net would need to be cast even wider if I were to consider Sentinel or the Elite, the agents and handlers too."

I let out a low grunt. "Fabulous. Well, let me know when you begin your investigation. I'll be busy that day."

Mom smirked and shook her head, the movement squishing her cheek into the pillow for a moment. "I'm not sure there is any point."

I scowled. "We need to know how deep Division 7 has their claws into the paranormal community, investigative agencies or not." Then I paused. "How sure are we that this is Division 7? What confirmation do we have that would have convinced the Chief?"

"The lab databases, though simplistic in terms of programming, were extensive, and the forensics people found the purchase details for the batches the facility bought. The crumbs were followed all the way to a shell company that was traced back to another shell, all the way to Division 7's Washington Branch."

"That's quite the investigative trip," I murmured as she paused to take a breath.

Mom nodded. "Either way, that's where the trail ended. Even if we can stick a label on it, Division 7 itself doesn't truly exist. Properties, leases, bank accounts, they all lead to shadow corporations and shell companies and nameless agents working for nameless handlers who answer to more nameless and untraceable people who give the orders. I've been working at this for too long," Mom said with a deep sigh as she rubbed her forehead, fingers pressing hard at the curved bones above her eyes. "They're able to lead you around in endless circles. You have no idea how many times I've given up and abandoned the search when the trail went dead. And how do you think we catch a break? When *they* pop their heads up again. Not because *we've* actually done anything constructive. It feels a lot like we're playing fetch, with Div 7 throwing the ball, and we're doing a bang-up impression of Fido."

I felt her frustration like a living breathing thing, and I shared the taut tension that coiled deep within her. "How long have you been on their trail?" I asked, aware that this was the first time we spoke of her work, her missions, the things she did behind the veil of lies and shadows and secrets.

And for the briefest moment, I wondered if she'd blanket the truth with warm smiles and evasions.

But she didn't.

Her lips thinned into a fine line as shadows played on the curves and hollows of her face. The sun was lower in the sky now, the day filling with the promise of sunset. My first night during which I truly faced my existence.

In which I stared, eyes wide open at my mortality, as there were things I myself had not yet revealed, to Chief Murdoch, to Chloe who had gotten so, so close to seeing it while she'd helped me heal, to my father whose cursory physical hadn't been sufficient but who'd demanded I head straight to the Elite Medcenter for an MRI—just in case.

Those had been his words—just in case.

Had he suspected?

I pushed the thoughts back down deep into the darkness that had settled within the very center of my being. The scales had been tipped, but I wasn't yet ready to take stock.

For now, I focused on Mom, whose low honeyed tones filtered through the web of my inner turmoil, forcing me to focus as she said, "When I first saw the signs of your abilities, I didn't think much of it. I'm a mage, so genetically there was nothing to be surprised about. But I'd earned a reputation through my years of working as a hunter, a reputation that I was hardly able to shake. And soon those who observed from the sidelines began to make connections between my power—the golden glow which I'm sure you already know all too well—and I soon became known throughout the DarkWorld as The Hunter. Uppercase with the requisite inflections when spoken out loud.

"People talked of The Hunter with a sense of reverence, and I found myself a tiny bit proud, believing they respected me and what I'd been doing for the people across the realms. I'd tracked and hunted demons, eliminated terrible threats, infiltrated factions whose aims were destruction and war. I'd made alliances and enemies too, but that was par for the course.

"Over the years my power only grew, and I was very much in demand. I was known for being swift, silent, and deadly so I could have sold my soul to the highest bidder, but I didn't. I worked for the Supreme High Council and by virtue of that, solely for Sentinel. And now, more recently, for The Elite. I suppose I may not have drawn attention so quickly had I not married and had children."

"Did your power fade when you were pregnant?"

"Not at all. It was Celeste who faded. My focus shifted to my family, first to my son and then my daughters, though I did work in between. I very much believed in being close to my babies in their early years, and now I treasure those times so much."

"Did you work at all while pregnant? Somehow I can't picture you going into confinement and knitting and sewing and doing...what's that thing where you make those tiny crosses that form a larger picture?"

"Cross-stitch," Mom supplied, affecting an elegant half-bodied shudder what with the fact that she was lying on her side.

Still, her disgust shone in her eyes, and I shook my head. "That bad, huh?"

"Yup. And yes, you are right. I worked until I began to show, until the Paranormal Medical Board advised that strenuous activities could harm the baby."

"Paranormal Medical board?" I frowned, having never heard of such a board.

Mom nodded. "To put it bluntly, they presided over cross-breed births. In Ancient times, they were a sort of judge and jury, the way humans used to treat unwed mothers, and often with the same result."

"Huh? You mean the babies would be taken away from the mothers?"

"Intermarriage in those times was officially frowned upon,

and unofficially taboo. Hence the board which was instituted for the express purpose of overseeing births and separating mother from child and in separating the couple. There were ancient horror stories of mothers who were killed for returning to their lovers, and parents sentenced to death for searching out their babies and stealing them back."

"And here I thought those were fables."

CHAPTER 12

KAI

Mom chuckled. "Even in the human world, fables have a thread or two of truth in them. Thankfully, in our case, the Board had evolved to a more scientifically acceptable outlook. They were doctors and scientists from every paranormal realm and across all species. Their job was to study the genetic combinations, predict possible problems and oversee the pregnancy all the way to a healthy birth.

"Mothers are assigned a Medical Unit comprised of doctors with knowledge of her species and powers, and of those of the father. They draw on historical cases—as well as the individual medical histories of the parents—to come to conclusions that ensure the health and wellbeing of both mother and child."

"Sounds intense," I supplied, only as a means to fill the long, tense pause in which Mom's gaze shifted to something unseeing where I knew she was held within the grip of some past memory filled with pain.

Mom blinked, and her expression coalesced as she focused on me. "It *was* intense. Especially with shifter births. In ancient times, shifters transformed into their animal form and gave birth to babies who would remain in animal form until their teen years. It was the other way around to how things are today; affected by centuries of interbreeding, the human form became dominant."

"Maybe it's something in the evolution of the genes though," I said, thinking about Logan. "The Drakyr, the Djinn, the gargoyles, they're all from different realms, and yet they too have a human form and shift after they've grown to a certain age."

"Perhaps you are onto something there. Or perhaps cross-Veil travel may have had some influence on the evolution of the species of the outer realms."

I pursed my lips. "Good point. You may continue."

Mom smirked. "Coming from a fully human mage genetic line, I had little to worry about in terms of my own gene code. Your father though, was a different story."

"He was?" I frowned, my head heating up at the thought of what new revelation Mom was about to drop on my unsuspecting head. "Okay, maybe I'm not all that surprised. Grams is just too hot for an old lady. She's an Immortal, isn't she?"

"Kai, you can calm down. It's not that life-changing." I sighed, relief filtering through me like a warm tide. And then Mom said, "But you're not far off."

"I'm not?"

My eyes narrowed as I studied my mother's face, now certain she was about to tilt my world a little more. I only hoped that whatever revelation she laid before me wouldn't tip the scales too far. I had a number of other things to deal with first.

I pursed my lips as she remained silent, not yet offering a clarification. "Mom?" I said, my tone sharper than I'd intended, but Mom didn't appear offended by my rudeness.

She blinked and gave a half nod—a tiny jerk of her head that I'd have missed had I blinked—and said, "Sorry honey, it's been so long since I've delved into these memories. It feels like I'm crawling around in a dusty attic and opening boxes filled with pieces of my past."

I snorted. "If your mind is like a dusty attic then I guess there won't be much hope for me in my old age."

Mom rolled her eyes and let out a weary sigh. "You watch it, young lady. I brought you into this world. Means I can also take you out. Mother's rights," she said with a sniff.

I grunted. "Nice. In case you didn't know, infanticide doesn't look so good on one's CV," I said curtly, somewhat offended at the thought of being taken out by my own mother.

"You're not an infant."

I huffed, wishing I had my phone on me. Why could I not recall the right word? The harder I tried, the more the word evaded me. In the end, I had to admit that perhaps I hadn't known the right term in the first place.

My expression dark, I said, "Childicide, then. Or Kailinicide. There, that sounds more accurate. And anyway," I said airily and waved a hand at Mom. "That's splitting hairs, and you know it."

Mom smirked and said, "Right, getting back to what I was saying, Ivy isn't a purebred Walker, though she did inherit a very strong Alpha Walker DNA. The other half of her genetic contribution wasn't Immortal, but it may as well have been."

I rolled my eyes and sighed heavily, as I'd imagine Atlas would sigh when one day the weight of the world was taken from his tired shoulders. Then I said, "Fine. I'll play." I wriggled in place, shifting carefully until I was lying on my back again. "Grams' mother wasn't one of the Immortals, but she contributed DNA that was as good as immortal. So, if you count the species who were long-lived enough to be considered immortal, you end up with two options: Fae and Light Elves."

I tilted my head to meet my mother's eyes, pleased at the smile growing on her lips. "Very good. Want to guess which one?"

I bit the inside of my lip and then shook my head. "Well, she doesn't have the whole pointy-eared thing going on," I said, stroking my ear as if to check for any subtle physical difference. Then I waved a hand at my shoulders and said, "Nor does she have the whole faerie-wing deal, but even both points are a little irrelevant because...yeah...glamor." I pursed my lips and stared Mom down.

At last, she chuckled. "Okay, fine. Grams is half-panther Walker, half-Faerie."

I nodded slowly, impressed that she'd kept that piece of knowledge a secret all these years. "How come she doesn't talk about it?"

Mom shrugged. "I guess it's a past she'd rather not delve into. Her mother was a powerful Fae who broke many rules in order to be with her father. But the pain in the tale is more in what happened to her mother than the fact that she was Fae."

I sighed deeply. "Mom, you have no idea how to tell a story. You've got to work the tension, yes, but those overly long pauses...they totally kill the suspense."

"Brat," said Mom with a light laugh that filled her eyes as she shook her head. "Ivy's mom was taken away. It's quite a dramatic story, likely something that will be told as a fairy tale in years to come. Trieste had eloped, for want of a better word. Her family refused to give their blessing for the marriage even though her father was an Alpha and possessed a senior status high enough for the Fae Courts to treat him with respect.

"But there were other things at play, perhaps political but, it was never made clear. And though Trieste went home with her husband and they were married in a grand ceremony befitting both their stations, the Fae Court's displeasure only increased with time. And then Trieste was with child, which had no doubt been a turning point."

"What? Did they think she'd marry him and get it out of her system?"

"Perhaps. Fae live long, long lives. Both Trieste and Alexander knew their time together would end when he died, and she'd be forced to make a life for herself without him."

"And then as her children grow old and die, she'd need to move on from them too. Man, that's an awful life."

"But it was the life they willingly chose. But, a year after the child—Ivy of course—was born, Trieste's family descended upon the town—"

"Descended," I scoffed, amused at the use of the word. "You make it sound like they flew above the town and lowered themselves onto the ground all over the city."

"Exactly."

"Huh," I said, eyeing my mother in search of even the smallest sparkle of amusement. I found none.

"A whole host of them arrived, swarmed in the air above the alpha's home and then drifted down to the ground, walking the lands of Alexander's family as though they owned the place. Trieste's parents demanded her return, or they would wipe out the entire town."

"And they would have done it? Killed an entire town because of one rogue-Fae Juliet?"

"Of course, they would. When that Juliet is the sole heir to the throne of the Water Fae, they certainly would."

I gasped, eyes wide as I whispered, "Shut the front door!"

Mom giggled at that, then composed herself. "At first, even Trieste didn't believe her family would carry out the threat, But she learned fast how brutal they could be."

I swallowed hard, afraid of what Mom was going to say next, but then heard myself asking, "Who did they kill?"

"They killed a traitor."

I let out a frustrated groan. "Again with the cryptic twists. Although, I have to say I'm intrigued. But, I must add that this would be so much better if it were a novel. The whole tense pause and revelation of a cryptic twist thing works way better on paper." Mom sent me a stern glare, and I took a breath and said, "Shutting up now," before pressing my lips firmly together.

With eyebrows raised, Mom continued, "Trieste was never alone in her decisions, both before she left her family and after she arrived in the EarthWorld. Parts of her family had given her their full support, as well as many of the noble families who'd sworn fealty to her as the future queen. Though I suspect things were a little tense with her father ruling the Water Fae and still knowing he'd have to pass the crown over to her when she came of age."

"Someone warned her that the Fae were coming?"

Even as I spoke the words, I knew I'd guessed correctly.

CHAPTER 13

LOGAN

With Lyra and Sienna gone, the old general sat back and let out a sigh, the sound drawing Logan's attention to Vyrian's bowed shoulders as he stared down at the table.

"Uncle?" asked Logan, tilting his head to inspect the man's face.

Vyrian chuckled. "Don't worry about me, Lyandr. I'm merely a tired old man."

Logan pursed his lips. "Was there nobody else who could have taken on the duties for you?" he asked, his tone insistent.

Vyrian sighed and lifted his gaze as he shook his head. "Not anyone we can trust. There was a long line of people who raised their hands for the role when you and your sister disappeared. But even then it was clear that far too many of those men had intentions other than keeping the seat warm until the heirs were returned to their rightful positions."

Logan frowned. "But isn't the role that of a custodian? Surely they would have known their rights would be limited? Sienna mentioned a joint decision-making process with both custodians as a means of avoiding any wrongdoing."

Vyrian smiled and shook his head. "Any position of power is a temptation. A number of interested parties even went so far as to contest my custody of the role. Two decades of watching one's back gets tiring rather fast."

Logan nodded. "So how do you plan on showing me around without alerting those interested parties of my arrival?"

The general sat back and pursed his lips, eye gleaming. "You shall be the Emissary of the Council of Elders. It will not raise too many eyebrows to know that the Elders wish to ensure all is well here after Elan's attempt to take over. And it's quite likely to reassure the people that Drakys is not being held responsible for the horrible acts the fae prince committed."

Hiding a smile at the old man's delight in his plan, Logan said, "So when do we begin? And where?"

Vyrian nodded and got to his feet, the fabric of his uniform crackling as he straightened. "First, I will give you a short tour of the city, on orders, of course, to assure the Elders that we've strengthened our defenses and have put measures in place to prevent another spy like Elan from weaseling his way into our realm."

Logan followed the old man as he walked stiffly toward the doors. Just before he reached out for the handle, Vyrian looked over his shoulder at Logan. "You will use an assumed name. But not Logan. There are a few ambassadors who were privy to the revelation of your existence. They, of course, believe you are still recovering in the EarthWorld, and I plan to keep it that way."

Logan nodded and took a breath. "How about Jordan? Jordan Cassidy?"

Vyrian smiled and opened the door. "Come, Emissary Cassidy," he said loud enough for a passing couple to hear. "We must show you around the city. I hope you will be able to assure the Elders that we are upholding the Treaty agreements."

The couple faltered in their steps as they glanced over at Logan who inclined his head and gave them a thin smile. The man's bushy brows waggled as he returned the silent greeting, but he kept walking, though the woman spent a little longer studying Logan from head to toe.

Vyrian waved Logan along. "That's Don Esvin and his wife Elira, both supporters of the Fathers. I'd keep an eye on them, though as Emissary they aren't likely to spend too much time on your activities."

The old man proceeded to guide Logan down the long halls and out to a large courtyard where a carriage awaited them, drawn by an unusual creature similar to the eight-legged Sleipnir of Norse myth. The animal's soot-black hide reflected a rouge blush from the strange light of the heavy blood-sun. Another strange to add to his already growing pile of strange.

A guard stood beside the open door and bent to place a stool on the ground as Vyrian approached. He climbed inside, and Logan understood then how much pain the man was in. Vyrian let out a deep sigh of relief as the guard closed the door and the carriage began to move.

"As you can see, my boy," Vyrian wheezed, "my physical strength is fading. I must say your timing was quite perfect."

"I can assure you my timing had little to do with how I would have wanted it. Had I known the truth, I would have come earlier," Logan replied, the truth of his words warring with the portion of his heart held by Kai.

Vyrian slammed a hand into his chest, coughed again and then cleared his throat. "Now tell me how you are feeling. Is that mind of yours well on its way to being whole again? I must confess that the explanation Synestra gave us seemed quite far-fetched at the time, but she's endeavored to educate me on the intricacies of how both of your memories have been manipulated."

Logan pursed his lips as he glanced out the narrow window at the view of the city that flickered on and off like freeze-frames. They passed between tall buildings of white stone, under bridges carved from dark rock, the stone roads twisting this way and that one moment with a view to the towering heights of the palace and the next to the vista of the valley outside the city walls. Such beauty, and he wasn't sure he had the time, or the presence of mind, to enjoy it.

The topic of his memories was one he'd rather have not discussed, but Vyrian had spent two decades looking after Logan's birthright. If anything, Vyrian would be one of the first people to deserve an explanation.

"To be frank, I know only as much as the MindMelder told me. The magic enables them to sift through a person's memories, the way one would flick through a stack of photographs. They are then able to remove the memory, either completely, or by redirection."

"Redirection?" Vyrian frowned.

"Yes. The mage takes the memory away, of perhaps your face when I was young, and attaches it to a different memory, so that when I think back to the day, I will not see you, as a result, my recollection won't include you. But the mage who treated me was deliberate in that she mixed the memories up in such a way that they would be so inconsistent that my mind would question it, and then look for connections on its own."

"So that MindMage left crumbs for you to follow. By that, I'm assuming he did not want his work to be permanent."

Logan nodded, thinking of Darcy, and of her attempts to explain her actions. "That's exactly what *she* did. She performed the memory wipe against her will, and she wanted to ensure that someday I would have my true memories back."

"And now they are," said Vyrian with a smile as the carriage rolled to a bumpy stop. He slid across the seat and was at the door as the guard opened it from the outside.

Logan followed the old man out into the dull sunlight, and found himself in awe of the building before him. The black stone walls of the small house gleamed, reflecting the sun's red-tinged rays in hundreds of faceted shimmers. A house built with obsidian was something Logan had never considered as possible. But then, being a dragon shifter had been just as much of an impossibility to him, so he wasn't about to question his eyes.

Old Vyrian closed in on the double doors, pushed them open, and waved Logan inside. "Welcome to my humble home."

Logan entered and found himself inside a small, sparsely furnished room, a stark contrast to the glittering beauty of the exterior of the home. A large table sat against the far wall, where the light from the windows ran a coppery track upon the rough wood surface.

Vyrian headed for the seat behind the table, and then paused to meet Logan's gaze. "I declined to use the official General's Quarters as my base, but given that the role is truly yours, I ought not to sit in that seat."

"General Vyrian, as Emissary, I cannot," Logan replied with a soft smile, grinning wider as the old man guffawed then thumped his chest again.

Logan took one of the stools in front of the table, and took his time studying the room while Vyrian shuffled over to take his seat. The windows were bare of drapery, the mantelpiece over the fireplace holding not a single ornament or sentimental object.

The floors were bare, uncarpeted, and unvarnished, as was every piece of furniture in the room, the only object of any interest being a set of black armor standing silently in one corner.

Vyrian shuffled in his seat and leaned toward Logan. "We must keep up the pretense of a debrief meeting, at least for a few minutes. Then I shall take you on a tour of the city and then an inspection of the barracks." Logan had barely nodded when Vyrian yelled, "Crostes! Refreshments for our guest please, and be quick about it."

Logan blinked at the volume of the old man's voice. Feeble? Logan had heard nothing feeble in the man's vocal cords. Footsteps drummed the floor outside until a guard came to a barreling stop, a tray held aloft. Logan was impressed that he hadn't dropped everything when he'd skidded to a stop and entered the room.

Vyrian smirked as the boy handed out lidded tankards and placed a platter of unidentifiable baked goods between them.

Logan grinned and reached for his drink. Something told him his tour of the city was going to be very, very interesting.

CHAPTER 14

KAI

Mom had waited only seconds—in which I'd both marveled and been appalled at the breadth of skeletons currently spilling from the Odel closets. Now she nodded. "A close friend, a fae of the same court from what I was told. His name has been lost in the telling of the story, and I'm pretty sure that Ivy wouldn't know it either. But he'd come ahead of the Fae contingent, giving her enough time to hide the babe because her friend had known that there was a good chance that the fate of the child was in question. Trieste's father was a ruthless man, though he'd appeared, until then, to have had a soft spot for his daughter."

"Until she developed a mind of her own. Oh, the horror," I said dryly, my expression of fake-shock probably not doing my words justice.

I *was* shocked. A part of me was listening, enthralled by the romance of this story that was my heritage, but the other part of me was grieving for what Trieste would have gone through, horrified at the danger the infant Ivy Odel had faced.

"Trieste was forewarned and had arranged for the child to be taken away and that she wouldn't know where. The King was also known for his elemental magic, and for his mindreading ability. Trieste knew he'd extract the child's location from her, no matter how hard she resisted."

"In much the same way that he'd taken the truth from the friend who'd warned her?" I said, already knowing this part of the story.

"Exactly. The King drew the memory from the boy and then killed him in front of Trieste. The horror of it was often the highlight to the tale, but when it's a part of the grotesque history of your own family, it tends to lose the glow."

"Tell me about it," I muttered then shuddered. "The fact that I have some of that creepy Fae King's blood running in my veins kinda makes me want to puke."

Mom smiled so sadly it hurt to see the pain she felt for Grams' mom. "The King brought the fae boy to stand in front of Trieste and then created a column of liquid around him that appeared to be water—but from the stories was described to be thicker and stickier. Trieste watched him drown, and when the boy stopped moving, the King touched a finger to the column and turned it into ice."

"And she agreed to leave with him."

"She agreed. But as she left, rising into the air with the rest of the Fae contingent, the Fae King exacted one last punishment. He sent a bolt of lightning into the column of ice, shattering it into a cloud of tiny shards. Then he spun the cloud of ice crystals into a tornado which lifted into the air until it reached the Fae. It is said that he's kept the cloud of ice spinning in an eternal hurricane, and when he returned to his kingdom, he set it up in the palace courtyard where a grand fountain used to play."

"He sounds like an asshole."

"Apparently he was."

"And what happened to Trieste?"

"Nobody knows."

I blinked. I felt like I'd been run over by a steamroller, the revelation of Gram's true heritage and a part of our family's sordid history settling heavily within my mind and heart. I felt like I wanted to explode, an amalgamation of disbelief, sorrow, and anger twisting into a ball inside me.

"Not even Grams?" I asked, my stomach twisting.

"I wouldn't know. Perhaps one day she will tell us."

"So that's why our births needed extra observation?" Mom nodded, her expression sober now. "But wouldn't revealing that Dad has Fae blood have alerted the Fae King? Or even Trieste—wherever she is?"

"Possibly, but we had little choice in the matter. The doctors took blood samples, and at the time—pregnant with Iain—I'd had little idea of my mother-in-law's true genetic heritage. Only when the results came in, and they questioned us did we check with Mason and Ivy. And then they finally told us the truth. Let's just say that Corin and Niko were not pleased with having been kept in the dark all that time."

I made a face as Mom's mention of Niko hit a sore spot. "Do we know if Great Grampa Creepy King was a little effed in the head?" Mom raised an eyebrow in question, and I said, "Well, if he was a psychopath, then that could explain Niko...and maybe even Greer."

Mom stiffened, and I bit my lip. "Sorry. I didn't mean to say that."

Mom shook her head. "Honey, I wasn't blind to Greer's issues. Ivy sent me news, and I have to admit I wasn't surprised. But I was helpless. I couldn't do anything to help her."

"I don't think there is anything anyone could have done for her. At first, I wondered that maybe it was something to do with being Pariah. Uncle Niko and Greer both shared the same traits, but Dad pointed out that other Pariah, like Lily, aren't mentally unbalanced. He'd said then that there must have been some reason and maybe one day we would find out why."

"And Ivy? How did she handle it when Niko was caught?"

asked Mom, a frown puckering her pale forehead. "At the time, she did tell me, but she'd kept her voice free of emotions. I knew I'd have wasted my time trying to get her to talk, especially given that I was too far away to do anything to help her other than pick at her scabs and make them bleed again."

I gave Mom a sad smile. "That was probably for the best, Mom. Grams had a lot to deal with. And even if she suspected that something was up with him when he was younger, it wouldn't have meant anything to anyone." I paused and looked at Mom who now appeared drained.

"So where exactly were you headed with this revelation?"

Mom chuckled. "Guess we got a little side-tracked, huh?" I grinned, then shrugged the one available shoulder. Mom smiled and said, "Where I was headed was the explanation of how my pregnancy with Iain started a few balls rolling that nobody really had much control of."

"One of them being Grams' history, but the other one? Something to do with your children? Or did it have more to do with your absence?"

Mom chuckled. "Each of the pregnancies and births was placed under intense scrutiny, especially with the three of you bearing Mage, Fae, and Walker DNA. The doctors were all on the edge of their seats waiting for some amazing thing to happen but thankfully each pregnancy and birth went off without much trouble. But you were onto something there. My absence allowed a number of key people to register the kind of power I possessed. I'd been The Hunter for so long, but my absence made my power seem something more."

I squinted at Mom, wondering where she was headed with this line of thought. I had a sneaking feeling that I knew but I remained silent and allowed her to speak without my annoying interruptions.

"The years between each of your births were periods in which many interests shifted their focus onto me. Until one day when a strange old man paid me a visit." Mom paused, and I stiffened, though I drew a mask of curiosity over my face, needing to hear more before I admitted to anything.

There was a good chance that Mom was testing the waters in order to verify if I was one of the Ni'amh, and even such an attempt made me feel uncomfortable, especially having seen a ShapeChanger up close and personal. Especially one who'd worn the very same face I was staring at, and I hadn't known a fricking thing.

My own mother and I'd had zero clue that she wasn't real.

That fact made me hesitate, the traitorous thought that this person I'd been speaking to, confiding in, cuddling with, could also possibly be an imposter.

I struggled with the suspicion, quelling the urge to move away and leave the room before she saw my mistrust, because either way, my suspicion would cause trouble—I'd insult my mom, or I'd tip off the imposter.

I blinked slowly and breathed slowly and then smiled. "You get many visits from strange old men, then? Is this something we should be discussing with Dad?" I said with a wink.

"Silly girl," Mom said, batting my arm. "I'm just not sure how to broach the subject. So I may as well just barrel on and see where that takes me." Mom paused, and when I gave her a reassuring smile, she continued, "So I received a visit from a strange old man. Not at all creepy, despite what it sounds like. He visited me at my office in the Sentinel building, making it past security with far too much ease. His calm, easy manner and bashful smile won me over far too easily—now that I think about it." Mom paused and scowled at the memory, then shook her head. "Anyway, he approached me saying he had information for me that he was certain I would want, given its nature."

"Cryptic."

"Then he handed me a letter. He was pretty clear as he explained that he'd bypassed a few security levels in order to bring it to me personally, but that he had to do it himself because he felt he needed to provide me with more than a cursory explanation. When I read the letter, I understood what he meant."

My eyes widened, and I was unable to hide the reaction from her. She paused a fraction of a breath then continued, "The letter contained a prophecy which detailed the importance of a special woman who would help the DarkWorld weather what the Ancient described as a 'near-annihilation event'."

"The Ancient?" I whispered, staring at Mom's face.

She tilted her head and shrugged. "Strange old man turned out to be a being so old he may likely be older than the universe."

I snorted. "Don't let Darian hear you. It may go to his head."

Mom's expression flattened as she hid her emotions from me. "You know Darian?"

I nodded slowly, aware that it was too late to take the slip of his name back, aware too that this dance of lies and omissions was a total waste of time. As wary as Mom was, I was beginning to suspect that she must be the real deal.

An imposter would be more confident in their own knowledge as they'd have likely come already armed with whatever they'd managed to unearth about my family and our history and our lives.

I sighed. "Yes. I know Darian. So tell me about this prophecy he gave you. What made you so important?"

"It wasn't him, actually. It was Darius who came to me, but over time I had the opportunity to meet the other Ancient. And, to answer your question, the mention of the Hunter was what had Darius convinced the prophecy was about me."

There was a hesitation in the rhythm of her voice, a subtle hitch which would have gone unnoticed had I not been on the lookout for some sign that proved Mom was Mom. But what her tone meant, I wasn't entirely sure. Although, for what it was worth, I was less and less sure now that I was speaking to an imposter.

That could just be wishful thinking.

I squinted at her now. "You don't sound all that convinced. Did you not think you were who he said you were?"

Mom shrugged. "I admit I did at first. The version of the prophecy that I had read had been a previous iteration, one where the translations hadn't been as accurate as it ought to have been."

I grunted. "They gave you the wrong prophecy?"

She chuckled. "Yes. But it wasn't their fault. The interpretation of this particular prophecy was entirely dependent on who was translating and from what language to what language."

"Brings a new dimension to the phrase 'Lost in Translation' doesn't it?"

"You can say that again," said Mom laughing softly. "We learned later—after much research, investigation, and a few more iterations of translations—that the prophecy did not speak of one woman, but rather five different women, each independently powerful and important."

I swallowed hard, my throat pulsing as though my nerves were a ball in my throat. "A quintet of powerful women?" I whispered.

"Yes," Mom said softly.

And even as she spoke next, I was saying the name too, our hushed voices merging into one whisper.

"Ni'amh."

CHAPTER 15

KAI

Well, that had certainly gone swimmingly.

Inside my bathroom, my legs were suddenly a mass of jello after another flash of stabbing pain to my brain. I sank onto the side of the tub, still careful to ensure I didn't make any sudden movements, my mind still focused on the skeletons in the Odel family closet.

I'd gone to find out how Mom was feeling, and I'd come away with two enormous, life-impacting revelations.

Grams was Fae royalty.

And Mom knew about the Ni'amh.

And not only did she know, she'd been instrumental in figuring out that the prophecy wasn't about one woman but rather a quintet.

We'd spent a few moments discussing how the suspicion that she was the Ni'amh had made things difficult for her, and that the revelation that I'd inherited her power had sealed the deal for her, confirming that she wasn't the one the prophecy was talking of.

I shook my head again, this time ignoring the pulsing of pain, so focused was I on the strength of the revelation, the meaning of it.

But the pain was far too insistent, and its weight on me pushed hard, forcing me over until I was bent at the waist, elbows on my knees.

Slow breath.

Slowly, steadily, I focused and breathed, in, out, in, out. And then, with movements filled with languid agony, I shifted until I was leaning against the cool porcelain of the tub.

Heat surged at the back of my eyes, and I cursed the tide of weakness that seemed to rush over me.

I had a secret.

And I wasn't sure for how long I'd be able to keep it. And I didn't want to face my father when he did eventually find out. Because this secret wasn't something I'd be able to hide forever.

Earlier that morning

Dad waved me upstairs as he'd done with Mom not minutes ago. In fact, he'd taken her up to her room and had likely tucked her in, then had returned for me, a steely determination glinting in his eyes as he waved at the stairs and waited.

Man, he could be hard.

But he had a point.

No matter how much I'd love to deny that I was exhausted, such a claim would be mere words. The truth would be that I was well past the point of no return, so tired that I should no longer have been able to stand without assistance. In fact, there was no certainty that I wasn't in fact sleepwalking.

After bestowing my stern-faced father-doctor with an innocent smile, I hobbled up the stairs as gracefully as I could, aware that he was watching my excruciatingly painful journey without saying a word. So, when was it that I'd graduated from child who needed babying not three days ago, to someone who he'd didn't offer to help despite how obvious my suffering was.

Had he seen some change in me, had he sensed that if he so much as touched me to help me up the stairs, I'd have fallen into a million hopeless pieces?

A breath and a step, and then repeat, was what I focused on while Dad hung back a few moments, giving me a head start. When I'd reached the halfway mark, all of ten risers up, he sprinted past me saying, "Meet you in your room. I'll just go grab a few things."

I grunted and took a step. "Fine, just don't even think of taking my temperature."

"That's okay," he called from the hallway near the door to his bedroom-slash-lab. "I think I have a rectal thermometer somewhere in the lab. If you can't handle it consciously, I'll wait until you're asleep. Done it plenty of times." His voice was even, but I wasn't stupid. I knew what Dad sounded like when he was struggling not to laugh.

I let out a ragged grunt. "Huh, rectal thermometer, my ass," I muttered as I reached the landing and turned to head to my bedroom.

Dad's voice drifted down the hall from behind me. "Of course, honey. Where else would one put a rectal thermometer." Only when he'd delivered his line did he dissolve into a fit of chuckles, not even caring to keep the volume down.

A disgusted snort escaped my throat as I reached my bedroom. "Everyone's a comedian," I grumbled, entering the room, distantly aware that Logan had slept in that bed only this morning.

A blink later and I found myself standing beside the bed, surprised that I'd reached it without moving. Then I took a slow breath.

That wasn't a good sign—losing time was always a problem whether it was related to one's health, one's mind or one's paranormal powers.

My body heavier now than ever before, I sank gratefully onto the bed, and then Dad was in the room, bustling about, wrapping my arm, the plastic crackling, the Velcro tearing as he repositioned and tightened the band. I sat there, half-aware as the pressure on my upper bicep increased almost to that point of unbearable, and then it was over, and Dad was waving a thermometer in front of my face, a wide grin splitting his mouth.

I narrowed my eyes but couldn't muster any more than half an eye-roll, the pain, and fatigue taking over. And that very disinclination to fight back must have put my father on alert.

He'd quietened then, his movements slower, more careful, his conversation ceasing as he became all too aware that I'd stopped replying to his questions.

I knew I'd worried him, and in a brief moment of clarity, I managed to smile up at him. "Thanks, Dad, but I'm fine really. Just need to sleep."

He paused to study my face, then seemed convinced as he gave a slow nod then repeated the movement three—maybe four?—times.

Then I lost track of him again, and when I opened my eyes, he was gone, and I was still sitting on the bed, bathed in sunlight, blinking and squinting.

Had I fallen asleep in a sitting position? Was that even possible?

I shoved the thoughts away and pushed slowly back to my feet. Toilet first. Then sleep. I'd had about enough of being a patient; I had no intention of undergoing the added degradation of having to wear adult diapers.

The journey to the bathroom was slow, as I moved with infinite care, timing each barefooted step with the rhythmic pulsing and beating in my brain that echoed in my throat—along with the niggling threat that I was about to throw up.

Thankfully I didn't, and I was never more grateful. As a migraine sufferer, I could confirm that vomiting when you had a headache was a bitch.

I used the toilet, brushed my teeth, paused to consider a shower even as my body resisted.

I never got to make that decision. The bathroom shifted, blurred, tilted. Something pressed hard against the side of my face, something solid and cruel and cold against my skin.

I had the vague sensation of my body thrashing, registering on the edge of my awareness that my hand hit the side of the tub, my knuckles cracking loudly against the porcelain as pain splintered my fingers.

But even that pain faded as my body bounced and my mind tilted, and my vision swam.

And then I blinked.

A second blink and I slowly became aware that I was still in the bathroom, that I was lying on the cold tiled floor beside the basin. My cheek was icy cold, and something sticky made my face slip and shift against the tiles. I swallowed hard, tasted bile as I moved slowly to sit up, back pressed heavily against the cabinet below the washbasin.

I blinked again, the throbbing in my skull growing ever stronger. My fingers pulsed, the joints on fire and I glanced down to inspect them. No swelling thankfully, so I hadn't broken anything. The cheek though was another issue.

Shifting to my knees slowly, feeling the ice of the tiles eat into my bones, I used the washbasin and the muscles of my arms and shoulders, and hoisted myself up to stand before the mirror.

I was barely conscious of the quivering muscles in my arms, spent and useless after their intensive efforts.

The bruise was quite beautiful, I had to admit. Purple and blue now, dark colors of night and shadows. Probably indicative of either my life or my mind.

My dry, hard laugh rent the air, the sound shattering on the tiled walls around me.

And that laugh was the very essence of a revelation.

I'd been staring into the mirror, wincing against the bright fluorescent glow of the ceiling lighting, when I'd let out that unamused barking laugh, but what had been reflected back to me was odd—my face was all wrong.

My mouth and lips had moved as I'd laughed—as I'd expected they would—but only one half of my mouth had performed the bitter, almost angry half-smile, the wobbly curve of my lips, and the unamused narrowing of my eyes.

Or rather, my eye—as in singular.

The left side of my face drooped, features slack, skin pulled down by gravity as though all the muscles had refused to function.

I knew what this was.

The moment I'd seen my reflection, I'd known.

All that electricity driven repeatedly into me, and with such malicious strength? Was I even surprised to see myself this way? This twisted version of my physical reality?

And as I stared at the dark-haired, tired woman in the mirror, the image blurred behind a sheen of tears—which I blinked away, fists clenched hard, ignoring the throbbing of injured knuckles, suddenly awash with fury.

I was furious with the world, with my life, with everyone—including myself.

And along with fury came that insidious, unadulterated fear of the ramifications of my condition.

But there was one thing I did know.

There was no way in Hel I was going to tell my father and mother that I'd just had a stroke.

A stroke.

What in the name of Ailuros was going on? I sucked in a ragged breath, ignoring the bite of the lip of the bathtub as it pressed into the backs of my thighs. I'd been sitting there for a while—how long exactly I wasn't certain—almost relishing the cold pain of the porcelain for no reason other than the cold bite of it was a reminder that I was still alive.

Silly really, since a stroke was what it was. Nothing I could do to change it. Nothing anyone could do to change it. Which was enough of a reassurance that silence was the smartest option for now. Just until I knew what was going on.

In the wake of the staring match between me and the damaged creature in the mirror, half-formed thoughts flitted through my mind, ragged images barely formed, spurts of fear that refused to identify their origins, just fading in and out, one moment crowding my mind, and the next leaving it a hollow cavern, a vacuum of blackness.

And I relished that blackness.

I wasn't entirely sure what it meant that I'd enjoyed the dense nothingness of what was likely the beginning of some form of mental incapacitation, wasn't eager to define it either. And yet, even with everything I had to do, all that I was responsible for, my deepest desire was...nothing.

Was it the freedom I yearned for?

The thought flickered through my mind as I blinked, vision blurred then cleared, then sharp enough for me to wince. Then gone again. But that desire returned, a shadowed creature lurking in the darkness, its low purr an almost seductive siren call.

And then I gasped softly.

Frantic now, I searched for her, sinking deep, breath catching, heart tripping, terrified this stroke could mean more than just a physical destruction, that it could mean something worse than being swallowed by that darkness without a fight.

Where was she?

But even as the thought writhed within my mind, I felt her again, a low purr, a soft reassuring vibration that sent waves of calm over me.

She was here. She was alive.

I let out a slow breath and moved to my feet, each action unhurried, deliberate, all the while holding tightly to the thread I'd latched onto that assured me she was okay. Swallowing hard, I checked the condition of my face and was relieved to find the signs of the stroke had dissipated.

I'd regained control of my face, and I looked normal.

Or as normal as a person could look with a cheek that I was sure was broken. But injuries were okay given what I'd just been through. If Dad asked, I'd just say something about makeup and forgetting about the pain, and then I'd pray to Ailuros that he wouldn't figure out that something was wrong.

But such concerns, no matter how strong, were no match for my fatigue. Maybe it was brought on by the stroke—who am I kidding, it was most definitely a result of the seizure—and was hitting me like a wave, full force, sucking the energy from me so suddenly that I almost didn't make it to the bed in time.

To be honest, I wasn't sure how I'd made it there at all, but I did. I found myself, moments later, sitting on the side of the bed, head lolling to the side.

I didn't fight, just flexed and tightened only the muscles needed to allow me to follow the direction of my falling body, to land on my pillow. The last reserves of my energy were used to bring my feet back up onto the bed.

The last reserves of my consciousness regretted the inability to pull the covers up over me.

It didn't matter though. An unconscious person wouldn't really miss a blanket. She'd be too busy enveloped by...nothing.

I shivered, the fear an icy web enveloping me slowly, steadily. Then I clenched my fists around the edges of the tub, tightening the grip of my white-knuckled fingers. I looked down, cheeks throbbing, head sparking pain, and I knew then no matter what, I couldn't fathom a life without my panther.

That inner creature defined me just as much as my human form did. As much as I'd run from my duties, and rebelled for so long against the use of my feline form, I'd grown to understand how important it was that I embrace who I truly was.

And how strange it was that the person who'd convinced me to accept myself had given that advice on the assumption that he knew who *he* was—and that *I* knew who he was.

Logan had been wrong on both counts.

And how strange it was that I found this moment, within the ragged black hole of fear that I'd lost her, to think about Logan's love and support—something I didn't have right now. Something I didn't have even though I desperately needed it.

Needed him to help bolster me against the rising tide of fear as I cast about for my panther and found only dark silence.

Still frantic, my mind spun as I forced myself to slow down, to breathe and pull a shroud of calm around me which—though fashioned of a breathless desperation and a tattered calm—seemed to have helped.

For the first time in a while, I wasn't sure again how long—I sensed the low rumbling purr of my panther, the warm throb that told me my inner cat was still alive. Though I couldn't be certain of the physiology of a walker brain and how it functioned in terms of the connection between human mind and that of the creature that resided within me, some inner fear screamed out in warning—What if the seizure had severed the connection?

What if I can't shift again?

I shook my head and focused on showering and dressing, finding fresh clothes inside my closet, everything neatly folded or hung meticulously alongside Logan's clothing.

Heat seared my eyes, and I blinked it away, fueled by a blend of anger and loss and hurt, and ignored his clothes as I grabbed black tights, an oversized jumper and a pair of fluffy knee-high boots.

Soon, dressed in my comfy clothes, I left my room and walked slowly, carefully toward the landing, sending up a prayer to Ailuros that I'd make it down the stairs without falling on my face, or at least without breaking something.

Ailuros heard my prayer.

I didn't fall. Neither did I break anything.

Thank you, goddess.

CHAPTER 16

KAI

A low hum of conversation drew me to the kitchen where seemingly the entire family was busy with dinner—the preparation, the production, and the presentation of it.

Only Mom sat away from the mob, ensconced in a rocking chair and covered in a large red-and-blue tartan blanket. She was leaning against the backrest, allowing the chair to rock slowly back and forth, though she did control the movements with the tip of one toe placed solidly on the floor.

Even in relaxation, Mom needed control.

Although, when it came to the rocking chair, I didn't blame her; I still had nightmares from my spectacular altercation with the thing—yes, a bit of an exaggeration but given the circumstances, I figure I'm allowed.

And it seemed I wasn't the only one who was taking that particular trip down memory lane. Dad looked up from the open door of the oven where he'd been inspecting the crispness of an overly burdened thin-base pizza.

He had a smudge of flour on the edge of his nose, and a scattering of polenta on the left side of his head where he had the tendency to fidget with the strands when he was thinking too hard.

Or, from the looks of it, cooking too hard.

Now he laughed softly. "Welcome back to the land of the living," he said, voice loud and brimming with amusement to match the mischievous look in his eyes as he glanced over at Mom—who'd turned to smile her welcome at me—then said, "Hey, kiddo. Want Mom to let you go for a spin in the rocker? Just make sure the chair doesn't capture you again, okay?"

Mom sent him a ferocious glare, though she failed to hide the slight up-tilt of her eyes that hinted at hidden laughter.

Dad, on the other hand, slammed the oven door shut, weaved his way between Lily—who was rolling out pizza dough and only took a quarter of a second to throw me a sneaky wink with one generously floured eye—and Grams who stirred onions in a pan at the stove, her expression determined as though the vegetable needed to know who was boss.

Dad scurried back to the other side of the table and fiddled with something—the identity of which was hidden by Baz's torso as he bent low and cut impossibly thin slices of jalapeños, anchovies, and sun-dried tomatoes.

"Baz? I hope you didn't use the same knife to cut the anchovies *and* the tomatoes," I said, my tone containing a fair amount of a threat.

Baz lifted his head slightly, looking up at me from the tops of his eyes. "Eh?"

I sighed—fatigue hitting me hard within the space of a few seconds—but I allowed the expulsion of air to fake exaggerated weariness with the vamp's lack of understanding. "Anchovies, Baz. Did you use the knife, contaminated with that…" I made a face that I knew conveyed my disgust with striking clarity, "… stuff, and then cut the tomatoes? Or did you—like a normal person with a modicum of common sense and taste—use a clean knife?" I raised an eyebrow, discreetly reaching for the nearest barstool and sliding onto it while still maintaining my stern glare.

Baz blinked, still motionless in his half-stooped position. "Huh? Oh. You don't like anchovies?" he asked, staring at me now, as though I'd grown another head. Eyebrow still curved, I tilted my head in a what-do-think motion. To which Baz replied with an eye-roll, a snort and then, "Who in their right mind doesn't like anchovies?"

I huffed. "Who in their right mind *likes* anchovies? It's a fricking bunch of stinking rotten fish stuck in a jar of gloopy oil. That stuff wasn't made to be eaten by modern people. It belongs back in the ancient times...where it came from."

Baz chuckled, then bent back to his task, slicing the rest of the jalapeños before dropping them into a small white bowl. "I think you're confusing anchovies with rakfisk. Now that stuff will put hair on your chest and then some."

I rolled my eyes. "Listen, kid. I know the difference between anchovies and rakfisk. I'm just sad to see that your taste buds fall into the category of malfunctioning. I honestly thought you were better than that," I said mournfully.

Lily choked on a laugh, Baz grunted then mumbled something I was sure he'd have gotten grounded for—though Dad seemed amused rather than stern and ready to serve him a plate of discipline—and Grams giggled. Then she snorted.

Yes, the immortal-fae-walker-secret-agent-daughter-of-a-queen succumbed to a fit of very-unroyal, decidedly un-adult giggle-snorts.

"Well, that's just fabulous. Thanks, Grams."

Grams composed herself long enough to say, "Whatever for, dear?" then spluttered into a laugh again, eyes sparkling as she waited for a reply, all fake innocent.

I waved a hand at her. "That thing you're doing…the whole laughy-snorty-chokey thing. It just killed the argument." I sighed, unable to hide my grin.

"Oh, I'm sorry dear," Grams said, "I just couldn't help myself."

With a snort inelegant enough to top Grams' most recent performance, I said, "Not like it was all that funny. I don't see why you're like almost dying with amusement over an argument about stinking fish."

Grams—now done with her onions which had probably been stared into submission faster than their usual cooking time—took her saucepan off the flame and set it beside the stove, in line with the rest of the toppings all prepared and waiting for the next pizza. Then she dusted her hands, wiped them on her apron and said, "Oh I wasn't laughing about the anchovies," glanced over at Mom in the rocker, then giggled some more.

"Ugh, not you too," I groaned and was about to drop my forehead to the table when a hand appeared in front of my nose bearing a tall glass of orange liquid. Thick orange liquid from which wafted the sweet-sour scent of yogurt, cardamom, and mango. "Oh wow! Lassi," I said, wrapping my fingers around the glass and inhaling the aroma.

The kitchen was silent for a few moments as everyone paused to watch me sniff the mango-flavored drink. I straightened, glass in hand, staring from face to face as I frowned. "Now what?" I asked, my voice snapping at them.

Lily cleared her throat. "You just sniffed the lassi," she said, holding back her laughter. "There's this picture in my head right now…I can't get it out."

I shrugged, refusing to smile. "If all I have to do is get zapped a bunch of times and that gets me a lassi, no sweat. I guess I earned it. And earned the right to sniff anything I want."

"Long as it's anything and not any*one*. I just got a new cologne, and I've heard it's like pheromones in a bottle," Baz said, expression dead serious.

I choked on my first sip of lassi. "Seriously Baz, you do realize you don't need pheromone-laden cologne to have the ladies falling at your feet, right?"

Baz scowled. "What are you going on about? I thought members of the fairer sex were quite entranced by a gent whose scent was attractive," he said in his gentile British drawl.

I nodded. "You're quite right, Baz. A *gent's* scent plays a key role in reeling in the birds. Only thing is, you don't need anything artificial. You can have every woman—and guy, whatever floats your boat—you want. All with a mere crook of your finger."

Baz stared at me, then looked over at Dad. "Are you sure that shock therapy she got didn't scramble her brain? She sure sounds like it to me."

"No, she doesn't," Lily said, chuckling. "You're a vamp, dummy. What has your secret vampire mentor-person been teaching you anyway?"

Baz straightened, looked from me to Lily and back again. Then, all he said was, "Oh."

Everyone laughed. I sipped my mango lassi. And then I *sniffed* my mango lassi.

And I smiled, feeling a lot less like I wanted the safety of the black nothingness.

Here, in the kitchen of my childhood, with Mom back and healing, and the family—blood and not—gathered around me, I was home.

And I felt the shroud around me grow a fraction warmer.

Maybe there was hope for me yet.

CHAPTER 17

KAI

Dinner was a rowdy affair, part of it spent listening to my reputation being dragged into the mud as Dad regaled us with a retelling of my altercation with the rocking chair, way back when I was eight and was made up of long skinny limbs and not much else.

I watched faces around the table and smiled as they heard how I'd demanded to be the first to sit in the rocker which had been made by my father in an attempt to find a way to channel his stress and calm himself. He should have taken up a different hobby, at least then I wouldn't have been embarrassed to death.

He'd put the chair together and announced it done, then called us around to have a look at his creation. I was impressed and excited and demanded to be the first to sit in the chair, and promptly received the old have-a-little-patience speech.

Bad idea.

The intrepid carpenter had forgotten to glue the rods for the backrest, and he'd made a couple of miscalculations during the cutting process. Long story short—I sat, I rocked, the chair crumpled a little.

I rocked more.

And I rocked faster.

Too fast.

The meager glued-together spots snapped, the pieces of the legs shuddered on the forward swing, and as I put my weight into the backswing, the rocker tilted a tiny bit too far back.

Okay, let's be real. It wasn't a tiny bit. More like a whole heckuva lot back.

Enough to tip over and deposit me against the backrest where my arms and legs ended up twisted among the narrow rails, entwined so badly that I was unable to extricate myself and had to wait for five hours before someone wondered what had happened to me.

Greer found me, intertwined with wooden rods, skin coated with sticky glue, unable to move. My sister laughed all the way to fetch help, returned with Grams who attempted a removal and failed for fear of breaking bones.

In the end, I spent another three hours waiting for Dad to return home, screaming my refusal to call in the fire department.

And I waited, finding that I possessed the unparalleled art of consuming a full meal while trapped between rods of wood. I discovered too that a girl's body can hurt in the strangest of places when braided together with a rocking chair. I also found that a girl's body had the strangest ability to contain her bladder for hours while within the chair's embrace, though that same bladder could lose all control all of three steps away from the toilet.

The story had spurred a round of the most embarrassing stories as dinner progressed and I understood that nobody wanted to broach any subject that required the necessity of being serious or considering life-threatening ramifications.

I found I quite agreed with them, and I found too that I was able to take their good-natured teasing in my stride—and give as good as I got.

All in all, that dinner was one of the best meals I'd had in months.

And I discovered then that a girl was well capable of keeping an awful secret, even in the face of all that love.

Or perhaps because of it.

"I thought I'd find you out here." Lily's voice wafted toward me, and I sighed, shifting from the shadowed depths of the gazebo and into a buttery band of light that shone from the living room window into the little wooden rotunda.

I'd come to find a place to hide from the bustle of people, but I knew it wouldn't last. I was amazed it had taken Lily all of twenty minutes to find me.

She scurried inside and plopped herself down beside me. Despite the apparent uncaring flailing—which was normal for the lynx shifter—I hadn't missed the way she'd been ultra-careful not to bump me with her hip, or the way she'd curved her torso in order to avoid hitting her elbow or arm against mine.

Kid gloves from everyone.

Lily smirked, honey eyes glowing bronze in the golden light. "You do know you have easier ways to escape doing the dishes than head-butting a billion volts of lightning, don't you?"

I sighed deeply. "Shit. Could you not have given me a heads up?" I gave her a glare filled with mock-reproach. "Could have saved all the parts of me that got fried. Repeatedly. What a waste," I said with a long morose sigh.

"Aww." Lily rubbed my back, holding back her laughter. "It can't be all that bad. You still have your lady bits. And a whole lotta people—and I mean like *aaallll* the cops in the CPD who were on the extraction team—will happily verify the non-fried-ness of the...er..."

Lily made a swooping figure eight motion with her hands in

front of my chest, and I swatted her palms away. "They're called boobs, you ninny. And quit the whole wax-on wax-off action before you really do injure the non-fried parts of me."

Lily snorted and said, "Girls," with a very straight face.

"Eh?" I frowned, feeling the throb in my cheek again and wanting to massage the area, yet knowing it wouldn't do to set Lily off on the subject of my wounds.

"Girls," Lily repeated, then re-enacted the hand waving this time in front of her own chest while also arching her back and sticking her boobs—or distinct lack thereof—out a little more, as though for emphasis. "You know, your BFFs, the bosom buddies you can never leave home without." Lily burst out laughing at that and hunched over as she moaned and squeezed her stomach.

I shook my head and smiled at her. "How are you feeling, kid? The treatment getting you back on track?"

Lily nodded. "The transformations have been easier lately. Your dad says in a few weeks I'd have learned how to control the shift much better. And when he's happy, he'll start weaning me off the drugs."

I frowned. "That sounds like it's a bit soon," I murmured, making a note to check with Dad what the real deal is with the treatment.

But Lily smiled and shook her head, confident and happy—two things I hadn't seen in her in a long, long while. "It's not as bad as it sounds. Your dad said it's almost like a one-step-forward-half-a-step-back thing. I'll stay on my doses, for now, keep practicing 'cos my brain needs to learn stuff that you guys already have in your muscle memory. And then, when I reach the next milestone, we taper the dosage back by ten percent. It'll mean less drugs, so I'd need more control, so I'll fall back in my progress a little. But if I keep at it, I'll be fine."

I raised my hand and curled it around Lily's shoulders, pulling her gently against me. "You're so brave, kiddo. I wish I were around more…so I can be with you for your therapy," I whispered into her hair, my heart warming as she snaked her own hands carefully around my waist. She didn't tighten them, just rested the comfort of her arms against my waist. It was as good as a squeeze.

"You really need to stop thinking you have to worry about everyone," Lily said, her voice scratchy as she held her tears at bay. "You were with me, right at my side when I needed you most and maybe I didn't say it then, but that meant more to me than a hundred therapy sessions. And besides, I know you're a snooty alpha princess, and a killer demon-hunter all rolled into one, but you're not infallible. Or immortal." Lily ended her monologue with an eye-roll of epic proportions, and I was partly amused. But the other part of my mind was stuck on her mention of immortality.

Given what I'd just been told about Grams, Lily didn't have a clue.

CHAPTER 18

LOGAN

The Previous Evening

Logan watched the sunset, the explosion of bloody flames on the dull blue horizon. He hadn't registered how long he'd been standing there until he heard the light knock on his door before it opened to reveal a sliver of Kai's face, features drenched in shadows.

"It's so beautiful," he said softly, holding out a hand to her.

Her skin was pale, shadowed beneath her eyes. She was being run through the mill and there was nothing he could do about it. He dragged his gaze from her face as she stopped beside him and wrapped an arm around his torso then rested her head onto his shoulder.

Where she belonged.

But something was wrong. Logan knew her too well, was well able to detect the tension writhing within her, tension...and something else.

He let out a sigh and ran his hand up and down Kai's back, as though the movement would infuse her with the strength she needed. He'd done it once, a long time ago, using his fire to heal her body.

Logan laughed silently, mocking his fantastical thoughts as he said, "I heard things with you were a little insane."

"You can say that again." Kai smiled and laid her hand against his cheek, the caress gentle and filled with concern for him. "How are you feeling?"

Logan studied her face, watched the uncertainty, the disappointment that shimmered there. And yet she didn't ask him why he hadn't called her at the hospital, why he hadn't even sent a message. A text would have sufficed, yet he'd done nothing.

"I'm better now. I had a small episode," Logan said, then nodded at the burn mark on her bedroom wall where the shock of Kai's injury, exacerbated by his inability to help her, had elicited an uncontrollable ball of fire from deep within him. A warning perhaps, that she was his weakness, and that he was also hers. A weakness that she couldn't afford right now.

He'd considered repairing the damage before his departure, but he hadn't. It was as though he needed it there to remind him of why he had to go.

"What was that?" Kai was grinning, her mouth twitching with amusement. "Did you burp, or was it a sneeze?"

Laughing softly, Logan replied, "It was a fireball that went a little wrong, and I ended up passing out as soon as I threw it. I wasn't conscious for the rush to put the flames out, but from what I was told the fireball's bark was worse than its bite."

Concern flared in Kai's eyes as she shook her head. "When did that happen? You look okay to me."

Logan gave a nonchalant shrug. "Early hours of yesterday morning. I was out for almost the whole day, but I've been fine since I got up."

Oh how easily the lies do slip from my tongue.

Kai shook her head and frowned. "Sienna came by to see me at the hospital. She didn't say a word."

Guilt twisted its blade inside Logan's cowardly heart as he lied. "Yeah. I didn't know a thing about your little hospital adventure until this morning, and then they were telling me you were already discharged. I had to cancel my Get-Well-bouquet too. Pity." Logan's attempt at lightening the mood got him a smack on the forearm. "Hey, don't abuse the patient."

Kai wasn't in the least apologetic as she shifted to face Logan, then wrapped her arms around his neck. "You do not appear to be very patient-like right now."

"Oh really?" Logan asked, his voice gritty now, a blend of guilt and desire. "And what is it that I appear to be."

"Kissable."

The kiss was enough to tempt Logan to change his mind, and he had to remind himself of his duty.

When they parted and caught their breath, Kai said, "I came to see how you were doing. And..."

Logan cursed himself for the pang of relief that she'd only come to check on him, and not to help him figure things out.

Silencing her with a finger to her lips, Logan said, "I don't need you to explain to me. You do what you have to do." He felt a rush of emotion, mostly pain, and regret. He was being an asshole; she *was the best thing to ever happen to him and yet he was still going to leave her.*

"I love you, Logan Westin. Or whatever your name is," Kai said softly.

"I love you more, Lady Kailin Odel."

Logan sucked in a breath, then bent to kiss Kai briefly. And when she stepped away, he didn't stop her.

"I don't have any more time, or my ride will leave without me," Kai said, her eyes filled with emotion. Then she walked to the door where she paused. "When I get back...we have a thing."

"A thing?" Logan asked, glad the shadows in the room had deepened so she wouldn't see the sadness in his eyes.

"Yeah. I don't have time. But it's to do with Saleem, and it's crazy dangerous and crazy important so rest up, soldier." With a brief wave, Kai was gone, leaving Logan wondering what the heck was going on with Saleem. And why nobody had told him until now.

"Take care of yourself," Logan yelled after her, "and don't do anything stupid."

"Why does everyone keep telling me that?"

~

Logan was jolted out of his memories as the carriage hit something on the cobbled pathway. That conversation with Kai—in which he'd hurt her deliberately—remained at the forefront of his mind, even now when things were changing so drastically around him.

Kai's parting words filled Logan's mind, and somehow her voice was filled with accusation.

And Logan deserved it.

The fact was that despite everything he was experiencing since arriving in Drakys, his mind continued to filter back to Kai.

Guilt has its own form of power over the soul of a mere mortal.

Logan had spent the last few hours with old Vyrian proudly showing the soon-to-be General of all Drakys around the capital city of Dyr. Logan had to admit that he'd never seen anything so astounding before. The architecture of the ancient city was an amalgamation of ancient wood, gleaming gold, and a deep obsidian, that melded almost seamlessly in a construction of elegant spires and sturdy towers and sprawling estates.

The entire city had been built upon a low mountain, the scattered homes of farmers just inside the great walls, to the densely packed homes of the lower city, then the elevation increased as the cobbled roads wound along the sides of the mountain like a bowl of spaghetti, all of which ended in a wide expanse around the palace grounds.

All in all, the city was like something straight out of one of those fantasy stories that Sienna used to love. Logan stiffened, breath stilling for a moment as he frowned—the new memory flickered through his mind, like the pages of an ancient tome, a little fuzzy, a bit faded around the edges, and yet still thick with emotion. With...joy.

Logan took a slow breath and straightened himself in his seat. He tugged at his coat, glad Vyrian had endowed him with the identity of someone from the EarthWorld, as neither Logan nor Sienna had had the forethought to clothe him in garments that wouldn't raise the odd eyebrow.

Now Logan studied the gilded towers outside his window, the ruddy sunlight casting a dull glow and turning the gleaming gold into a burnt copper. Vyrian had given Logan the glossed-over history lesson, one that hadn't contained any more information than what Sienna had already passed on.

The city sights had been one thing, giving Logan the feel of being a gawking tourist in an old and very romantic land. The army barracks though, had lent an entirely different air to his introduction to the men, and women, he would soon rule.

Rule.

Such an ugly word, the connotations of control winding around it like a serpent. But Logan had no intention of turning into the evil king. He only hoped he would be able to gain their faith and trust by showing them who he was and what he wanted for the realm.

As the carriage slowed to make the final turn on the serpentine cobbled roads and enter the palace grounds, Logan thought of the middle-aged lieutenant—Lorsit y' Geral was his name—who'd greeted him with fervent subservience, all the while failing to hide the cold resentment in his eyes.

A resentment he'd revealed again when Vyrian introduced Logan to the Captain Kyala y' Vell of the Dyr platoon, as well as Captain Vedra y' Dost of the Royal Guard. Both of whom had turned out to be female, a condition that appeared to have irked the steely-eyed, pale-haired Geral.

Logan had received a quick tour through the barracks, all sturdy wood and stone buildings housing those on weeklong and on-shift posts. The training grounds were expansive, and the weapons of a larger variety than Logan had expected.

What he had expected had been the dragons, and when he'd spotted them in the distance, arcing around the city on patrol, he'd glanced at his old uncle who'd merely given the tiniest of head shakes.

Logan's sheepish smile at the realization that the General of the Army of Drakys would hardly be providing detailed introductions to a visiting emissary, had earned him a light pat on the shoulder from the elderly dragon shifter, after which he'd curtailed the tour with a reminder that they had treaty matters to discuss.

Not long after, Logan had been bundled into the carriage with Vyrian waving him off with a word of warning to not delay. At the time, Logan had suspected something was afoot, and now, as he stepped out of the carriage to find a palace guard standing stiffly near the entrance to the building, he was not surprised.

The dour-faced man handed Logan a piece of yellowed paper closed with the fat red wax seal, then spun on his heel and hurried off without looking back. The letter required Logan's presence in the royal reception room as soon as possible, an apparent urgent matter only recently arisen required his speedy attendance.

Logan pursed his lips and hurried inside, finding his way back upstairs without much of a problem. He'd expected the summons to have royal or diplomatic reasons.

The last thing he'd expected was to be a spy.

CHAPTER 19

KAI

With Lily having unwittingly brushed on the truth, I found myself focusing again on Grams and Mom, and the past. As I headed across the small town of Tukats. I'd heard much of the tale in a state of semi-sleep, and until now it had all seemed like a dream.

The problem was, Mom had a somewhat convoluted way of telling a story. Still, in the end, she'd spilled it all.

And it was about time.

I wasn't sure how they'd kept such a secret all these years. Especially when those details had been relevant, not just to me, but to Greer and Iain too. I had to wonder—though it plucked a chord of intense pain deep inside me—if Greer would have been different had she known of our history.

There were many things in the family's story that could possibly have touched her, in whatever way she'd felt she'd needed it most—in ways that none of us were able to.

Almost automatically, I entertained the thought that Greer would have enjoyed the fact that she had royal blood in her veins, and perhaps that, combined with the Fae DNA, would have filled the gaping hole within her that her inability to shift had left.

Perhaps it would have been a way for her to feel a sense of belonging.

I paused as I left the rolling lawns of the park that sat at the edge of the shifter settlement where the accesses to the mountain trails, as well as the burial tombs, welcomed one and all.

Here, within the forest of oaks and elms and fir, I found a sense of peace I'd been unable to access these last few days. That connection to nature was a fundamental aspect of the walker species, a part of me that I'd ignored, denied, rebelled against for so many years.

I followed a path between the trees, here and there massive trunks seeping a golden sap, and breathed in the fresh scent of pine needles and moss and nature. The night was cool with the inky hills to the west having engorged itself on the sun hours ago, but here—within the dense forest—the sun rarely shone. And if it did manage to snake its way through the canopy of woven branches and leaves, it merely graced the forest floor with a gentle dappling of faded sunbeams.

Surrounded by the elements, the earth and the creatures who lived and thrived around me, my wild spirit fought for freedom, pulling, tugging at the barrier around her. I'd spent years caught in this battle with my inner feline, only recently coming to revel in the sensation of the freedom of the shift.

I shook my head and gave in to the deep need with a low growl, the sound careening out around me, sending birds aflutter as the predator called its warning.

Not that I'd indulge in an after-dinner snack of the feathered and beaked variety. Walkers had evolved over the centuries, no longer the feral creatures of legend, no longer the predator who sowed fear and mayhem wherever they stalked.

Harmony.

We'd become a people of harmony, a species who lived alongside the humans, who would even marry and breed with them—a transition born of the desire for peace among the EarthWorld's people.

And, as with many attempts to sow the seeds of peace, trust, and a happy coexistence, it failed. The crumbling of the foundations of peace had come slowly, over decades, perhaps even centuries, given that much of our past had been lost to war, raids, and annihilation.

And those shattered bonds of trust had shifted something within the nature of the walker species, something that had, over time, festered and turned one too many to seek justice in their own way, in the solace of claws and teeth and the slick warm arms of fresh blood.

To my left, leaves rustled and whispered, stones scattered and rolled, and I snapped my attention toward the trail, spotting the flutter of a bushy feline tail as a small cat disappeared into the brush. I squinted, an odd sense of familiarity skimming my awareness. Strange, as I'd barely seen enough of the creature to even feel any sort of recognition.

I blinked and focused, working my jaw now as the panther undulated within me, the heat of the shift rushing through bone and blood and flesh, cresting to fill my mind with her visceral, animal desire.

Ears burned, cartilage shifted, lengthened, thinned jaw and cheekbones, the plates of the skull all vibrated, set alight with the flame of the change, parting and performing the age-old dance of rearrangement, of the almost-magical separation of cell from cell, the inexplicable dance that saw them seek out new bonds, like birds migrating to an alien destination, a journey controlled by a magnetism that was not seen or known, but that was destined, unavoidable, unstoppable.

This I'd learned through the long years of fighting my truest nature.

And now I slipped my feet from my boots, followed soon by

my socks, tights and the rest of my clothing—all of which I rolled into a bundle and tucked up in the hollow of a nearby oak.

Little packages of clothing littered the forest, a communal offering to shifters on the prowl, to those who wanted the freedom to shift on the spur of the moment without having to worry about being caught running nude through the forest by the random ranger or hiker who ventured into the mountain range. For centuries, the hills had been guarded by the magic of the shifters, a ward that caused the human eye to skim over and not see, to take a fork in the road without knowing why, to avoid a stream or glade, a copse or a falls, repelled by some strange force and perhaps to never ask why.

Now, naked, the cool air of the forest caressing my bare skin, the call of the night birds enveloped me, urging me to be, to just be. To stop questioning, analyzing, weighing the why's and the wherefores and to surrender to myself, eyes closed, arms spread wide, falling, trusting in my nature to protect me.

And my nature complied.

The shift rippled through me, lengthening limbs, thinning bones, skin sprouting dense, smooth body fur. And then the very sight of the world shifted, colors danced and split and swirled, swaying and evaporating, to leave behind the hues of the night vision—the feline sight.

On all fours now, I surged ahead, loping along the narrow path before me—allowing my panther to make her own choices —I abandoned the worn strip of sand and rocks created from years of passage, and sprang over a fallen log to land in a dense copse thick with leafy bushes and saplings. With barely a pause, I skittered past a shattered trunk almost hidden by a thick carpet of pale orange mushrooms, the fungus too large, too ugly to even hint at its tantalizing aroma and delicious taste when sliced just so, then braised with onions and garlic and thyme.

But very soon, the thought of food evaporated as I became one with nature, with the forest and its residents, as my paws slammed into soil and grass and mud, claws skittering, gripping, sending stones cascading as I made my mad dash across the forest.

As I ran, I caught sight of the pale cat, loping along a parallel path to my left and I wondered where it was headed, and why it hadn't yet fled from the company of a predator feline ten times larger and about an order of magnitude more deadly.

One moment it was there, and then it was gone, a feline wisp, a furred shadow flitting between the trees, teasing my awareness before it was gone, as though it hadn't been there in the first place.

I didn't know where I was headed, not until I arrived at the edge of the tree line, where the moon filtered in through the columns of the straight and tall sentinels of the elms guarding the wide, lush green lawn that surrounded the entrance to the Burial Tombs.

Panting softly, I scrambled to a stop, my claws scraping the flat stones marking the beginning of the paved pathway leading to the broad stone entrance to the burial ground of the people of Tukats and those of the shifters living around the settlements for up to a fifty-mile radius.

Though the goddess Ailuros presided over the caves and the great number of panther souls occupying the warren of caves and alcoves, these burial grounds have never, and likely will never, deny entry to the dead of a different sub-species of SkinWalker.

Or perhaps to any species, considering the number of fae and djinn and humans currently languishing at an address within the cave's halls. Odd that, despite the fact that the walkers knew full well that everyone was equal in death, many had supported the Walker Council's attempts at reinstating the taboo against inter-marriage.

I sniffed, tossing my head up and down as I scented the air and scanned the lawn with a sweep of my head. A throbbing sound and a subtle scent told me that the lone occupant of the burial grounds was no threat to me, and likely never will be the one to threaten or endanger my life.

Fluid heat seared my form, bones cracked and splintered as though shattering beyond a state of repair. And then, in a patch of silver moonlight, I was standing, sweat coating pale skin, the night bathing the expanse of my hot—and very naked—skin.

I threw my hair over my shoulder and hurried to a nearby elm, marked with a small green glyph, its unusual, seemingly natural long irregular lines filled with a twist of three types of moss, making the sign appear to have been born of the natural curve of the rugged bark.

Just above the sign, in a lee formed by two branches and an umbrella of overlapping leaves, I found a plastic Ziploc bag.

Inside were what appeared to be dozens of rods, narrow and supple, and the white one I selected drooped as I lifted it away from its companions.

The pale fabric had been tightly rolled in order to save space to ensure the stash of garments would be large enough so walkers from the area wouldn't need to be checking to restock the caches more than once a month. A quick glance confirmed more than enough remained to cater for a dozen shifters making a trip this way once a day for an entire month.

I gripped the ends and let the garment roll free, grabbing it as it flapped wildly in a gust of wind that seemed to have appeared out of nowhere. I dusted the fabric out and bunched its length up to draw it over my head.

Seconds later, I'd fastened the loops and knotted the ties of the long floor-length Roman-styled garment. The white silk was soft and smooth and settled in elegant folds over one shoulder, before swirling around my torso, leaving the other arm bare then sweeping around my waist and dropping to the ground.

The elegant toga resembled that of the goddess Ailuros in her mother form, and many a walker women enjoyed the formal, yet comfortable, garb. Now, dressed and decent enough for company, I made my way across the lawn toward the wide entrance to the burial tombs.

And my steps faltered as the high-pitched yowl of a cat echoed in the trees and filled the clearing, the sound roosting in the trees and slipping between crevices and cracks. It was as though the creature was issuing a warning, not a message filled with danger, but one that said it would return, that I hadn't yet seen the last of it.

And oddly, I felt somewhat bereft as a sense of coolness settled into my flesh, as though I'd been wearing a warm shawl which had just now been swept away into the black night, taking with it the comfort and the inexplicable sense of security.

With the cat having departed, I focused on the wide entrance to the caves, trying to ignore the green lawns around me, blinking away the vision that seemed to overlay my sight, as though determined to make me remember the funeral.

Not so long ago, and not long enough to relegate the day to a faded memory, white folding-chairs had been scattered across the grass while a priestess had presided over the gathering, sweeping gestures and words that performed a whirling, intertwining dance designed to comfort, to envelop, to support. Perhaps the tradition had helped lend me a calm I hadn't felt at the time, or perhaps it hadn't—I couldn't recall all that well.

What I felt now was a lilt of pain, a hot river of shared grief as I thought of the woman who now stood in the Odel mausoleum, the salt of whose tears I could scent with a twitch of my nose and a light huff of the mountain air.

I reached the threshold, wary, swiping aside my thoughts as I approached the entranceway. The main door was closed, but a red light blinked on the security panel to the left of the threshold —and confirmed the presence of someone who lurked deep within the caves.

My panther nose had already identified the visitor, a rush of warmth and familiarity filling my heart as I punched in my personal code and waited for the panel to give a soft beep—the perimeter alert confirmed the surroundings clear of intruders, ensuring the comings and goings of any visitor to the burial grounds didn't endanger the security of the place of rest of so many SkinWalker dead.

The panel chirped a third time, and the door clicked, letting out a soft hiss as the seal released and it swung open. I didn't wait for it to widen, just slid through the narrow opening and hit the button to shut the door behind me.

CHAPTER 20

KAI

The door shut behind me with a soft hiss, as though it too wanted to preserve the peace and serenity of the burial place. Many of the ancestors of the Walker community, going back at least three hundred years, were entombed within the heart of the mountain.

All those centuries ago, the first walkers made the trip to the Americas only to find that a small group of their brethren had arrived some decades before them, finding the cave system and setting down roots in the surrounding area.

From the annals of the Chicago Walker history, we knew that the walkers themselves had formed strong bonds with the tribes of the area, trading, and hunting alongside them. The elders surmised that perhaps it was the firm belief within the tribes in the existence of SkinWalkers, humans who turned into spirit animals.

Though there were inherent differences between the stories of the tribes and the truth of the walkers' nature, both groups found a common ground on which to live while sharing the myths—or realities—with a deep mutual respect.

And from that bond rose the name by which many walkers

went, more especially on the American continent—the name of SkinWalker, a nod to the ancient tribal beliefs. In fact, with the extent of intermarriage through the years, the lines between the ancient stories and the clans' realities had tended to blur, with the children of those marriages often revered as they manifested the natures of their parents, thus increasing the prevalence of the SkinWalkers within the tribes.

These new children were of a different nature, and perhaps even of a different species than that of the SkinWalkers within the native tribes. I'd often discussed that history with my father and Grams, each of us adding opinion and question to a growing pot. The current belief was that modern history had relegated much of the tribal reality to a more censored version; a more palatable reality for the colonizers as they forged their way through the continent.

I understood the political need; would settlers have come had they been faced with a hard truth that the natives also comprised of paranormal creatures who shifted into dangerous animals, that the cougars and wolves and bears most likely to cross their paths were possibly humans in animal form? Probably best not to highlight such dangers, especially not when the divide between the strongly spiritual and the native pagans was an ever yawning void filled with darkness, distrust, and judgment.

As a community though, our story was woven irrevocably with that of the local ancient tribes. A fact reflected strongly on the walls of the central passage of the cave system where one painting after the other depicted the evolution of the walker history from before their arrival on this land until most recently.

The painted scenes of the two first waves of the walker arrivals still evoked a depth of emotion every time I saw it. The first to step on the shores, of what is now known as Boston, was a small shipload of Norsemen, a mismatched company of traders, farmers, and warriors lost on the black oceans in their search of the northern reaches of the British Isles.

The stories of their arrival and settlement were ones filled with a curious blend of disappointment, expectation, fear, and discovery—emotions which had managed to filter down through the ages. Or perhaps those feelings were inherent in the nature of exploration that could be applied to everything new a person experienced in their lifetime.

The soles of my bare feet made no sound on the cool stone of the cave floor, though I was confident Mom would be well aware that a new visitor had entered—a fact which would not have been a concern as many walkers came and went daily.

I followed the corridor until it curved slightly left and reached the entrance to the Odel cave. As an alpha line with roots reaching back at least two centuries, the family had been granted a section of their own. In fact, I was pretty confident there were even larger caves within the mountain which belonged to non-alphas—likely having been granted to those with bigger families.

Guess it paid to procreate.

I hovered at the entrance to our mausoleum, eyes scanning the shadowed interior, and spotted Mom, her spine slightly curved as she sat, hands clasped and resting on her knees, fingers threaded together, the grip white-knuckled and almost gnarled. There was a long and pain-filled tale in the cruel braid of her fingers, perhaps a chord of guilt too that would have strengthened whatever other emotions intertwined within it.

The scratch of my heel on the stone brought Mom's head up, eyes snapping to me, filled first with annoyance, then surprise and relief. Guilt buzzed through me at the awareness that perhaps Mom had wanted to be alone to say her words to Greer, but I suspected she'd been here a few times anyway, given she'd returned home a few weeks ago already. This visit though seemed to mean something more.

And when I saw where she sat, I understood immediately.

She smiled and patted the stone beside her, and I weaved between the sarcophagi whispering blessings to the long-dead as

I went. The cave was an irregular rectangular shape, the uneven rock-faces of the walls having remained as untouched as possible, the only change being the seating.

Along the walls were six- to ten-foot lengths of hollows gouged out of the stubborn rock, narrow and shallow, only as wide as your average chair, only as high as needed to accommodate a seven-foot male. The seats had been smoothed down so as to glimmer with an unusually shimmery shine, an effect a result of the tiny particles of silver and gold that streaked the rock which had blended together during the smoothing process to form a shallow translucent layer on the stone's surface.

Bracketing each of the seating spots were white carved statues of the gods of the ages, each representing the various shifter deities of the cultures of the world through the ages. From Ailuros, Roman goddess of the Cat, to the Egyptian Bast and Anubis, to Asgard's Fenrir, Buddhist and Hindu Narasimha and Hanuman, to Chinese Huxian, the walls of the Odel crypt, like the rest of the caves around us, made obeisance to every shifter god with even the most fragile connection to the family's history.

I moved closer, the white fabric of my toga-dress whispering as I walked to Mom's side and reached for a candle from a narrow recess carved into the bottom of the seat nearest the wall. I selected two fat green candles and then two ruby pillars—that looked a lot like blood in a solid column—and proceeded to place them before each of the statues, and then in front of two sarcophagi, Greer's and a broader darker one which seemed to exude strength and power even in the absence of the spirit of its occupant.

I placed one green candle before Greer and the other within the open palms of Ailuros, beside a dark purple candle that flickered in a slight breeze. This for Greer, I lit and raised my face to Ailuros, asking her to keep Greer's spirit safe, to hold my sister within her arms in ways Greer had never been held in her lifetime.

Then, blood-red candles in hand, I walked silently over to the rugged coffin and knelt to settle one on the floor, beside a squat white one—no doubt offered by Mom. The movements silent and soft and reverent, I turned and walked over to the left side of the seat occupied by Mom, to a tall statue of the god Fenrir whose part-benevolent part-vicious face was tilted down as though ready to hear our prayers.

Fenrir had been the god which Grandpa Mason had raised his palms to—being a walker of both species: panther and wolf. He'd shared his respect with both Fenrir and Ailuros—in her Bast form as did many of the older generation. Candles lit beside Mom's, and now flickering in invisible air currents, I went to her side and sank down next to her. She reached an arm out and wrapped it around my shoulders, drawing me toward her, offering me her comfort, her protection.

It was hard to ignore the fact that Greer had experienced so little of that love, and had lived her life as though she believed that nobody truly loved her, despite the assurances of those around her.

My low sigh echoed around me as I stared at my sister's sarcophagus a few feet away, the sound earning a brief squeeze from Mom. She leaned her head toward me. "Do not bear her burdens on your shoulders, honey. Greer's load was her own, in choosing and in shouldering."

I shook my head, images of my sister in the Graylands flickering in front of my eyes. "You know what was funny?" I asked with a dry laugh—a question that hadn't needed an answer. I swallowed the twist of pain in my throat as I said, "She was probably the best sister I could have ever wished for..."

Mom glanced up startled, and I gave her a rueful smile. "In the last few minutes of her transition through the Graylands, before she entered the light...she was...I think she was at peace. She seemed to have accepted how she'd behaved, maybe even understood how her anger and fear had colored her perceptions of the people around her."

Mom moved her hand and ran it up and down my back, offering me comfort even within the web of her own grief and pain. "What did she say?" Mom asked, even though we'd both touched on this before, when Mom had first been returned to us after Greer's death.

I swallowed and replied, "She said 'Death removes the barriers to truth, that when you die you see clearly all the things you've done that were wrong and right.' And that she regretted so very much. That she pushed me away, that she'd spent time hating instead of loving. And she was so sorry. Even her last words were the apology to you, that she was so sorry she didn't allow you to explain because she was so consumed by anger."

My voice drifted away, and I glanced up at Mom, surprised to see her eyes bright, though her tears hadn't yet fallen. She shook her head, the movement so small I'd almost missed it. "And how do you feel about her words, how she was in the end?" I squinted at Mom; the question seemed so odd in the face of my understanding of Greer's feelings. I exhaled slowly.

"Angry? I guess I wished she'd seen it all before she'd taken the paths that had ultimately led her to her death. Disappointed that I'd only had a loving older sister for a few minutes before her death when I'd had contempt and anger for every other day of our lives. Sad that she'd never had the opportunity to sit among our family and be enveloped with the kind of crazy we'd just shared at dinner, the teasing and the laughter and the love." I fell silent, my throat tight.

A long moment went by, the silence thick and dark, and then Mom said, "I'm angry too. I'm not sure if it's anger at Greer or myself, but it's intertwined. I'd left her in charge of you, the older sister to take care of and protect the younger, and she failed at her task. So simple, so easy, and she'd failed. And worse, she hated instead of loved, she hurt instead of protected. I'm finding it hard to come to terms with that." Mom fell silent, and I swiveled slightly to look up at her.

Staring into her green eyes now, I was achingly aware that I saw three people—Mom, the woman who left me alone, and Celeste the Hunter, the woman who fought for her children, and now Celeste the human, the woman struggling with her emotions, struggling the way I myself did. She was no longer just a mother, because as I studied her face, I saw her clearly—more clearly than I'd ever seen her before.

She was a fragile being, filled with strength and weakness, hope and regret, fear, indecision, doubt, love, passion, sacrifice. She was strong and weak all at the same time, indomitable and fragile.

And she was the best representation of a mother I could have hoped for. Despite all those years of anger at her abandoning me, rage that she'd never returned, never called, loneliness and self-blame wondering if it had somehow been my fault because she'd left after *I* was born, not Iain and not Greer.

Now I stared at her and saw that all those years didn't mean anything, those years and the pain they held faded away, replaced by this deep understanding that Mom was as fragile and as real as I was.

And there was an intense power to this feeling, this emotional connection with my mother, the bond that encompassed mother and daughter but had expanded to be filled with sister and friend.

And in that moment, all the anger and blame I'd harbored against her fractured into a million pieces, leaving me filled with a peace and an understanding that I'd never before experienced.

And leaving me filled with an immense understanding of the true meaning of daughterhood.

CHAPTER 21

LOGAN

Logan tried to keep a straight face as he swallowed a groan. He wore a dull gray cloak, the deep folds of the hood shielding his face, as he watched the proceedings below him.

Lyra had provided Logan with the cloak, and he'd drawn it over his shoulders, somewhat confused with the very brief details he'd been given. With nobody to question, given that the queen regent had hurried off muttering something about being required in ten different places at the same time, Logan had dressed and waited for Sienna to arrive—which when she did, he'd found her also encased in a dull cloak.

Hers, to nobody's surprise, was a dirty coral rather than a dirty gray.

Sienna had explained that they were to attend a public forum in disguise, as a means of understanding their subjects at a grass-roots level. What she'd meant was they had to spy on the competition.

Now, Logan listened as the members of the Fathers argued their case against Lyandr and Synestra taking their rightful places on the throne. The crowd buzzed, many onlookers shaking their heads, staring in disbelief at the speakers.

The crowd appeared reticent, which Logan counted in his and Sienna's favor. Something he'd noticed about many of the people he'd encountered on his *seeing of the sights* earlier in the day. Vyrian had often pointed out that meeting the citizens eye-to-eye was what would win their hearts, not ruling from a palace on the mountain and throwing down decree after decree.

The meeting soon disbanded, with Logan disappointed that he couldn't get closer to gauge better the men who'd arrived unannounced to give the dinner crowd an impromptu end-of-days warning. The contents of the man's speech had been vague, and almost inconsequential, but Logan suspected he'd only been part of the plan. This had no doubt been a testing of the waters, a quick gauging of which way the people of this particular district were swayed.

Sienna nudged Logan, urging him to follow as she led them out into the warm sunlight and down a stone street to what appeared to be a tavern. Inside, he and his sister took seats in a far corner, where they sat enveloped by shadows awaiting their orders of meat broth and buttered loaves of bread.

Various groups of customers made rowdy conversation, subjects ranging from the rains and the bad harvest, to the dangerous word the Fathers were spreading, to the secret behind why the twins were taken.

One visit to a public watering-hole was enough to convince Logan that those responsible for rising up against him and Sienna did not have a strong support base—which still didn't negate the danger the two factions posed. The latter Logan could find a way to deal with, but the Fathers and their awful cultish ways would have none of Logan's support.

Seems like this lot actually might like their rulers.

Not everyone is going to oppose us, replied Sienna.

Thankfully, the Fathers don't appear to have the entire citizenry supporting them.

Small mercies, Sienna. We have no idea what we've stepped into. Not until we are ruling the place. Until then we can only guess as to support and outcomes.

Sienna snorted. *I've been here long before you brother. I know the people well enough. The Fathers may not garner support from the layman, but the Equals might. Two decades without formal rule has made Drakys vulnerable to attacks from inside and from beyond the realm's borders.*

Was Aunt Lyra such a tyrant? asked Logan, knowing the answer even before Sienna replied.

It had nothing to do with her. It was just a reason for the people to express their worries. Concerns Lyra had no power to address. Not until the true heirs took their positions.

Which brings me back to my initial question, replied Logan. *Who killed our mother and stole us from our home? And why? What were they after, and could any of it have to do with the Fathers or the Equals?*

Sienna nodded as she sipped from her beer mug. *Exactly what I was thinking. But let's just get through the ceremony and the blessing. Then we can begin our own investigation.*

Sienna was right, and Logan agreed to bide his time.

But if there were anything he was going to do first, it would be to hold the murderers of his Mother responsible.

CHAPTER 22

KAI

The rest of the time I'd spent with my mother in the tomb had been filled with memories of Grandpa Mason, who to me, was a large man, in both memory and spirit. That he'd died protecting Mom—though I was still yet to hear the specifics of those circumstances—had made him seem even larger than life.

I'd left her there, assured that she would not be attempting to return home by foot as Dad was meant to come up to fetch her. Entering the tree line, I removed my dress and bundled it up, then tossed it into the crook of a nearby tree bearing the requisite markings.

Then, with liquid ease, I shifted back into my panther form and settled into a loping run that fell somewhere between a sprint and a trot. I was in no rush to return home, even though I'd felt the pull of fatigue as it reminded me that I ached for rest. I'd get that rest, of that I was sure—I just needed a few more minutes to myself.

And as I ran, I caught sight of that cat, at first a blur in my peripheral and then a flash of gold as it crossed my path, bolder now, as though she'd decided to reveal herself on purpose as a message to me.

I slowed to a walk and studied the trees into which she'd disappeared, eyes focused on the thick brush which rustled and shivered in the breeze. The wind had picked up...or had it?

I looked around the forest, beyond the clearing in which I'd been standing so still, and confirmed that whatever the breeze was it didn't extend beyond the area surrounding me.

Odd as it appeared, I didn't default to a state of fear; the cat was certainly no danger, its size hardly that of a predator that would make me afraid. Besides, its bearing and behavior didn't lend itself to announcing a threat either.

Even so, I didn't drop my guard as I wavered in place, unsure of whether I ought to leave now or wait to see if she'd reappear. I wasn't far from the spot where I'd left my clothing, and I was tempted to shift, but my panther body was by far more conducive to tracking any form of prey.

I scented the air and began to follow the trail, moving between bushes and plants, making my way ever closer to a scent that remained elusive.

And so, I soon came to a halt and turned away from the trail, tired now of this game of hide and seek that seemed to have only one player.

But, as I turned, the trees blurred, wavered, colors bright now and then dark, so dark that the reds and greens appeared neon. I hissed a low breath and sniffed, now unsure of what I'd walked into, almost certain that I'd been dumb enough to allow my curiosity to lead me straight into a trap.

And this time there's no SoulTracker to come in and save your ass.

I shook my head, blinked again and scanned the trees, letting out a low whine as my vision stuttered. A blood-red bird called from a low branch as though he'd sensed my worry. But as I glanced over at him, the bird itself flicked out of sight—as though it had slipped away through the Veil. I coughed, the sound low in my throat, aware now that something was terribly wrong.

And then, just as I was about to shift back to human form—the need to stand upright seeming to overpower me—a red spot shimmered on the branch and the bird returned.

I tossed my head, confused now as around me the trees and grass and plants shivered and wavered, feathered pixels merging and splitting and then joining again. I took a step forward, and later I wasn't at all sure what I'd intended to do, whether I'd meant to race off into the trees or if I'd moved in order to shift back to human form.

Either way, I never made it; I blinked and found myself lying on my back in the grass, one arm flung out, knuckles grazing the dirt, the other resting on my abdomen, fingers fisted. I grunted and lifted my head, eyes inspecting every shadow, every tree, every movement. I shivered, cold having sunk deep into my bones.

I bit down on my jaw to stop the trembling. Twisting around, I was placing a hand to the ground to boost myself up when a flicker of gold blinked from around my wrist.

The hand on my stomach threw off that shimmer, and one glance down had me drawing a breath of shock.

A bracelet. Bronze, carved, wrapped around my wrist.

And so very familiar.

Familiar as though a new image had slid in front of the old, and I knew in that instant why the cat had seemed so familiar.

I knew her. I knew her very well.

Cat, the cat.

Grams' mysterious little feline sidekick.

I frowned, struggling to recall what had happened to the cat, aware that in my memory she'd been there one moment and then had evaporated from my mind, as though someone had taken an eraser to her.

I cleared my throat and then forced myself back to my feet,

spinning around to check the trees around me. There was little chance that I was truly alone, and I'd dropped my guard despite all my best intentions.

And now I stood in the forest, naked as the day I was born, staring around like a madwoman, wondering when a flickering shadow would spring out at me.

I took a step back, blinking as the second memory hit me.

Not only had Cat been a part of my life, but so had the bracelet which had miraculously appeared around my forearm as though it had never left. I stood there for a moment, staring at the intricately carved armband, remembering how it had protected me from the wraith lord's blade...well not entirely; a shard had embedded itself inside my arm despite the armor. Still, my injury would have been infinitely worse had I not been in possession of the armband.

And then...and then I'd removed the armor.

I struggled with my memory, trying hard to recall what had happened when Logan had removed the bracelet from my hand, and we'd seen then how badly the poison had infected me, poison from the wraith's sword.

I caught a flash of a memory, the bracelet in Logan's hand, his scowling face, eyes shadowed with worry, the soft clunk as he let go of the bracelet and it hit the bare wood floor.

And then...nothing.

I hadn't even thought of the armor, hadn't spent a moment wondering where it had gone and how—even though it had fallen at my side in my bedroom. How was it even possible that every single memory of the bracelet had been wiped from my mind?

Limbs now stiff, fingers wrapping around the bracelet, my thoughts flittered to Darcy. Was it possible my memory had been tampered with without my knowledge?

There had been too many instances in which such an intrusion could have occurred, and I would have at least registered the skipping of time. And even then, what kind of mental manipulation was capable of allowing memories to return at the same moment that the armband reappeared out of nowhere?

I shook my head, fingers tracing the bumps and grooves of the carvings, then I let out a sigh. The cold of the night was apparent now, in the ache of my skin and my bones, and I shivered, turning on my heel and heading off at a run.

I navigated through the forest and made my way to the tree hiding my clothing, then dressed quickly, my mind not for a moment leaving the new mystery. Not even later when I was lying under my covers, freshly showered and changed, the blankets wrapped around the armband so I wouldn't keep staring at it.

Eyes focused unseeing at the ceiling, I bit my lip as I clenched my arm, the bulge of muscle touching the warm metal of the armor. Where had it come from? And what did Cat have to do with the bracelet?

It appeared that an innocuous little housecat was more than she had seemed to be. I nodded slowly, acknowledging that Cat had never been consistent, and would often disappear for long periods of time, where Grams would merely shake her head and say that it wasn't right to stop any living thing from doing what nature intended.

Even now my mouth curved in a grin at Grams' implication, but now it didn't seem to be so cut and dried as answering the mating call.

And that brought me right back to the one person I was sure would be able to answer a few questions.

Grams.

My lips narrowed, mouth forming a thin line as I turned to reach for my phone. My aching body had grown less achy, and I was pretty confident that the shift from human to panther—and then back again—had something to do with the multiples of throbbing. My cheek, too, had repaired itself, shattered bone reknitting as human bone had shifted to animal and then back again.

The shift had often been used as a method to repair broken bones and other injuries, a secret magical power within the transformation also encouraged cell repair. There was a working theory that perhaps it was the very act of shifting that ensured the SkinWalkers were a long-lived race—maybe not immortal, but definitely possessing an extended lifespan with some of the oldest of our community still sprightly at the ripe old age of two centuries.

Now, as I tapped out a message to Grams and then waited for her response, I had to wonder how much the fae-walker knew? And even if she did know anything, would she tell me the truth? Grams had always been mysterious, but now that secretiveness was a reason for me to wonder if I could honestly trust her.

The little dots at the bottom of my screen began to bounce as Grams typed her response. Seconds late the phone pinged as her answer appeared, a simple statement of place and time to meet.

The Corner Cafe, 10am. Don't be late.

I snorted. I was the one who'd requested the meeting, why would I delay my arrival? I shook my head, reminding myself that I had to stop being so suspicious, that I had to give Grams the benefit of the doubt.

So I took a breath, calmed down, sent off a hugging face emoticon and tucked the phone under my pillow.

Within seconds I was asleep, my questions regarding what Grams would have to say remaining unfinished as darkness swallowed me whole.

CHAPTER 23

LOGAN

Logan was pacing the carpet of his room, his mind a whirl of everything General Vyrian had shown him. He was finding it a little hard to wrap his head around the fact that he'd been immersed within the city of Dyr for only half a day and yet he felt as though he'd been here for weeks.

Everywhere he'd turned, he'd been impressed beyond belief—the castle, the city and its construction, and of course the army. The might of the Drakys military was incomparable, and the reality was that should the dragon realm decide it was time to take over the EarthWorld, they'd take the realm with such ease it would be painful to watch.

But, other than the breadth of their military might, Vyrian had also revealed details of security issues within the realm, small skirmishes in the outer reaches with ancient clans who didn't bend to the rule of the regent queen.

And Logan's brain buzzed with the words of the Elders he and Sienna had spied upon. The fact that there were two powerful groups threatening to overthrow centuries of rule made for a very volatile situation all around.

The door opened behind Logan, and he spun on his heel as

Sienna stalked inside, her face flushed, eyes sparking with fury.

"What's wrong," Logan asked, frowning as she shut the door and leaned against it, eyes closed, exhaling deeply.

Sienna let out a groan. "Don Eridyn is too damned persistent. The man thinks he's the best thing since Morid's Tart."

"What?" Logan snickered. She'd been meant to bathe and change, then meet him for dinner—which was still waiting on the table near the balcony doors—but it appeared she'd been waylaid by a passionate suitor. "He wants to marry you?"

"He wishes." Sienna pushed off the door and hurried inside the vast room toward Logan who had paused in front of the open balcony doors, with its grand vista of the valley below the castle. She stopped at his elbow and let out another breath, this time the sound filled with something akin to rapture. "It never ever gets old, Logan. Every time, this view reminds me that it's all worth it."

"Marrying an old git called Eridyn is worth this view?" Logan smirked.

Sienna hit his arm. "No, you idiot. You know what I mean. This place was beautiful when I thought it was my prison. But knowing it's my home? It makes the beauty all the more impressive."

Logan was silent as he studied the view alongside his sister. He could see what Sienna meant, but somehow, the beauty of the view faded when he thought of Kai and what he'd left behind.

Sienna sighed and leaned her head against Logan's arm. "I know, brother. Just give it a little time. Fix things here and then go fetch your panther." Then she moved away, almost skipping as she walked over to the table and lifted steel lids to inspect the array of food the palace kitchens had provided. "Mhhh. Come, let's eat."

Sienna had already half-filled her plate with roasted potatoes and grilled meat, the color deep and red, and making Logan's mouth water.

He grabbed a plate and hovered behind her. "You think it's that easy?" he asked as he waited for her to make her next choice. "That I can go back and get Kai to follow me home all because she loves me? What will I be asking her to give up? She's an alpha panther, destined to look after her people."

Sienna poured a dark gravy over her roast and skirted the table to slip into the nearest available seat. "But her brother is looking after things just fine, last I checked. And her father's still alive and kicking. Corin will take up the reins if Kai isn't around."

Logan grunted, staring at the food, then dishing out everything his sister had selected. "I'm pretty sure it's more complicated than both you and I can understand," he said, licking gravy off the back of his finger as he sat beside her.

She tossed him a warm bread roll. "So what about giving *Kai* the choice?"

Logan scowled at his sister as she stared up at him, eyes narrowed, holding the butter dish hostage as she waited for an answer he didn't want to give.

Sienna snorted, shook her head and handed the butter over, giving him a dirty look. "Typical. You're going around assuming you know what Kai will say, and yet you haven't even given her the courtesy of making her own choice? You've just gone on an assumption and made her choices for her."

"You think giving her that choice makes it easier?" Logan asked before he forked a pile of roasted meat into his mouth, then chewed and swallowed. He'd only half chewed his mouthful when he continued, waving his fork in the air as he said, "If I did that, Kai would make the choice of her heart."

"Which is?" Sienna had almost cleaned her plate and was wiping up the gravy with one end of her overly-buttered roll.

Logan paused to concentrate on his food, a little annoyed that Sienna was insisting on having this conversation during their dinner. He swallowed and eyed the buffet as he replied, "She'd choose to come with me and leave her responsibilities behind.

And then she'd resent me for the rest of our lives. And believe me, walkers live just about as long as dragons." Logan got to his feet and went over to the buffet to fill his plate for a second time.

"Logan, you're forgetting something," Sienna said sharply.

"Which is?" he asked, teasing Sienna with laughter in his eyes—though he was wondering if the thing he was forgetting was Kai-related or food-related.

At this point, he wasn't sure given that Sienna was poking her fork at the air in front of her as she replied, "The option for her to turn you down. Are you afraid of giving her the choice in case she chooses not to come to Drakys with you?"

Logan winced as the question hit him deep, but as he parsed his feelings, he found himself shaking his head. "No. If she said no, I'd be okay with that," he replied and returned to his seat. "I just don't want her to stay because she was afraid of breaking my heart."

Logan made a deliberate attempt to eat slowly and not shovel his food down like Sienna was doing. Plus, the conversation had succeeded in somewhat dampening his appetite.

"There's no easy way, Logan," Sienna said, rising to fetch a bowl of what looked like lemon meringue pie. As she returned, she said, "You need to lay down all the cards for her, and accept what happens either way. You can't sit here and bear the burden of a decision that Kai hasn't yet made. That's insane, brother."

Logan took a breath and focused on Sienna, his food forgotten. "So what's our situation with the Ascension? When is it scheduled for? How do we prepare for the ceremony, and what in god's name am I supposed to do about flying?" Logan whispered.

Sienna rolled her eyes and pointed at the door to his suite. "Don't you read your messages?"

Logan grunted, then reached for his phone. But, seconds later, his cell phone in his palm, he paused as Sienna's barking laughter drew his gaze. "What?" he bit out.

"No cell service here, remember?" Sienna smirked, tilting her head. "Messages come in paper form. Usually left in the waiting room outside, on the hall table."

Logan shook his head. "Well, it's not like you gave me the full orientation, you know."

"Yeah. Things are going a little faster than I'd expected it to." Sienna's smile faded. "So it's been scheduled for sunrise tomorrow morning."

Logan gulped, eyes wide as he stared at his sister. "You can't be serious."

"Sorry?" Sienna offered, lifting one shoulder.

"So what's with the rush anyway? Why do the Ascension so quickly? Lyra did give an explanation, but it wasn't really detailed enough."

Lips pursed, Sienna nodded slowly. "The thing with the Ascension is that once it's completed, no other Ascension can be performed until one of us dies. And even then, the regent who takes over won't be given the full powers that us—as the 'Fated Pair' long foretold."

"Oh? So, our rights as rulers cannot be taken away once we go through with this Ascension?" Logan's question received a quick nod from Sienna who was eyeing the buffet again. "Okay, I get the rush, but now what? It's tomorrow morning, kid. A handful of hours away?"

Sienna grinned and nodded at Logan's plate, waving at him to eat. "We do the only thing we can. We practice. So eat fast."

Logan decided that it was best to move to the how instead of pondering the why. Brow furrowed, Logan dunked a potato into his gravy, popped it in his mouth and chewed saying, "And where the hell are we supposed to do that?" around his food. He really had lost his manners since arriving in Drakys. Logan swallowed, wiped his mouth and said, "I think a few people will bear witness to their ruler falling from the sky half a hundred times before he actually manages to fly. *If* he manages to fly." Logan concentrated on finishing what was left on his plate, then hurried off for a piece of that pie before Sienna went for thirds.

When he returned to his seat, Sienna was pursing her lips, a feat that was admirable considering her mouth was filled with pie. "You'll fly. Even Darcy said the block was gone and you've healed. You just need practice."

Logan snorted and polished off his pie, feeling a little too full, and a lot lethargic.

"Don't worry," Sienna said, her voice a song. "I have the most perfect solution to get you flying."

"Which is?"

Sienna smirked as she pushed her plate away, got to her feet and raced for the balcony. Just as she flung herself over the railing, she yelled out, "Easy. Just throw you off the side of a mountain."

CHAPTER 24

LOGAN

Sienna had not been joking.

"You threw me off the frickin' cliff, Sienna!" Logan screamed as his hands cartwheeled, legs pumping the air as he just kept falling.

All he could see were jagged black cliffs topped with caps of white snow, every single peak sharp and deadly as a thousand knives, all waiting to impale Logan when he finally hit land.

"Sienna!" Logan yelled as the rocky blank ground drew closer and closer.

And, just when he knew he was going to faceplant into the ragged boulders, Sienna swooped down and scooped him up, whooping loudly as she lifted him back up to the top of the mountain.

Sienna transformed and dropped Logan to the clifftop just as she also found her footing, taking short, sharp, excited breaths. "Wanna go again?"

"Not if you're going to throw me off the mountainside again. We already know *that's* not going to do anything."

Sienna clicked her tongue then paced back and forth dusting out her hands as she caught her breath. "You're no fun."

"No. I'm not. Not if you throw people off mountains. Look, this isn't working. Maybe we need to tell Lyra and Vyrian to hold off on the Ascension Ceremony. It's not likely that I'm going to learn to fly overnight."

Sienna stopped in her tracks, hands propped on her hips as she glared at him. "Logan. This isn't a game. If you can't fly by Ascension, or at the very least by Blessing, our legitimacy to the throne will be in question. We give the Fathers and the Equals a better chance at taking it from us."

Logan laid his own hands on his sister's shoulders and squeezed gently. "Sienna, please. We can only do what's within our power. Nothing more. Now come on. Let's practice some more, but how about we try from the ground first, okay?"

Sienna pursed her lips. "Fine. Let's start from the ground. But I warn you, it's not going to be as effective."

Logan smirked. "I think I can deal with less effective if it means staying more alive for longer."

Sienna rolled her eyes and jumped off the cliff, swooping smoothly into the air as she transformed into a shimmering golden dragon, the sight like nothing he'd ever seen.

As he watched her glide low and then rise, shimmering scales flickering in the fading reddish sunlight, Logan wondered for the first time what his own dragon would look like.

Then he shook his head and focused on Sienna. The golden dragon swung about and flew straight at Logan, then transformed and landed in one smooth fluid movement.

She hit the ground and placed her hands on her hips again, the movement, the curve of her eyebrow and the tone of her voice as she said, "Now you," all overflowing with smartassery.

Logan shook his head. "How?"

Sienna remained silent.

"How, Sienna? How did you learn to fly? Did someone chuck *you* off a cliff, too?" Logan asked, his voice rising.

And Sienna laughed. "That's it," she said, clapping her hands wildly.

"That's what?"

Sienna's eyes sparkled as she drew closer to Logan. She looped her hands around his waist and grinned. "Hold on," she said softly, then stepped back over the edge of the cliff.

"Sienna! What the hell?"

"I figured it out. It was a life-or-death situation," she yelled up at him.

"Sienna, you stupid idiot. Shift into a dragon, now. Before we're both roadkill," Logan screamed.

But Sienna wasn't listening. "Shift, or I die too," she said, a stubborn glint in her eyes.

"Sienna, I swear if we live through this, I'm going to kill you."

"You have to shift to do it," she sang out, taunting him.

Beyond Sienna, Logan could see the ground racing up to meet him. What the hell was she thinking putting her life in his hands when he couldn't fly.

Stupid, stupid kid.

"Shift, Logan!" Sienna screamed, tilting her head to look at the ground, her voice now edged with fear.

"I can't," Logan yelled. "I don't know how."

"Shift. Logan, shift!" Sienna screeched. And then her eyes changed to a golden hue, and she blinked, dark dragon eyes glistening as she screamed, "Save me!"

Something in her voice drove deep within Logan, and blasted through a wall in his mind. And then, ten feet from the ground, he heard a rush of sounds, a flapping of something large and leathery, the whistle of the air in his ears.

And the trilling of Sienna's laughter as she whooped and screamed from below him.

And then he dropped her.

"Logan, you idiot," she screeched.

But Logan only laughed as Sienna spun around and shifted

fluidly into the golden dragon. Logan skimmed through the air, the knowledge of flying, of riding the air currents, seeming to come from somewhere deep within his mind and soul.

Logan swooped low, then surged up into the sky, spinning in the air as he rose. His dark gold, almost-but-not-quite-bronze wings flapped around him, the scales on his hands and feet glistening in a multitude of iridescent colors.

"You're beautiful, Logan!" Sienna screamed. "Goddamn, brother! You're so damn beautiful!"

Logan grinned as he glided to meet her, unable to deny her words.

He never would have called himself beautiful, but he couldn't help but agree with Sienna.

His dragon was goddamn beautiful.

With the Ascension Ceremony planned for sunrise the next day, Logan and Sienna had cut short their flight training. As they flew back from the border of the Black Mountains, Logan found himself nostalgic, aware that this was the last day of his life as a normal person.

He'd been about to think the word *human*, as mages were essentially human in origin, just born with magical abilities. But Logan was, of course, not human. If he'd been in any doubt, he'd just proved it to himself an hour or so ago.

And now, as he and Sienna glided in toward the balcony of his bedroom, Logan scanned the city below him, studying the flames that flickered to light the way for travelers and watchmen.

The land of Dyr was an unusual combination of magical and advanced, and Logan was slowly getting used to it.

"Now *that* was exhilarating," said Sienna as she shimmered into her human form inside the room.

Logan, on the other hand, skimmed the balustrade, scuffed his clawed toes on the stone balcony floor, tripped over a rug where his human foot caught on a fringe, and tumbled at the foot of his bed, slamming his skull into the hardwood base.

"Oh gosh," Sienna called out as she ran to him. "Logan? You okay?"

Logan groaned and pushed to his elbows, then felt the small bump at the back of his head. "I'll live. You can stop with the fussing. Remember, not too long ago you were only too happy to toss me off the edge of a cliff?"

Sienna smirked and crouched beside him as he righted himself. "Don't be such a baby. It worked. You should be thanking me."

Logan grunted. "Remind me to keep you away from training your children to fly. You're likely to be the first queen of Drakys to fly her children to their deaths."

"Gosh, you're so dramatic." Sienna got to her feet. "Lyra's going to be on time tomorrow morning. If she's anything, she's fastidious and prompt. So best we get some sleep and be up early."

"What?" Logan mumbled as he got to his feet.

"Nothing. Go have a bath and get some sleep. Your muscles are going to need a soak again after you wake up too, so I'll knock on the door a half hour early. And don't be smart and ignore me or you'll be limping around the city all day. We can't afford that."

The door clicked shut behind Sienna and Logan sank into his mattress. As tempted as he was to dive straight under the covers, Logan did as instructed and headed into the bathroom.

And boy was he glad he'd obeyed his brat of a sister.

CHAPTER 25

KAI

The thing with the benefit of the doubt was that all too often it was undeserved. Grams stared at me from the other side of the table, our teas and cream-and-jam-drenched scones sitting between us like a cheery friend attempting to avoid a battle to the death.

I blinked and said, "You can't be serious."

Grams' mouth thinned, and she reached for her tea. "I am serious. I don't know."

I opened my mouth, then closed it before shifting my gaze to stare out the window. I had to control my anger, or my panther would think she was getting the go-ahead to surge forth.

Also, yelling at one's grandmother in a public place was unseemly, and even more so for an alpha. So I took another breath and leaned closer, reaching for the hem of the cardigan that I'd worn over my long dress. I'd decided that the morning was warm enough and I was not awake enough for complicated fashion decisions, so a simple cranberry-red, ankle-length shift dress and sneakers did the trick.

Now, I reached for the sleeve of my cream chunky cardigan and resettled the cuff—which I'd worn tugged all the way down over my wrist to hide the armor which was annoyingly unremoveable.

My grouching this time around was no different from when I'd first worn the armor and had discovered I'd not be able to remove the darned thing until *it* was ready and willing to come off.

I'd found out this morning before my shower that things had not changed, and I'd had to scrub around the bracelet then slide the exfoliating cloth as far beneath the armor as I could. Thankfully, it didn't fit too snug, or I'd have happily chopped off my arm to get rid of the damned thing—I was never the type to enjoy bondage, and the bracelet certainly did feel as though I was imprisoned somehow.

I sipped my tea, ate a few bites of scone, then plopped the remains back onto the plate. I'd had about enough of this craziness. And from the curve of Grams' eyebrows as she studied me over the top of her teacup—from behind a veil of steam—I could tell she knew I was close to exploding.

Still, she said nothing.

I shook my head and leaned forward, the edge of the table pressing into my ribs. "I'm sorry if I come across as a little rude, Grams. But I'm tired, I'm sore, I'm reeling from truths I've heard that have changed the very fabric of my life. I'm feeling a little abandoned by the sudden, very conveniently timed, departure of a certain fire-mage-turned-dragon, and I'm also," I shook my wrist pointedly between us, "possessed by a freaky piece of jewelry with a mind of its own. A little help here?"

Grams had been staring at me while I'd spoken, her expression bland, but at the mention of Logan, her features tightened and she stiffened, almost as though I'd hit a pause button on her. Then she relaxed, and her shoulders slumped. Whatever inner battle she'd just fought, the case for truth had won her over with an argument based on Logan.

How very curious.

Grams sighed and bent closer as well. "Fine. I guess I owe you a little of something. If I get put to death for this indiscretion, then I guess it would have been worth it."

I lifted an eyebrow. "Thanks, Grams. But I don't think you need to worry about dying. I think you pretty much have the immortal thing covered."

Grams was nodding, and—almost as though she hadn't heard me—she replied, "The armband is a token from the gods. Literally. It belongs to the goddess Ailuros, and she gifts it to those whom she believes have a deep need for it. Especially when that need has a wider impact on the lives of the people around the recipient, or on the DarkWorld as a whole. Which is why it does the arrival and disappearance thing."

Eyes wide, I paused for a long moment. "Oh." Grams remained silent as I let her words sink in. "Ailuros. Okay. I can deal with that...And the cat? The one that followed me in the forest...that was Cat...but she was really Ailuros? Was I just visited by the goddess herself?" The words all came tumbling out on a whisper as I stared at Grams.

She smiled. "Take a breath, dear. It helps you know, with the living and breathing thing."

I rolled my eyes, glad that the action didn't threaten to render me unconscious again. "Come on, Grams. This is...huge."

"I know, dear. But one does get used to the strange and bizarre...when faced with it often enough."

"So again, no clue as to why she's sent me the armband?" When Grams shook her head, I squinted as a memory hit me. "But wait a sec. When you gave me the armband...it was in this fancy chest and...you made it seem like a gift. How did you get it?"

Gram's face tightened, her expression flattening. "It wasn't me."

I blinked at her words, the memory of the day returning in a flicker of an eyelid.

. . .

Grandma Ivy's door was shut, the sound of the shower confirming she was home. Ailuros knew how long she'd be around though. The Odel matriarch never stayed for long.

I grinned and headed for the kitchen. With the kettle boiling, I busied myself cutting up coffee cake and setting out plates and cups.

A few minutes passed, and then Grandma Ivy emerged, fresh and beautiful, her bright blonde hair moist and frizzed from her shower, looking far too young to be anyone's grandmother.

"Kai, darling," she murmured, and squeezed me into a deathly tight embrace. The woman may look fragile, but the blood of an Alpha ran strong within her veins.

"Grams, you're home." That was all I could offer before my throat closed up. With the week from hell just behind me, all I wanted was to let her hold me, to forget everything and just be a kid for five minutes.

She held me.

And then, she grabbed me by the arms and thrust me away from her, studying my face in scary silence. "How have you been? Anything interesting happen while I was away?" The hardness in her question gave me the eerie feeling that she knew exactly what had happened while she'd been gone.

Which was probably why I spilled everything. I skimmed the wraith hunts, detailed the dead SkinWalker and the abductions, the Alpha visits, and Omega's paranormal investigations, and skimmed my near-death experience with Brand.

Grams sat in silence until my monologue was over and when I sat back, she slapped the top of the table with a flat palm and said, "Well, I think I have just the thing to make you feel better."

Odd thing to say.

Odder still when she scurried away and returned to place a rectangular box before me. Not a box—more like an artifact.

"Hope you like it." Grandma Ivy plonked herself back into her seat

and shoved a piece of cake into her mouth. The action didn't hide the strange expression in her eyes. Concern.

I hesitated. What did Grandma Ivy have to be so worried about? When her gaze didn't waver, I turned my attention to the small, bronze chest. Beautiful flower-shaped rivets held the box in shape at each corner, hinges that curved and curled into viper heads, carvings on each side reminiscent of Roman Gymnasts, and great ancient battles.

I opened the lid.

The hinges didn't dare to squeak. Within the box lay a piece of armor, a bronze armband which looked much like a gladiator's trappings. Carved into the inside of the armband was a set of letters, surely something so ancient the likes of me would never understand it. What an odd gift.

"Wow, Grams. This is insanely gorgeous," I whispered. And it certainly was no lie; the light glistened on the carved surfaces, and the images seemed to dance. I had to blink as it became too entrancing.

"It's a really special piece, Kai." Grams' voice lowered, a dead seriousness colored her words, and a shiver crawled up my spine. She sounded so serious. Too serious for a simple gift giving. "Put it on."

Didn't sound like a request, and yet I felt like once I submitted there was no turning back. My gut twisted as instinct agreed with me.

"Once you accept this, it belongs to you." Grams was getting weird on me. I raised an eyebrow and was about to giggle when she continued, "And you belong to it."

"Grams, what in Ailuros' name does that mean?" My fingers had stilled in their movement toward the armband.

Grams sighed. "Once you place it on your arm the bracelet will sense whether you're right for each other. If you are, then the locks will jam, and you won't be able to remove it."

"Okay, forgive the girlie question, but what about showering?" I looked at the band—its size would dwarf my hand from elbow to wrist. "And how will it ever fit me?"

"I don't know dear. I just know the bracelet chooses its wearer and gives him or her a special strength." Grams leaned toward me and

gripped my fingers in hers. "You and I both know you need all the help you can get."

There were too many unsaid words in that one sentence. Grams knew more than she was letting on.

"So, what's this thing supposed to do for me, make me invisible? Give me super-strength?" The whole story was so far-fetched. What was Grams thinking?

"Protection," Grams said, her eyes so sad I felt an answering clench in my heart. "If you were mortally wounded, you would survive."

The silence which followed rang around the room on painful echoes. How could she seriously expect me to accept what she'd just said? I teetered on the verge of hysterical laughter.

"So, definitely no try-before-you-buy?" This is so crazy.

"Nope. No returns once purchased either."

Beneath the banter lay a stone-cold seriousness I found disconcerting.

"Anything else it will give me?"

"Each of its wearers has been granted...a different sort of...ability. Some, who already possess power, have had it multiplied beyond their comprehension. Others have acquired a new power altogether."

"Maybe this isn't such a good idea. How do I know it won't hurt me? Maybe I should think about this."

"Kai, this is hardly the time for you to go away and have a good think about it. You have only this one chance."

I raised my eyebrows; I didn't appreciate being pushed into a corner even if it was my Grandma doing the pushing. I stood barely an inch away from the glowing bronze armor, my fingers almost touching the metal.

Almost.

When they made contact, my twinge of fear was lost within the swirl of electrical energy and iridescent light enveloping both Grams and me. From my fingers to my shoulder, aquamarine light sparkled and twirled around my arm and the band, coils of intangible color which wound from elbow to wrist in a magical embrace.

Within the blink of an eye, the band absorbed my arm into it. Or maybe it was the other way around. Perhaps my arm had called to it. Either way, band and arm now seemed as one.

I blinked and breathed deeply, drawing in some of the swirling green light too. It didn't matter. It didn't seem to have any adverse effect on me. I felt the warm weight on my arm and remembered what had just happened. I remembered, too, that I should be royally pissed off at Grams, but something within my soul had erased those negative feelings.

The weight of the band felt permanent. Forever. I felt the fear of what I'd gotten myself into.

"What just happened?"

Grams looked affronted, as if I'd asked why I'd been molested by the heavenly talisman. Grams cleared her throat. "Kai, this bracelet is now yours, forever. Or until the day someone else needs it far more than you do. It has chosen you."

"Why me?"

"I don't know." She raised her hands in defense. "All I know is that you needed help, and this was the best way I could help you—to pass the armband on to you. Hopefully, you will find a use for it."

"Where did you get it?" I shook my head, trying to figure it out, and hoping Grams had some answers. "Is it yours?"

"No, it wasn't mine. All I can tell you is that you can trust it. It won't harm you. Its job is to protect you, and that's what it will do."

I stared at the golden bronze carvings. At that moment, though, all I could understand was some ancient adornment had taken possession of my arm. It felt warm against my skin. Molded comfortably around my arm. My heart jittered as I felt its embrace. This band wasn't going anywhere.

"Okay, so what's it meant to do? How does it work?"

"Look, Kai, I can't tell you anything more. You will know what you need to know in good time." Grams stood up, her eyes unreadable. "I can't stay, Kai. I've got to be going again."

And then she strode to her room, grabbed her overnight case and headed out the door with a wave.

I took a breath and stared Grams down. "What do you mean it wasn't you?" I asked slowly.

Grams pursed her lips. "Sometimes, Ailuros will deliver the gift in person. She's been known to assume the form of humans in order to deliver her gifts. I have a memory of giving it to you, but it's more like something I saw happen than something I did myself."

The silence was thick and cloying, almost like the cream that now settled at the back of my throat. Coffee-shop sounds rose and fell around us, and Grams sipped her tea which had likely already cooled to undrinkable.

"Okay then," I said, casting my eyes around me, my tone slightly higher than normal. "Well. I suppose I have to deal with it then. Wish I knew what it's meant to help with."

Grams drained her cup and set it back on its saucer with a little chink. "Hold on a second," she said, her eyes sharp. "Back up a bit, young lady. What was that you said about me having the immortal thing pretty much covered?" Grams' gaze held me firmly, and I had nowhere to escape to.

With a grunt, I said, "I'm so busted."

CHAPTER 26

LOGAN

"Lyra has sent her riders ahead with some of the supplies that we'll need," said Sienna, her face sober.

She'd arrived only ten minutes after Logan had emerged from the bathroom. He'd taken a second soak in order to loosen up his muscles, glad he'd obeyed her command. Thankfully the hot water had done the trick.

"Can we trust them?" he asked Sienna, wondering how trustworthy Lyra's men would be given this ceremony was meant to be secret.

"I believe so. She's been exceedingly accommodating so far. If she hated us, surely she'd have revealed some of her dislike by now."

"Maybe," said Logan as he grabbed his duffel and followed Sienna toward the balcony, wondering why she waffled when it came to deciding whether or not she trusted Lyra. From what Logan had seen so far, Lyra was honest and straight-up—what you saw was what you got.

Even Vyrian had had the same opinion, but then he was her uncle so he may be biased.

Reaching the balcony, the siblings launched into a run,

jumped the railing, and flew off in the direction of the Black Mountains.

"So where exactly are we off to?" asked Logan once they were aloft, his great wings slicing through the air.

"It's a temple, an almost holy place called the Hollow of the Life's Blood. Or the Aurul i'Drysht. It's on the northern faces of the Black Mountains, and it is said that the temple has been there all the way back to the beginning of Drakys history. It is where the Drysht, or the Ancient Egg of Life, has been kept for centuries. Apparently, it has never been moved. Not since it was first found. And every year they celebrate the power of the egg in the Rebirth Ceremony. It's called the Sirin 'a Drysht."

"So what's so special about this egg?" he asked, staring at the thin glimmer of burnt-orange and gold rays as they scarred the horizon in the distance, promising a new day. He scanned the city below and watched as homes came to life along the streets, as people awakened and prepared for the day long before the bloody rays of the red sun lit the horizon.

"The egg is considered magical. It's believed to have life-giving properties," said Sienna, her voice lilting on the currents. "The priests tell tales of the stream below the Hollow being imbued with the magical healing properties of the egg, and of the waters curing illnesses and fevers, helping women fall pregnant... you know the drill."

Logan smiled. No matter the realm, superstition and old-wives' tales never changed.

Sienna banked right and followed a shallow rise of jagged black mountains, gliding up toward the sharp ridgeline that touched the clouds. They flew over the ridge and down again where Logan knew he would find the next chapter of his life.

Lyra and Vyrian had come dressed in their finery, which made Sienna roll her eyes and sniff. "Good thing I prepared something earlier," she muttered and handed Logan a cloth bag. "Go change and get back here quickly." Sienna pointed at a shallow cave to their right as she too headed for a spot to change.

Before long, the siblings were dressed in tailored garments of blood-red silk and shimmering gold thread. Satisfied, Sienna gave a nod and led the way around the rocky outcropping inside the cave toward the cavern where Lyra and Vyrian stood in somber silence.

The old man wore a smile that implied he was enjoying the formalities and Logan had to force down a grin. He'd grown fond of Vyrian so quickly that he'd been surprised—it wasn't often that he grew close to another person so swiftly.

And then Logan soon forgot about everything as he followed Sienna down a stony path and into the cavern, which turned out to be nothing less than a cathedral lit by hundreds of little fires blazing away in every nook and cranny along the walls.

The Drysht sat upon a stalagmite pedestal. Above it a giant stalactite aimed its point at the top of the egg, dripping water onto the amber relic—water which washed down the egg and into a dark, silent pool that formed a moat around the base.

"Looks festive," said Logan softly as they neared the egg, which turned out to be a large amber pendant holding within it a form that wasn't entirely definable. Not in this light at any rate.

Sienna's eyes shimmered with mischief, and Logan shook his head. She'd known the egg was a fossil all along.

Sneaky kid.

Lyra waved at the siblings and inspected their clothing, nodding in approval as though she hadn't at all intended on outshining them. Still, what did it matter when this ceremony was meant to be a secret?

"Come. We must hurry," she said, clapping her hands briskly. "The sun will rise in a few minutes, and you must both be ready."

Vyrian and Lyra helped to position Sienna and Logan, feet in the moat of water, hands on the egg, palms flat so the warmth of the amber fed into their bodies.

Sienna looked over at Logan and smiled. "Ready?"

"As I'll ever be," said Logan softly.

As he spoke, a strange ruby glow filled the dark cave, making it feel like the very air was bleeding as the red sunlight shimmered through the cracks and channels in the roof of the cavern above.

A thin line of sunlight fell on the amber, and the egg glowed as though it pulsed with blood, with life. And Logan found he could understand the fascination of the people when it came to this fossil. It did appear quite magical with the rays of the red sun bathing it, enveloping the mysterious form within.

Lyra and Vyrian were speaking words Logan did not yet understand, and the sounds undulated around the cavern like a sad lament. He felt awkward with his feet planted in the water, palms placed on one side of the egg, but he glanced at Sienna to find her giving him a confident smile.

Seconds passed, and then Lyra and Vyrian walked toward the siblings, both bearing bowls made of gold. They reached down, dipped the bowls into the pond and then poured the water over first Logan's, and then Sienna's head.

Then, as the water sluiced over their heads, the sun's bloody rays bathed the egg, and Logan felt a strange heat beneath his hands. He glanced over at Sienna and recognized the consternation on her face.

Logan shifted his palms, as though he intended to move away, but Sienna shook her head at him. She didn't need to worry though, as Logan found he was unable to let go of the egg; it seemed to be holding onto him with a force that he couldn't understand.

The scarlet light brightened and dulled, swirling around them, and within the egg. And in the same moment, Logan saw something move inside the amber, and Sienna gasped. Logan didn't look at his sister to check what had caused her shock.

He was looking right at it.

Within the egg, the movement proved to be a pair of eyelids cracking open, then slowly widening until he found himself staring at a single dragon eye.

And before he could take a breath, the eye closed and a bolt of scarlet lightning struck the egg, sparks flying as the branches of the energy bounced off the amber and sought out both Logan and Sienna.

Within seconds, the pair were enveloped, immersed, impaled by the lightning and Logan had to wonder if this experience was anything like what Kai had endured.

Perhaps not, as he found he felt no pain.

Just a million thoughts and images filling his mind.

Though the water was icy, and the lightning continued to spark around them in a living web, neither of the siblings made a sound. Not until the eye blinked again and the lightning faded, as though it had never been there at all.

And then it was over, and Lyra and Vyrian were stepping back out of the water, smiling brightly as the twins let go of the egg and turned to face them.

As Logan and Sienna stepped out from the water, Lyra and Vyrian bowed low, then straightened, faces aglow with an almost palpable joy.

"All hail the new Queen of Drakys, Synestra of the House of Yl. All hail the General of Drakys, Lyandr of the House of Yl."

Both a little stunned, Logan and Sienna shared an uncomfortable smile, though they nodded graciously at the older members of their family who had both looked after the realm in the absence of the rightful heirs.

Logan only hoped that in the days to come, his aunt and

great-uncle would remain loyal, because he suspected that he and Sienna were going to need all the help they could get.

And from the knowledge now surging within his head, he knew things were only going to get worse.

Talk about an information overload.

CHAPTER 27

KAI

Mel had left with Steph a while ago, and I was still standing in front of the fire in the living room, my mind churning on a whole bagful of issues—Mom's revelation of the possibility of betrayal which implied a mole in our ranks, the fact that Mom was instrumental in discovering that the Ni'amh was five women and not one, that Grams was half-fae and royalty to boot, that Saleem was not just in need of help in Mithras but captured and being tortured and needing an extraction sooner than anyone had expected.

And that I was still weak, still suffering bouts of shakes—though thank Ailuros, there had been no further strokes.

And Ailuros.

How often does a girl get a visit from a goddess?

I mean, we all knew the gods existed, but many had withdrawn from interacting with the general population and few still retained the elemental power to influence events or even people. But the armband on my wrist was a solid reminder that this wasn't just a gift from a goddess, but that it was take two.

Maybe I was just that lucky.

Or, maybe I was so deep in shit that I actually needed a god to help me get out.

Now *that* wasn't a thought I wanted to ponder.

Good thing something else was turning around and around in my head—I was trying to convince myself that I really had no other choice but to go to Drakys and speak to Logan.

But a small part of me didn't want to go.

Logan had left behind that letter. He hadn't even been there to know what had happened to me, or to Mom—though, considering the contingent of spies within our home, I couldn't be certain he didn't have his finger on the pulse of my life at any given moment.

And when I finally came home, injured and weak, needing to be surrounded by my family, and when my thoughts had turned to Logan, to how much I needed his arms around me, what I received was not the man himself to offer his comfort, but instead, a letter of goodbye with Grams acting as courier.

I couldn't deny that I felt somewhat betrayed, and yet the contents of that letter weren't enough for me to give up on him. Though it was enough for me to simmer with hurt. Simmer and try not to think about it.

He hasn't said goodbye, I reminded myself firmly. I suppose I could take that as a sign, and as a reason to refrain from losing my shit altogether.

And I wanted to lose my shit. I really did.

But, a voice in my head said that there was too much to do to waste time losing my shit when I wasn't altogether sure that Logan had given me a reason to.

Sure, he'd left without saying goodbye to my face, but I knew him well enough to know that he was hurting. He'd not have made that decision to leave lightly.

And Logan was no longer the man I had met all those months ago. A fire-mage paranormal-operative for Omega? Omega didn't exist anymore, and neither did that sexy fire mage who'd walked into my office at the Rehab Center all those weeks ago. Because Logan was a freaking living breathing dragon.

And a royal one at that.

How much irony was there in the fact that the djinn and the dragon were partners with neither knowing how important the other was?

Until it was too late.

I let out a sigh and spun on my heel to find Lily and Baz hurrying into the room toward me. I picked up my crossbow—which I'd been cleaning when Mel had arrived—and my soft cloth which I tucked into my back pocket.

"When do you leave?" asked Lily, barely catching her breath as she came to a stop in front of me.

"Really, Lils? Give her time to breathe at least," said Baz, throwing his hands in the air.

I smiled and patted Lily on the shoulder as I peered over at the vamp-demon. "It's okay. I know everyone is eager to get moving. Especially when a life hangs in the balance."

"But are you up to cross-Veil travel?" asked Baz, his lips thinning. "You've only had a few hours of proper rest since you got home. I'm not sure that's enough."

"I'm fine, Baz. Seriously."

He snorted. "You had your insides fried, repeatedly. I'm not so sure you're as fine as you think you are."

I lifted an eyebrow as I met the challenge in Baz's eye. He was so much a part of the family now that I had no choice but to consider his point.

Eventually, I let out a sigh. "I swear I'm fine. But I'll have Dad check me over one last time before I go."

"I'm going with you," said Lily, straightening her shoulders.

"You are most certainly not," said Dad as he passed the living room doorway and stopped in his tracks.

"But—" Lily began.

"No buts, young lady." Corin Odel waved a finger at the lynx walker, and I stifled a snicker as Dad said, "If you think you want to travel to Mithras with the team when they're ready to leave, then you're getting a full physical and some rest. Even with the batch of Krisl stamens, the Elite managed to find for us, your recovery isn't a magical snap of the fingers. Cross-Veil travel is hard on a person's body, and I'd like to keep the number of trips to a minimum, if you don't mind."

I grinned at Dad's stern, paternal monologue but then he looked over at me and when I saw his expression my smile fled. "You too." Dad sent me a threatening look. "Alpha or not, you're going to need an assessment before you travel."

I caught the smirk on Baz's face, but I knew when I had lost the verbal battle. Little did Dad know that he was in for a full-scale war if he thought he'd get me sitting still long enough for an in-depth medical scan.

The thought reminded me that there was also the matter of a certain MRI for which results would be ready at the Elite HQ very soon. I had to figure out a plan to waylay those results.

And fast—if I knew what was good for me.

With a quick nod, I said, "Sure, Dad. I'll come up soon. I'm just getting a few things together."

Dad's eyes narrowed. "When are you leaving?"

"As soon as I can. Saleem can't wait. The longer we leave him there, the worse he gets. The last thing I need is to dawdle and have him die on us."

Dad gave a nod, expression inscrutable. "And how are you getting to Drakys?"

"I have the seal Horner gave me when I first went to Drakys. It's still keyed to me so that part is easy."

"What about traveling from the portal to the city? That journey isn't like catching a cab, Kai," Dad said, his tone cool. "I know you went out last night, and yes, the shifting would have helped immensely, but you're getting at least another six hours of sleep before you leave. Am I making myself clear? I have enough sick people in this house. I don't need you adding to my list of patients."

Dad gave me one more glare—one edged with concern and a touch of what I suspected was fear—and then stormed out the door, slamming it behind him.

Oh dear.

"What did you do now?" asked Iain from across the hall. He stood there, golden hair shimmering in the sunlight, cup of coffee in one hand, bran muffin in the other.

I'd barely seen much of Iain these past weeks, what with his traveling across the country, and his trips to various European council meetings. Something big and very secretive was going on with him, but I didn't have time to wrangle it out of him.

"You're back?"

He looked down at his dark-suited, well-muscled body and nodded. "Looks like it."

"Smartass," I said, hurrying over to give him a hug.

"Hey, watch the hot liquids," he protested, before setting the cup down to give me a one-handed hug. "Wow, I haven't been gone that long, kid. I just saw you in the hospital—like what?—a couple of days ago."

I shook my head. "A lot's happened since then, bro. Keep up."

Iain's expression sobered. "I heard. I just checked on Mom, but how is she really? She seems okay, but..."

I smiled. "She'll be fine. She's more riled up with being forced to stay in bed." Then I gave an evil grin.

After our chat at the coffee shop, Grams and I had made a quick trip to the haberdashery across the road and had returned with a gift for Mom to pass the time. She wasn't at all pleased with the package or with the explicit instructions that she'd only be cleared as healthy once the needlework had been completed.

I could still hear Mom's horrified shriek of "You got me a bloody cross-stitch!!" in my ears and—

"And where did you just go?" Iain asked, quirking an eyebrow. Then his eyes narrowed. "What did you do?"

I smirked. "Not a thing, big brother. I've just been making sure our patient upstairs is behaving herself."

Iain guffawed. "That was you? The crossing stitches thing with the purple horses?" When I bit my lip and nodded, trying hard not to laugh, he shook his head. "Oh, you're so going to pay for that one."

"Nope," I shook my head. "Well, yes. But I'm not going down alone. That was a joint effort but, to be fair, the cross-stitch was my idea."

Iain chuckled as he gave me a look that was a blend of fondness and weariness—the quintessential emotional reaction of brothers to their sisters. "So, where are you off to? I caught the last bit about cross-Veil travel."

"I have to go talk to Logan. Saleem needs help. Life or death thing. We're getting an extraction team together." I tilted my head and studied Iain's face, well aware that he too had served his time as an intelligence operative for Sentinel. "Think you can lend a hand?"

Iain paused and looked over my shoulder at Lily and Baz who'd remained inside the living room. "They going?" I nodded. "Darcy?"

"What do *you* think?"

Iain huffed, then nodded. "Okay, let me clear the decks as well as I can. I'll try my best, but I can't promise. And even if I do go, there's a good chance I'd have to come back early if there's an emergency."

"Geez, Iain, you sound so official and important."

Iain made a face. "It is what it is. Alpha isn't your average job."

I paused as I studied his expression. "So what's the council going to do about Wade and Trapper? They being held accountable?"

I most certainly hoped so.

Iain nodded. "Most definitely. They'll serve their time. And the addendum Marsden and his cronies put through has been repealed. We're in the process of electing a new committee."

"Most of the old guard standing down?" I asked, somewhat satisfied, although justice was tasting a little lukewarm and bland.

"Yeah, they are. Whether they want to or not."

"And me?" I asked, holding my breath. I *was* a murderer after all, even if an unintentional one.

Iain smiled. "You've had a lot of very passionate vocal support. Justin's done enough already to ensure you're absolved of the crime. All my efforts have only boosted those he's made."

I bit the inside of my lip at the mention of Justin. His proposal still hung in the air between us, and I had yet to give him his answer. "I hope he's not lobbying on my behalf with marriage in mind."

Iain winced. "Geez, Kai. You really aren't the most tactful woman around." He let out a sigh and reached for his coffee. "And no, he isn't. He told me as much. He's just doing what's right, so you just give the guy a break, okay?"

My eyes narrowed. "He told you he proposed?"

Iain nodded. "He's my best friend, Kai. Of course, he did."

"Ugh, this is so awkward." I folded my arms, not sure what to do with myself.

But Iain patted me on the shoulder. "Not awkward, kid. Logan's a great guy...dragon...king. Whatever. As far as I can tell, you'll choose the right man. I've got no dog in the race, despite my affection for Justin. So may the best man win," Iain said before he stuffed the remains of his muffin into his mouth and disappeared down the hall to his study with a waggle of his fingers over his shoulder.

Baz and Lily had left, too, so I hurried upstairs to my bedroom. If Dad thought I was going to let him check me out, he had another think coming.

Ailuros only knew that the last thing I could afford right now was to have Dad do a full medical on me. What he'd find out would just be a huge obstacle to saving Saleem.

When the djinn was free, then I'd get Dad to give me the once-over.

And what if, by that time, it's too late.

I shook my head, avoiding the voice which whispered that I was being reckless. I had other things to worry about.

And my health wasn't one of them.

CHAPTER 28

KAI

The weight of the portal key in my jacket pocket was enough to shorten my stride, to slow my purposeful steps and transform them into a flurry of skipped beats, where doubt traced its insidious fingers through my confidence.

The ride over to the Elite HQ had been short—I'd taken Logan's bike again, given that he wouldn't be needing it in the near future—and I'd just toed the stand in place and removed my helmet. I swung off the seat and hiked my backpack up before making a beeline for the back entrance of the Elite HQ.

I'd at last been given an access pass for long-term parking at the rear of the building, which had turned out to be a graveled lot surrounded by neatly trimmed brilliant green lawns and a stretch of garages that likely held the agency's little fleet of limos.

Bike parked, and keys logged at the Rear Entrance Security station, I made way my through the house to the front hall, my mind nowhere near agency responsibilities.

I'd been so certain that Logan simply had to be included in Saleem's retrieval that I hadn't stopped to consider whether I was doing it more because I owed it to Logan, or because I was merely acting out of the selfish need to not be alone in the mission.

And yes, Logan *had* said he wanted to be included when we went to save the djinn's ass, but I had to wonder if I would be putting Logan in a difficult position. He'd only just returned home, and knowing what he likely faced, the expansive duties that he'd be burdened with now that he and Sienna had returned to rule, I had to consider the possibility that Logan may not want to take time out from his duties to go to Mithras.

Or worse, what if he had no choice in the matter? Things were never as easy as it appeared to be from the outside. And that was my current position in relation to Logan's life.

I was on the outside.

And Logan would have responsibilities, obligations. Running the military of an entire realm? *That's a slight step up from paranormal special investigator.*

Should he decline to join their team, would I really be in a position to judge him for it? My stomach tightened, clawed fingers curling into a painful fist, searing my spirit at even entertaining the possible aftermath of his possible refusal.

With a slow breath, I swept back the curtain of pain, impatient with my instinctively emotional response to something which was yet to happen.

I rolled my shoulders and shook my head, an admonition to the inner weakness that had snuck past my defenses to rear its ugly head. There was little point in exploring a disappointment that had not yet occurred, no matter how likely Logan's refusal may be.

And, whatever he ended up deciding, I knew all too well that any decision he makes, neither choice would be any more difficult than the alternative.

Tara would likely tell me not to borrow trouble; I already had enough to keep me busy for the rest of my existence. A smile slipped from my lips as I thought about Tara. Did she have any knowledge of Grams' history or family?

And if she did, would she have told me?

Plus, the Queen of the Fae had been radio silent for a while now—one of my many concerns that were currently sitting on the backburner for when I had a moment to think my options through.

That backburner is certainly getting crowded.

Other than Logan—and Tara going incommunicado—I had another more sobering problem to consider. As this trip to Drakys was being made without my father's confirmation that I was well enough to travel across the Veil, I had snuck out of the house within a few minutes of my conversation with Iain, without letting anyone know that I was leaving.

The whole sneaking out in the dark of night—daylight I mean—avoiding the squeaky stairs and evading any visitors to the kitchen, had almost ended up in my sitting on the hall carpet, crying until I had no more tears left.

How hilarious that I'd been reduced to sneaking out like a disobedient teenager when I was no longer a minor, when the responsibilities resting on my own shoulders were those of an adult alpha and a mythical persona come to life, a fifth of a whole, charged with saving the DarkWorld.

And neither alpha duties, nor Ni'amh responsibilities, drew the kind of fear from me that I felt when considering my lies to Corin Odel.

If I were to be honest, the man was likely worse to face than the Ancients, worse even than being framed for murder by the Walker Council and almost dying in the process.

But, despite my awareness of the line I was crossing, the last thing I needed was to be delayed with my father's nagging—nagging which would turn decidedly worse when he finally did discover the reason I was avoiding his medical probing.

Now I clenched my fingers to still the tremors, balling my fists so that I could at least pretend there was nothing wrong, pretend that I hadn't been on the verge of passing out on numerous occasions in the last few days, pretend that I hadn't had a grand total of three seizures since I'd returned home after the shadowmen debacle.

Whatever power the shadowmen had used on me had left a residual effect on my body, resulting in strange tremors in my limbs as well as blurred vision, light-headedness, and weakness in my limbs.

Or perhaps those were merely the result of those strokes you've been having.

There had been a good reason I was sitting on the living room floor when Mel came by. I had taken to remaining seated wherever possible to avoid any of my attacks being witnessed by my family. I'd managed to avoid their attention so far, but I didn't believe for a second that I'd get away with it for too much longer.

I tugged the strap on my satchel higher on my shoulder as I entered the front hall of the Elite HQ and searched the living room for any sign of High Councilman Horner.

I'd messaged him before leaving home with my request for a jumper to transport me to Drakys. Of course, Horner had been more than happy to help and had assured me that he'd have transport available as soon as I arrived.

But the living room was empty, much like the reception desk in the hall and I found myself pacing the carpet for a few minutes before I heard the sound of footsteps along the passage.

I spun on my heel and found myself staring at a very surprised Darcy. "Hey. What are you doing here?" asked the MindMelder, forehead creasing as she came to a stop in front of me.

I hesitated before replying, well aware that whatever answer I gave Darcy may find its way to the ears of my family.

Or maybe try trusting her?

I cleared my throat and shrugged. "I have an errand to run,

and I needed to speak to Horner. Have you seen him?" I asked my friend lightly, hoping Darcy would accept this was my business.

But Darcy tilted her head and frowned at me, eyes narrow and suspicious. "What errand is this that needs to be done so quickly? You have barely even recovered from your ordeal, and you're running errands? Has your father checked you out to give you the okay for normal activities like work and errands?" Her eyes were still narrowed as she fell silent.

I scowled and avoided the MindMelder's eyes. "When did you turn into my mother?"

Darcy shook her head. "The moment you became evasive—which tells me that you are up to no good."

And she didn't even need to read my mind.

CHAPTER 29

KAI

After Darcy left the living room, I sank into the sofa and let out a deep sigh. I'd been so close to revealing the truth to Darcy; just something about the woman encouraged me to confide in her. Funny how the MindMelder didn't even need to delve into my mind for me to be on the verge of spilling the real truth to her.

I would have to keep a tighter grip on myself if I wanted to make it across the Veil before someone from my family stopped me, likely seconds before I jumped through the portal.

I bounced my knee up and down, checked the time five times then boosted to my feet and began to pace across the carpet wondering where in Ailuros' name my requested jumper had gotten to.

Just when I'd almost given up and had been five seconds from sending a text to Mel, Larsson strode into the room a lukewarm smile on his face.

"Hey," I said, curious now as the usually cheerful jumper gave me such a subdued reception. "Everything okay?" I asked, a little tense now as I studied his face.

Larsson gave a quick shake of his head and lifted his hand in the air as if to negate the tension that seemed to flow off his body. "All good, Kai. Sorry, just a few things happening at the same time is all. Nothing I can't handle."

I paused at the realization that my request for a jumper may well have inconvenienced a mission in progress and I cursed myself for being so self-involved that I hadn't even considered how my sudden request would have impacted other Elite agents.

"I'm sorry. If this is a bad time, I can come back later," I said, giving him a smile.

Larsson shook his head and gave a dry laugh. "No, I'm just a little off-balance because Ash decided to ground your transport until she can come down and speak to you. Something about a *sensitive request*." He made air-quotes as he spoke the phrase, then rolled his eyes.

"Oh," was all I managed to utter before the subject of the conversation scurried into the room, her eyes scanning the space as though she'd expected me to have already left, despite her instructions to Larsson.

"You're here, thank goodness," Ash said as she rushed over, a small plastic bag in her hand.

Larsson scowled. "Where did you expect her to be? You just told me to tell her to wait for you," he said sharply, eyes flashing with irritation.

Ash grinned at the redheaded jumper and shook her head. "Sorry I held you up, okay? Look, I'll make it up to you. How about I cook you that lamb vindaloo you like?" she said, her eyes sparkling with fond amusement.

Larsson tilted his head, studied her face for a moment as though he wasn't quite sure if Ash was serious. Then he nodded and said, "Add garlic roti, and you have a deal."

Ash let out a low groan. "Ugh, you know I suck at making decent roti."

"No. You make more than decent roti. You only suck at making them round. And I don't know what the big deal is. They end up inside your stomach anyway, so you don't need to be so darned OCD about it." Larsson smirked, and I had to hide a smile. Seemed he'd gotten what he wanted out of the deal and I made a mental note to check back with Ash how her dinner with Larsson had turned out. Though something told me their relationship was anything but romantic.

The doc smiled and shook her head. "If I didn't know any better, I would say you maneuvered me into this deal just because of that greedy gut of yours."

Larsson didn't reply, although the smirk on his face made me wonder if Ash wasn't more correct than she even realized.

She turned to me now and held out the bag, giving me little choice but to take it. Inside were a handful of plastic bags, gloves and tweezers, and a few airtight tubes for degradable samples. It appeared to be a specimen-collection kit.

"You want me to grab specimens of something while I'm in Drakys?" I asked, frowning as I stared inside the bag, though I suspected what she was after.

Ash cleared her throat. "Yes. Larsson was supposed to have conveyed this information to Logan before he left, but it appears he forgot to *tell Logan* because in the end, the pair of dragon royals had no need for a jumper." Ash was glaring at Larsson as though it was his fault.

Larsson raised his hands, his shoulders and eyebrows rising in question. "Can I help it if it slipped my mind? They changed plans on me when I got there."

I scowled at the thought of Logan and Sienna's departure, then I stiffened. "Wait, what? How did they go if they didn't use a jumper?" I asked, glancing from Larsson to Ash and back again. "Mendenhall is the closest portal? Don't tell me they flew there themselves? Aren't there laws against revealing ourselves to the normals? Or dragons have glamor, right?" I slapped my forehead, mind awhirl with dragon-facts.

Ash snickered. "They may well have as long as they used their glamor to hide themselves. Although, I wasn't aware of Logan having broken his wings in as yet."

I fell silent at the mention of Logan's wings, well aware that *I* had even less knowledge of what was going on in Logan's life than Ash did—a position that didn't sit at all well with me.

I forced a smile onto my face, determined to ensure that my personal concerns remained exactly that, and shook the bag. "What samples are you after? Black lily?"

Ash brightened at my question. "Yup. I need a couple more samples of the flower. I've also added in the vials for you to collect samples of the water in the river, and at least one other spot that's not contaminated. I have the instructions in the bag for you."

It cracked me up the way Ash ordered me around with that sweet, almost innocent smile, but I tried not to giggle. "You want samples from the trees nearby? I saw a few that appeared to have been poisoned. Dead branches, shriveled leaves, bark giving off this strange colored goo."

Ash nodded at my suggestion. "Yes, please. That would be great. I need the soil samples from the river banks and the surrounding area, as well as clean samples from maybe a mile or so away. The more samples I have, the easier it will be for me to do the assessment on helping rehabilitate the area."

I nodded and tucked the forensics-kit inside my backpack before gripping the strap and glancing at Larsson who had been looking on with keen interest at the mention of samples and poisons.

I gave Ash a quick nod. "Anything else?"

She shook her head and then clapped her hands. "Nope, I'm all done here. Larsson, she's all yours. Safe trip you two." With that, Ash turned on her heel and hurried for the door.

But when I called to her, she stopped and turned to me, a question in her eye. "Sorry, I need a small favor," I said, glancing briefly at Larsson.

"Sure. Anything. Text me before you leave, and it'll be in your inbox upstairs when you get back."

I flushed with guilt and smiled. "Thanks so much."

Ash waved and hurried out into the hall, her reply of "Anything for you, Kai," and the rapid tapping of her shoes on the wood floor, echoing toward me as she disappeared upstairs to her lab.

Larsson chuckled. "She's too easy."

I laughed and shook my head. "I'm guessing she's an amazing cook."

"Like you wouldn't believe. Michelin stars have nothing on Ash in the kitchen. The woman is *literally* the goddess of spices."

"It appears I've been missing out having never sampled the creations of this goddess," I said with a pout before I tapped out that text to the goddess in question.

"Okay, I'll make you a deal." Larsson was grinning wider now. "You keep my secret, and when she cooks me that vindaloo, you can come share my victory meal."

I laughed and shook my head. "You do know she's got your number, right?"

Larsson shrugged. "Doesn't matter, she's had it for years. But...I still get my food," he said, his voice filled with triumph.

I laughed softly and tapped the jumper on the shoulder. "Right. The faster we get to Drakys, the faster I get to taste it."

CHAPTER 30

KAI

My arrival in Drakys was much less uncomfortable than my last jump, probably because I'd been relieved of my concerns regarding travel from the portal access-point north-east of the Black Mountains to the city of Dyr itself.

From previous experience, I knew that the journey on foot—feline, that is—had been an overnight one for me, and I'd calculated it had taken around five hours to descend the cliff and follow the map through the Black Mountains and across the plains before arriving at the city gates.

I'd even come prepared with my panther-adapted rucksack to store my luggage and my clothes so I could shift and run as much of the way there as I could make it on foot. Panther speed, that loping feline flight, was decidedly faster than human.

But, now, when Larsson deposited us on the bright white ice beside the frigid lake on the Mendenhall Glacier, he hadn't simply flitted away with a reminder that he'd return every few hours, as he'd done the last time we'd both stood here, wrapped in icy sky and icy lands and icy gusting winds.

Instead, he gave me a sheepish grin—along with an exaggerated shiver at the frozen breeze that swept past—and then, one hand on the hood of his fur-trimmed parka, his voice undulating around us, he shouted, "I'm on orders to accompany you to the palace...remain with you until you need to return. Horner was all antsy, worrying about the distance you'd need to travel and if you needed to return urgently...he gave me 'permission' to go with you." I hid a smile as Larsson drew air-quotes as he spoke the word with a quick roll of his eyes. "He also procured us documents to allow us to formally collect the required samples that Ash needed—of which she had no idea, so you can't tell her. He said whatever your reasons for visiting, he was certain you'd appreciate a letter from the Supreme High Council should it smooth any wrinkles in your journey."

Though amused that he'd kept such a secret from Ash while still bargaining with her for food favors—and that he'd manage his monologue despite the wind plucking words from his lips as it swirled and whipped around us—I remained silent as Larsson handed over the envelope with a cheerful smile, one which evaporated when I did finally speak; I'd merely asked him if he'd thought to bring along some luggage as I wasn't sure how long I'd be in Dyr.

He'd grumbled as we crunched across the ice to the edge of the dock where the portal was located just over the freezing black waters, muttering something about how long he was going to have to wait until he finally got his lamb curry and roti. Then we jumped, me with my portal key, and Larsson using his teleporting skills, arriving inside the familiar, though still incredibly dark, cave. Not the nicest welcome for incoming visitors, in my humble opinion.

I'd enjoyed teasing Larsson, though after we arrived in the cave, I made a point of thanking him, and reassuring him that I didn't believe the trip would take too long. And we'd only remained in the cave long enough for me to say those words.

I was about to suggest stopping within the small forest of trees outside the gates of the city so I could give him an idea of where Sienna's rooms were within the enormous structure of the palace, but Larsson just waved a hand and smiled.

He curled his hand around my waist, a little awkward with the backpack mind you, and jumped us directly inside a small waiting room, its pale cream-and-blue decor and elegant, spindly-legged furnishings suggesting a woman's touch.

I grunted after we solidified, then tightened my hold on my rucksack. "Dude, where have you brought me? And how do you know to come here?"

The redhead smiled, eyes sparkling. "After the poisoning debacle, the SHC decided we had to have an easier method of communication with the council and the rulers of Drakys. That trip from the portal to the palace is a killer," I raised an eyebrow giving him an *I-know* glare, "and then Sienna and the SHC wanted to guarantee the safety of the next emissary. Between Queen Regent Lyra and Sienna, and the SHC, the decision was made to elect one teleporter who will have knowledge of, and access to, an arrival point within the palace. And this is it." Larsson thrust his hands out in introduction of the waiting room, his cheeks ruddy from what was clearly his enjoyment of his role.

I grinned. "And you were the lucky guy. Congrats," I said.

Larsson rolled his shoulders, puffing out his chest. "This place is amazing. They have the most divine chicken dish—though I'm pretty sure it's not chicken, so it's maybe chicken-like...chicken-ish?—" Larsson squinted, frowned, then gave a "whatever" shrug, "—and they throw in toasted nuts and the most succulents raisins...which I'm sure aren't really raisins..."

I left Larsson to ramble as I studied the small room, about the size of our living room at home and large enough to receive a small delegation from off-world. And then the door opened, and I never got to hear what the equivalent of a raisin was in Drakys.

Sienna hurried into the room, and as I peered around Larsson, I caught the cheerful, though distracted, smile on her face. "Why is it so hard to get rid of you, Freckles?" she asked as she walked over, the teasing grin disappearing once she caught sight of me behind him. "Kai? What…is something wrong? What happened? Is everyone okay back home?"

I wrapped her in a hug and squeezed her for a second. "No. Nothing like that. I just needed to speak to—" Sienna's eye widened in a deliberate glare, a silent warning perhaps? So, I amended my words and continued, "—you. And don't worry, Red over here has our papers from the SHC, the letter of authorization for collection of another batch of samples for Ash."

Sienna snickered when I called the jumper 'Red,' but all he did was glare at her, reach out and fluff up her glossy red curls. Sienna stopped snickering, threw him a glare, then focused on me. "That's fine. You don't need a reason to come visit, but the letter will appease the council if they get their panties in a bunch about the sample-collection."

I frowned, wondering why Logan's name was a no-no, but it was okay for her to refer to the council in a less-than-classy, and disrespectful manner. "But wouldn't the council want to know for sure if the land and the water are healing? I thought the halting of the Erulite mining would be detrimental to Drakys' economy."

Sienna smiled. "It is detrimental, but it's safer what with Elan still lurking in the shadows, not in Drakys mind you, just that he still hasn't been caught and he's got an agenda that he's yet to advise us of."

I had to agree with her. And I would have said so, but Larsson interrupted, "Got anything to eat? I'm stuck here waiting on Kai, and I'm hungry."

Sienna chuckled and turned to walk over to the door. "Come, Kai. Let's see about setting aside some time to spend with you. Perhaps we could take a short flight out to the mountains for a good girly giggle and catch-up."

Okay, then.

As we walked off, the jumper called out, "Hey, what about me?"

Chuckling and shaking her head, Sienna paused on the threshold and said, "I'll have Wylia send something up to your room. You remember where it is?" With that, Sienna walked off while I kept up, trying really hard not to laugh.

I failed.

"He's good fun," Sienna said, eyes sparkling. "I don't trust too many people, but he's definitely on the list."

"You asked for him, huh?"

"You bet," Sienna replied, waving me through a narrow vestibule into a larger waiting-room with three- and four-person seating-arrangements scattered informally around the space. The color-scheme matched the off-white-and-blue color scheme of the room I'd arrived in, and I had to say that the more I saw of it, the more I liked it.

Walls covered in floor-to-ceiling tapestries depicted what I assumed were fables or historical tales, all done in a combination of whites and varying shades of blues, and highlighted in gold and black. Such elegance was almost breathtaking, lending an almost artistic concept to paintings I'd seen around the palace the last time I'd been here.

Along one wall, a pair of open doors were guarded by two expressionless sentries. Leading me inside, Sienna waved at the men who leaned in simultaneously and reached for the door handles. They shut both the doors silently, leaving us alone inside what I had to assume was Sienna's private office.

Then, the Queen of the Dragon Realm let out a soft squeal, clapped her hands and threw her arms around me. "Oh gosh, Kai. I was really worried about you. I'm so happy to see you."

I chuckled and returned the hug with equal emotion. "I'm glad to see you too. How's everything going with the transition for the two of you?"

Sienna pursed her lips. "It's a bit complicated—"

I raised a hand. "Absolutely. Not my business so no need to explain."

I'd spoken with a gentle smile, but Sienna's face fell. "I'm sorry...I mean...no, it's not because I want to keep it secret or something." Sienna paused. "Well, it is a secret...but one that I will tell you. Just not," Sienna waved a hand around the room, clearly meaning the palace itself by the gigantic circle she attempted to draw around her head.

I patted her shoulder. "I'm serious. I don't expect you to share stuff. You're a queen-person around here. I think that's a big deal."

Sienna rolled her eyes. "Sometimes I have to wonder. We've—I've only been here a day, but it's been all-go." She paused and gave me a pointed look.

Raising both my eyebrows, I bit down my question as the pieces fell into place. Then I frowned. "So, when will I be able to see..." I gave up, unsure what I was supposed to say.

"Emissary Cassidy?" Sienna said a little too loudly. "Oh, I think he should be able to see you soon. He was out with General Vyrian earlier today, but I think I spotted them returning to the palace. You wait here, and I'll go look for them. I'm sure the General can spare a moment for you two to talk."

With another pointed look, Sienna left the room, and was gone for what seemed like ages. When the door opened again, I spun around only to find a smiling pixie-faced elegantly uniformed girl pushing a small trolley bearing what appeared to be pots of coffee and tea, along with a selection of cakes and savory snacks.

"Welcome to Dyr, Emissary O'Neill. I'm sure you must be peckish after your trip." The girl gave a quick curtsey and left the room while I stared at the closed door, wondering how it was possible a person could move that fast.

Then I shook my head. I was in the land of the dragons so even if she had wings, I wouldn't have been surprised.

I approached the trolley and selected a few morsels then poured a coffee. Taking my goodies over to the table, I sank into the soft chair and gave a sigh. Only then did I allow myself to acknowledge my fatigue.

Threads of sleep and pain pulled at me as I sipped my coffee in the vain hopes that the caffeine would help boost my energy levels. My early morning snack at the coffee shop had only been followed with more chatting, then Mel's visit and my secret departure from the house, then the realm of Earth altogether.

Boy, was I going to be in trouble when I got back home?

CHAPTER 31

LOGAN

Logan blinked rapidly before he entered Sienna's office, the fatigue of the Ascension Ceremony—or rather the whole direct-to-brain-information-download—was still pulling on him. He hadn't understood the effects of the ceremony on his body and mind. Not until he'd landed on the balcony of his suite, shifted into his human form, and almost passed out.

And he hadn't been the only one shattered by the process; Sienna too had been wobbly on her feet as she'd entered the suite, blinking as though her transition had made her lightheaded. Logan hadn't bothered her with questions, and had instead walked her to her own suites, down the darkened halls lit only with low-burning flames. Despite her assurances that she'd be fine making her way there on her own, she'd stopped protesting as they'd walked, Logan's arm around her holding her upright.

He supposed he himself had needed an arm, but adrenaline was a thing of wonder, both in human and dragon-shifter physiology it appeared. He'd only given in to his fatigue when he'd returned to his bedroom and shut the door. It was also a thing of wonder that he made it to his bed before he passed out.

The newly ascended dragon twins of Drakys had slept the

entire morning away. And when Sienna had hammered against his door, greeting him with a wide—though somewhat sneaky—smile, he'd been more than annoyed at her cheer.

Now he understood.

The last person Logan had expected to see when he entered Sienna's office was Kai.

She stood up slowly from the table where she'd been sipping at a cup of coffee, plate strewn with the remains of half-eaten pastries and cakes.

Her gaze flickered away from him and then returned, as though she weren't sure what to do with herself. Her expression flattened though, as soon as Logan closed the door, her green eyes darkening to a near-black.

Still silent, she watched him draw nearer until he reached her to stand close enough to stare into her eyes and see the pain undulating in her gaze—though she tried valiantly to appear unconcerned, to seem fine.

Kai cleared her throat. "I wouldn't have come if it weren't important." She blinked quickly, hesitant, and Logan hated that he'd turned her into this nervous, unsure, vulnerable person. Maybe Sienna had been right.

Now he shook his head in response to her words, aware that he'd need to keep up this secretive pretense. "It's okay. There's no reason why you…" Logan fell silent for a moment, then scanned Kai's shadowed face. "What's wrong?"

Kai took a sharp breath. "Saleem is in real trouble. Mel just stopped by...this morning...she was only conscious for a few hours before she came over. What she said...we don't have as much time as we believed we did. And now we need to go and get him out. Mel's rounding a team up, and you're the tactical specialist. We need all the help we can get. We need you to help us extract him."

Logan frowned. "Where is he?"

"Mithras. Held captive and being tortured." Kai said the words with an almost-accusatory tone. He knew she didn't believe him to be responsible for his best friend's incarceration, so he assumed the hurt and accusation in her voice had another reason.

One he likely entirely deserved.

"Do we know who we're up against?" Logan asked, keeping his tone even.

Kai nodded. "Mel thinks it's Omega. We need you...Cassidy. Saleem's life depends on it. Seriously, all the passion in the world won't save Saleem without knowledge of infiltration, and special ops. That's your department." Her eyes glittered as she spoke, as though she was already priming herself for a disappointment.

Logan was silent as he considered Kai's words. With the Ascension Ceremony over, there was one problem off the list. That still left the Blessing, which he knew could be postponed, but there were still the two rebel factions slowly inching closer. So the timing of Kai's news left a lot to be desired, and Logan wasn't sure what he should be telling her.

Leaving now would jeopardize his position in the realm, putting both him and Sienna in danger. Logan cleared his throat. "Kai, I'm not sure I can leave right now. Things here are...let's just say it's not the best move for me to leave Drakys right now." The look she gave him was so filled with pain that Logan took a breath and said, "Okay, let me look at how things are stacked up at the moment. I'll speak to you in a while, maybe for dinner?"

Kai swallowed, spine stiff as she recognized the evasion, but she let it slide and shook her head slowly. "That's fine with me. I could do with a couple hours sleep and maybe a soak in the tub." Then she paused. "I recall there being some amazing bathtubs here the last time I visited."

Logan grinned and said, "It's likely you'll get the same room this time too. Where were you located last time?"

She thought for a moment, the splotches of shadows beneath her eyes emphasizing her fatigue. "The north wing, I think. View to the city and of the Black Mountains."

Logan frowned at that. The Northern wing belonged to the General of Drakys, to him, his wife and his family for the duration of his reign.

Logan suppressed a grin. It appeared Sienna needed a good talking to.

CHAPTER 32

KAI

I felt somewhat off balance after my conversation with Logan. I should be angry with him, for his reticence, for his indecision. But I couldn't. Not when I completely understood his position, the weight of his duties on his shoulders, the pull between obligation and the call of ones' heart's desire.

As I walked off, following one of Sienna's staff—or was he Logan's?—my mind hovered on how calmly I was taking it all. Sure, Logan hadn't told me what I'd wanted to hear, but I had to wonder if I was hoping too hard that he'd change his mind before I left Drakys for home.

But I wasn't the type to bargain with the gods, or to cross my fingers and pray for the outcome I preferred. It came with being far too practical and logical.

I suppressed a sigh as I turned a corner and found myself in familiar territory as the staffer waved me toward a pair of double-doors. He scurried past me to open the doors, throwing them wide with a flourish as he gave me a cheery smile.

"Her Highness, Queen Synestra, welcomes you, Emissary O'Neil, to the Palace of Dyr. She hopes that you are most comfortable in your suite." The young man bowed low and then straightened, his expression a tad more serious as he flicked his eyes over the sitting room behind me. "Would you like a tour of the suite?"

I smiled. "No thank you. I've used these rooms before. I know my way around."

The man tipped his head in acknowledgment, nothing in his eyes revealing the slightest curiosity or question. "A light luncheon has been provided for you on the balcony." He waved a hand to the right of the room where the floor-to-ceiling doors were open, a light breeze ruffling the silky pale coral curtains. "Please ring the bell should you require anything else." Another bow and he was gone, leaving me with a quick, polite smile before shutting the door silently.

The suite of rooms was familiar enough, though the receiving room appeared to have undergone a redecoration. I smiled at the soft curtains as they swayed in the breeze, thrusting the fragrant scent of coffee at me. I'd just eaten before seeing Logan, but oddly I was hungry enough to sample a little sandwich slathered in something green and creamy that looked like avocado and tasted like smoked cheese. A few of the rich, fried balls of cheese-laden rice followed the sandwich, along with a second cup of hot coffee.

I'd drained my cup, and was standing at the balcony, staring out at the view of the city, the spiked turrets of larger buildings, the peaked roofs of rows of residential homes where colored drapes fluttered inside open balcony windows. I was slowly getting my head around the reddish sun—which sometimes gave the sky a somewhat macabre feel—and could now appreciate the view of the city of Dyr, bathed in red-tinged light.

A soft knock sounded on the outer door to the suite, and someone entered. From where I stood, I made out a slim, elegant form, body draped in dark-blue silk that traced the floor as she walked out to the balcony.

"Kai?" Sienna called out, smiling as she caught sight of me where I'd remained, hip propped against the stone balustrade. "How did it go with Logan?" she asked, her smile fading as though she already expected to hear bad news.

I made a face, aware that she didn't really know the whole deal. "I told him how important it was that he return with me," I said, shaking my head. "Saleem is in Mithras, held captive and being tortured as we speak."

"And you need Logan to return with you to help extract Saleem from his captivity," Sienna said, nodding slowly as she tapped a blue- and gold-painted fingertip against her lips.

"We do. He's the one who has the strongest tactical knowledge. We need to go in small and discreet, and we aren't too sure who's in bed with whom, so it's not like we can go knocking on Sentinel's door asking for their most talented operatives."

Sienna frowned. "You think the agencies are involved?"

I shrugged. "Omega is a certainty, but so many things have happened to raise flags in terms of moles within the other two agencies, so it's better safe than sorry."

"I agree. Better to do it quick and clean, get inside, get the djinn and get gone."

"Couldn't have said it better myself."

"And that brother of mine said 'No'?" Sienna asked, her tone now sharp, as though the meaning of Logan's response had just suddenly hit her.

I sobered then, being careful to ensure I didn't reveal my disappointment to Sienna. But when she let out a low—somewhat feral—growl, I knew I'd failed. I raised a hand, halting what I expected to be a tirade against her ignorant brother, as well as freezing her expression into one of angry frustration.

"He had every right to take all his responsibilities into consideration before making a final decision. I'm not going to try and sway him, Sienna. He's a big boy, and he doesn't need either you or me making his decisions for him…or maneuvering him into making the right move." I threw her a warning glower.

Sienna grunted, then let out a frustrated *oof*. "Fine. Though I will go on record to state that I disagree. Sometimes, guys need to be helped along in their decision process."

I rolled my eyes, and Sienna snickered as she poured herself a coffee and joined me at the balcony. "So how are you doing," she asked softly, giving me a sober look that said I won't be able to get away with lies.

I sighed and gave her my brave smile. Sienna's response was to drain her cup and lift mine free from my grip. Then she said, "What you and I need is a girl-chat. Let's take a ride out to the warm-baths and have ourselves some private time."

Sienna grinned and leaped from the balcony, in a very unqueenlike move. She dropped out of sight and then swooped around in a shallow half-circle, her dragon form glinting in the red sunlight.

As she glided back toward the balcony, I performed the same move, one hand on the stone balustrade as I swung my body lightly over it and flew into the air, landing almost expertly on the upper back of the dragon. I gave a low whoop, and Sienna's laughter rumbled through her body and into my bones.

She flew for a few minutes, crossing a distance of close on twenty miles in mere minutes while I lay with my cheek to her neck, studying the rocky landscape far below us. She glided left of the obsidian mountains, drifting among the clouds toward an area of undulating hills where plumes of what appeared to be smoke drifted from the ground.

As we drew closer, geysers and vents to subterranean pools came into view, all scattered across the stepped incline of a granite mountainside, which from our height resembled a dark honeycomb.

On closer inspection, I found the hollowed-out steps were

filled with steaming waters, likely fed by an underground system of geysers. Many of the pools overflowed, and waters rushed down from one level to another, hundreds of little waterfalls that filled the air with the low murmur and whisper of rushing water.

I found myself quite looking forward to the prospect of a hot soak, one of the reasons I didn't decline Sienna's offer of warm-baths before she'd decided to jump from the palace balcony.

Though, I hadn't exactly pictured this scene.

We drifted past the mountains a minute or so, and then Sienna began to glide lower and lower, at last landing on a clear spot of stone barely large enough to hold her bulk.

Sienna waited only long enough for me to slide to the ground along the gleaming scales at her left side. The moment my feet touched stone, the golden dragon shimmered away, and Sienna resumed her human form, a happy grin on her face.

I scowled. "Why do walkers have to get naked first to shift while dragons just magically go from big-and-scaly to dressed-and-ready-to-go?" I asked, pretending annoyance—although to be brutally honest, I *was* a tad put out with the cards fate had dealt me.

Sienna chuckled, and the sound echoed up the hillside. "Sucks, right?" she said as she pointed to a cave along the hillside, its entrance carved into a pair of dragons exhaling flames that intertwined to form the overhead arch of the doorway.

I passed beneath the impressive structure, marveling at the artistic ability of the stonemasons while Sienna pottered around inside what appeared to be a waiting room where oversized cushions, poufs, thick rugs, and pillows, were scattered across the carpeted floor of the rocky cave. Here, the slate-type black rock was as dark as the outside, creating the need for added lighting, which Sienna resolved with a few flicks of her fingers.

Tiny little flames and sparks flew from her fingertips and ignited the oil in a narrow channel cut along the top of the wall.

The recess ran all the way around the cave, and with a soft whoosh, the place was alight, a low golden shimmer of burning oil enveloping the room.

I turned on the spot, scanning the comforts surrounding me; such luxuries were hardly what a girl expected to find inside a mountainside cave.

And before I made the full revolution, the very cavern with its blast of bright colors and brilliant firelight, faded from view as I slumped forward and dropped to the floor. The last thing I remembered was my entire body pulsing, caught within another convulsion.

Oh crap.

When I opened my eyes, I found my head cushioned by a soft purple-and-pink striped cushion, while a certain dragon queen paced back and forth a few feet away.

"Ugh, my head," I muttered as I pushed myself up into a seated position, if my half-sprawl, half-slump against a pile of pillows could be described as sitting up.

"What the hell was that?" yelled Sienna, eyes flaming as her shrill question reverberated around us.

I frowned. "Geesh, that's some bedside manner you got there, Your Majesty."

"Don't you even give me that." Sienna let out another low growl. "What? Just? Happened?" Her voice had gone from frustrated to furious in the space of uttering those three words.

I shut my eyes and sighed. Then spilled the beans. There really wasn't any reason I shouldn't tell her the truth, especially if the telling ensured she didn't come to her own *incorrect* conclusions.

I filled her in on the mega-dose of electricity courtesy of the shadowman, and the resultant convulsions I'd experience, though

I kept my tone airy and unconcerned. "And I'm pretty sure I'll be fine soon. Just need some time to recuperate," I said, giving Sienna a serene smile.

My nonchalance hadn't had the effect I'd wanted. Sienna hurried over and sank to her knees beside me. "You need to tell Logan about this, Kai."

I shook my head. "Nope. Not a chance in Hel. If I tell him about my condition, he's going to feel obligated to come with me, just so he can look after me."

Sienna huffed. "So what? He's going to come with you if you tell him."

I pursed my lips. "No. This is about Saleem and Logan. I'm not going to make it about me. He needs to come back with the intention of saving his friend. And I'm not going to use my health problems to sway that decision."

Sienna let out a disgusted croak. "The two of you are so damned alike it's pathetic."

I lifted an eyebrow though I was still smiling sadly. I kinda got exactly what she meant.

Sienna bit her lip. "I don't mean that." She paused, looked around, then threw her hands up in the air. "Oh, who am I kidding. I do mean it. Can the pair of you just stop behaving like idiots and talk for once?"

I didn't reply.

Sienna stamped her foot. "You know what? I revoke my blessing." Her eyes narrowed as she pointed a slender finger at me. "But that doesn't mean you're off the hook. Grab a towel and come with me. You can consider that a royal demand," she said, flashing me a glare before snatching a gigantic bath-towel from a pile near the door and stalking stiff-spined out into the red sunlight.

I had little choice really. I did note that she hadn't coddled me, hadn't tried to force me to sit still and behave until I felt better.

Shaking my head, I followed her slowly, grabbing an enormous green towel for myself before following her outside. She'd selected a pool two levels down and was already immersed to her shoulders, her clothes strewn on the stone nearby.

I didn't speak as I undressed and slipped inside the super-hot water. She didn't talk either as she glared out at the scenic view as though the landscape had pissed her off.

A few moments went by, and then I said, "Thank you."

Her eyes narrowed almost imperceptibly. "What for? Did you realize I was right about you being too damn stubborn for your own good?"

I sniffed then swirled my hands around in the water in front of me. For a long moment, I didn't reply. Then, after sinking a few inches lower, I said, "Thank you for the fire treatment. I had no idea you'd learned how to do it."

Sienna winced, realizing too late that she'd revealed her guilt. She let out a laugh and shifted to look back at me. "How did you know?"

I shrugged, sloshing the water around me. "I was feeling a little too well after this particular episode." Silence stretched between us as the water bubbled and blipped. Then I took a breath. "I'm not going to tell him. I know you want me to, but I don't think it's fair to manipulate him. And I need you to promise me that you won't tell him either. If he comes back with me, I'll tell him. If he stays, then he really doesn't need to know. I'm not going to send a cross-Veil telegram every time I break a bone or get stabbed in the line of duty, so this situation with me…it's not all that relevant at this point."

Sienna stared at me, and I could see the emotions shifting on her face. Anger, sadness, frustration and then capitulation. She sighed. "Fine." She leaned her head back and looked up at the ruby skies. "If this is any indication of my royally diplomatic ability to argue my case, I really need to work on it, or I'll probably just give the entire realm away if the whole struggle-for-power thing depends on me."

I smirked. "Well, perhaps you won't be so bad. You're pretty scary when you want to be. Just make sure it's not me you're bargaining against, or I'll be the one sitting on that cushy throne of yours."

Sienna rolled her eyes and then smiled. It took her a few minutes before she began to ask for details—everything from how Lily and Mom were doing, to exactly what happened to me after I'd come to see Logan the night I'd been abducted.

Despite the topic, I found myself relaxing, letting go of my frustrations and fatigue.

Sienna would have made an amazing sister-in-law.

The soak in the bathtub, if you could call that monstrosity a tub, had turned out to be entirely unnecessary given my little jaunt to the warm-baths with Sienna.

As large as many a backyard pool, the mosaic-tiled, blue-and-gold sunken bath had been steaming when I'd returned with Sienna, the water giving off a gentle steam and the scent of jasmine and vanilla.

I smiled at the thought that Logan had likely sent someone around to fill the tub, and I felt somewhat sad that I'd let it go to waste. Even the promise of food hadn't swayed me from aiming myself at the bed, the hot pools having done their job to soak away my stress and pains.

I may—or may not—have passed out before my head hit the pillow.

I woke an hour later, confirmed from the time on my phone which still functioned, though, without Wi-Fi. It was late afternoon, and I knew I had plenty of time to have a second go at Logan in the hopes that his best friend's predicament would have some effect on him. I had to wonder though, what else was going on that would impact his decision, that was capable of stopping him from going to Saleem's aid?

I promised myself that I wouldn't be angry with him.

And you know what they say about promises, right?

CHAPTER 33

KAI

When Logan spoke the words, the very words I'd dreaded, I glared at him, knowing I'd appear like a harridan, eyes glittering with fury. I didn't care.

"And Saleem's life? Does the life of your best friend have so little value to you?" I shook my head. "I was so sure you wouldn't change now that you've taken on your rightful role. Should I be worried that I may be wrong?"

My words were hurtful, and I regretted their utterance the moment I spoke, but Logan appeared unaffected. His expression was that of a man who'd been expecting to be struck through with a sword, a man who felt he deserved it.

He reached out and held my arms, lean fingers gripping my skin in a tender vise. "No. I'm still me, Kai. It's just…things are...complicated." He sounded hesitant, and beneath his words was an undertone of regret and anger.

There really was more going on, but I couldn't get past his refusal. I didn't blame him, I really didn't, but on the back of his stupid letter, this refusal just seemed to compound my anger and disappointment with him.

I shrugged him off and stepped past him. "Then, uncomplicate things," I heard myself say, my mouth taking control. "Your friend will die if you don't come with us. I understand there are responsibilities here for you. Believe me, *that* is one thing I do understand. But there's no situation in life where you are left with no choice." The look I gave him would have revealed helplessness, a little anger, and absolutely no judgment.

I understood.

And I couldn't hide that.

Logan smiled sadly. "A choice between two shitty options is still a shitty choice."

Truer words were never spoken.

"Do you mind explaining why you're in such an all-fired rush?" asked Larsson as he stared at me, his confusion clear considering I had implied we could be in Drakys a while. He'd been summoned to the waiting room in which we'd made our arrival, and for the first time appeared flustered.

Strange.

I shook my head, not yet ready to share Saleem's current situation, not until I had the okay from Mel. "I have what I came for. And you did get an afternoon away in a fantasy city, didn't you?"

"Mmh," was the jumper's single syllable response.

I lifted a shoulder and offered an apologetic purse of my lips. "Sorry?"

To his credit, Larsson straightened his shoulders and gave a firm, businesslike nod. "So now we get those samples, right?"

"That we do. Do you know where?"

Larsson nodded as he reached out for my arm. "One riverside landing coming up. Just watch out for poisonous flowers and deadly waters."

I shook my head as we disappeared from the waiting room inside the palace and materialized on the banks of the river.

The sounds of water rushing off rapids filled my ears, and I glanced around me as Larsson let go of my arm. Ahead of us was the wide expanse of the river. With its steep banks bordered in overgrowth, and its roiling surface almost covered with dark lilies.

I really hated lilies.

A glance over at the jumper revealed his eyes focused on the flowers and I took the chance to grab a couple bags and thrust them into his hands. "Can you grab a couple of the flowers? I'll get soil and bark samples from the trees over here." I aimed a thumb at the trees behind me then did an about-face, heading to the small orchard, my fingers mentally crossed.

"Why do I always end up getting the dirty jobs?" Larsson was muttering behind me, and I let go of my breath.

"Think of the lamb vindaloo and the roti?"

What Larsson replied with was something rude and hilarious at the same time, and for a few moments, having forgotten the disappointments of the last few hours, and the fears I had for the next day coming, I was laughing, and for those few moments, I was carefree.

Needless to say, my freedom from cares didn't last.

CHAPTER 34

KAI

I swung my leg over the seat of my motorcycle—or rather, Logan's—and hesitated, the envelope left for me in my mailbox by Ash weighing down the pocket of my jacket. In the end, I sighed and dragged it out, not keen to wait until I arrived home before opening it.

I unwound the string from the little button thingie at the top of the envelope and slid out the papers, and the printouts of my MRI. My heart raced as I stared at the words, every damning letter telling me I'd been right subverting the journey of these result to my father.

The man had enough on his mind. He didn't need my health added to the weight he already bore. Heart still thumping, I shoved paperwork into envelope, and envelope into jacket pocket, then gunned the engine and sped off toward the outskirts of the city.

It was after ten at night, and it made little sense for me to go home first. Baz and Lily were driving over to Natasha's place with Grams, so they didn't need me to play chauffeur. It made sense for me to go straight there.

Or perhaps that was an excuse. All I wanted was some time to come up with a good poker face. How was I supposed to explain to them, especially to Mel, that Logan was a no-show? My mind was so filled with turmoil that I almost missed the dusty road that would take me to the witch's homestead, and I had to skid to a stop and make a sharp turn before taking the track up into the trees.

A few minutes later and I was knocking on Natasha's door, waiting half a second before it opened. The witch, with her platinum hair and pale skin, was a picture of serenity. Her eyes though, were nothing short of tumultuous.

Not that she shared.

With a wave, she led me to her living room where the fire crackled, and music played on an old gramophone. "You made good time. We have just over an hour and a half to go. I've got food for the troops, just in case. You should just curl up and give me the details of your little trip to dragonland."

I gave her a dirty look and was halfway to seating myself on the sofa beside her when my stomach grumbled so loudly that I gasped.

"Someone is hungry. Don't they feed people in the land of the dragons?" Natasha arched an eyebrow.

"You're so hilarious," I replied, giving her a cold glare.

Natasha boosted to her feet. "Well, far be it for me to let a hangry panther keep on being hangry. Come, kitty cat. Let's find you something to eat." Her laughter led the way to the kitchen.

I groaned. "You're so fucking hilarious."

Her only response was more laughter.

CHAPTER 35

LOGAN

"You said what?" yelled Sienna after Logan apprised her of the contents of his discussion with Kai.

They were standing in his sitting room, surrounded by the serenely plush white-and-gold decor, but Logan felt not in the slightest bit calm.

"I didn't have much of a choice, Sienna. You know full well what we're up against here. If I leave now, we'd be putting everything at risk. Our realm could be taken away from us even before we get the chance to rule."

Sienna shook her head. "And Saleem? What if he dies? You happy to have his blood on your hands? Happy with the choice you made? A crumbling kingdom paid for with the life of your best friend?"

Logan stiffened, his anger rising. But he had little right to take his fury out on his sister. She was right. He'd never be able to live with himself knowing his position as ruler of Drakys came covered in Saleem's blood.

Logan took a deep breath. "So what happens if I go? How do we hold back this crazy tide until I return?"

"How long would you estimate it would take?" asked Sienna, tapping her finger against her lip.

"That's the problem. It could well be an easy in and out. Or we could be looking at a week. I don't see it taking longer than a week." Logan nodded, confident what with his experience on previous missions—very few would take more than a week. Not unless they were undercover.

Sienna shrugged. "That's manageable. We'll announce a viewing of the Northern Reaches to check on the flooding. We're very concerned with the situation as it will affect the city as a whole."

"And leaving the capital unattended for a week? Not risky?"

"No. Because the Northern Reaches will be assessed by General Lyandr, who will be surveying the realm with old Vyrian. Tactical military assessments are seldom seen as opportunities for social interaction or for lobbying. They'll lobby me here in the city if they want." Sienna smirked as she folded her arms. "You'll have almost ten days, maybe twelve. Make them count, brother."

CHAPTER 36

LOGAN

When Logan arrived at Natasha's homestead, he didn't immediately reveal himself. He told himself that it was because he didn't want to startle them with his dragon form, but a whisper in his mind called him a liar.

He didn't deny it.

Still, he approached in silence and studied the gathering. Baz, Lily, and Steph were chatting, the younger group appearing to have formed a stronger bond. Lily's skin was pale, but she appeared to be in better health than when Logan had left Tukats. Corin's treatments must have worked, for which Logan was very glad.

Darcy and Nerina huddled close, conversation appearing light and free from tension. Drake crouched near the trees, his dark skin almost blending with the shadows, though his shoulders rippled with a tension that was reflected in his silvery eyes. Near the edge of the pond, the white witch chatted with Cassandra, both appearing polite, rather than friendly.

Interesting.

Logan shook his head. He'd barely returned, and already he'd begun to parse body language and assess moods. Guess being a detective was a natural instinct.

Mel stood at Ivy's side, both deep within what looked to be a serious conversation. Logan found himself smiling as he realized he'd missed Grams. It had taken him some time to get his mind around referring to her as a grandmother, what with her young appearance and her badass persona. The stern pale-blonde matriarch was a woman not to be trifled with.

Good thing Ivy seemed to have had a soft spot for Logan.

Kai sat across the clearing, her face half-hidden in shadows. But even from this distance, he could feel her tension, her disappointment, as she repeatedly scanned the trees discreetly. He'd let her down with his refusal to join the mission. And he'd hurt her too, when he'd declined to continue the discussion. He'd been cool, imperious, almost arrogant. But he'd done it deliberately, needing to make her leave, believing the choice his heart was making would impact his duty to his people.

How wrong he'd been.

Mel moved away from Ivy. "Ready when you guys are," Mel said before she and Ivy shared a brief but significantly conspiratorial glance.

Logan smiled—a mystery for another day. He focused on Mel, who strode toward the clearing and dropped onto a blanket. Fire flared at the center of the group, the white witch throwing warmth and light onto the sober gathering.

Logan wondered what Saleem would think if he could see this; so many people, all who cared for him in some way, all now focused on bringing him home.

"Wow, now that's cool," Baz said as he peered closer at the fire which gave his ashy skin a bit of a golden tan. "It's even hot."

"Be careful you don't burn off your nose, you idiot. The fire is real." Lily was rolling her eyes as she smacked the hacker on his arm.

Mel cleared her throat as she studied the faces around the fire.

"So I don't think we'll be here too long. We just need to go over a few things. The agreed time, as requested by Saleem for reasons still unknown to me, is tomorrow midnight. We've obtained a portal key to help us with access."

Mel's words drew a frown from Kai who opened her mouth to speak. But the jumper just nodded, and Kai fell silent. Logan wanted to go to her, but he decided it would be best to gauge the crowd first before he made his presence known.

"So for clarification for everyone," Mel scanned the group again, "the story is as follows, just in case you are missing any of the pieces."

She got to her feet and walked a few paces back and forth, confirming to Logan that though she was good at keeping her emotions in check, she was still a bundle of tension, and nerves. He didn't blame her.

"A couple of weeks ago—okay, maybe I need to go back a little further than that," Mel said, and was rewarded with a round of subdued laughter from the team. She inhaled sharply and said, "A couple of years ago, Queen Aisha of the Djinns was kidnapped while on a trip to the EarthWorld. Her sons were concerned—she's not the flighty or irresponsible type—and the elder son—who was also the next in line to the throne—came to our plane to investigate, hoping to find her. What he found instead was Omega, who recruited him with promises of helping him find his mother. What Saleem didn't know was that Omega themselves had taken Aisha and was holding her hostage…sort of."

Logan blinked, and his gut tightened. There was so much Saleem hadn't told him. Yes, the djinn had mentioned his responsibilities, and that he was searching for his mother, but the Queen of the Djinn? That was something a guy ought to have told his friend.

Logan shook his head. He was the last person to judge. How much of his own turmoil had he kept from Saleem? Granted, some of his omissions had been for pride, the stupid male ego refusing to admit to suffering from mental issues. And then, when things had escalated, there just hadn't been time to sit and have that heart-to-heart.

Was it too late?

Maybe. But even if it were, both he and Saleem had their own history, their own responsibilities. Which did nothing to detract from their duty to each other.

Mel's voice rose, cutting into Logan's thoughts. "—uncovered clues but kept getting stonewalled. In the interim, he became concerned about his brother who'd been left to control the realm. He's not known for having important character elements, like a spine."

Steph snickered at that, but quickly composed herself.

Mel's eyes though, had taken on a faraway expression. "But Saleem was also tied down by his agreement with Omega, and although he didn't say as much, I think he'd attempted to return home and was shut down by them—which is when he came to me. As far as Omega was saying, they'd been unable to track Aisha down, but it didn't take me too long to find her.

"Omega has a property out in Aspen where they are currently holding the queen. It took only one visit to confirm her presence, and I went in to speak to her at Saleem's request. That's when things got a little complicated."

Mel paused as she appeared to struggle with something and then her expression cleared.

"On my announcement that I was there to break her out, the djinn queen refused and promptly reminded me that her powers as queen of the djinn meant she could get out of her captivity whenever she wanted to. Omega was well aware of her abilities and had threatened her with something—this is another unknown variable that I hope to find out—and as a result, she refused to leave. It's possible the lives of her sons were threatened, but I couldn't figure out exactly how. Either way, Aisha has refused to join the mission."

"It certainly would have helped to have her guide us through the Veil," Kai said. Tension coiled around her, and her voice rippled with something—annoyance perhaps. Logan couldn't blame her. Seemed both Logan and Aisha—two people who should have cared the most for Saleem's safety—had summarily declined to help the mission when first approached.

"But you're a jumper?" Lily frowned, her lynx eyes glittering like liquid honey in the firelight. "Why can't you get us there? And we have Nerina as well."

Mel's nod was a sharp jerk as she replied, "Unfortunately we have it on good authority that cross-Veil travel has been shut down. Mithras has been quarantined, and we're concerned there may be protective wards set up. Not sure about that, but better to be safe than sorry.

"So to avoid setting off any wards, we've obtained a portal key. So we have our way in sorted. And we have the allocated time set in stone. Other things we need to be well aware of is the city is under the control of an as-yet-unidentified element, but I have my suspicions."

"Do tell." Kai boosted to her feet, then stepped to an ancient oak. She rested a shoulder against the gnarled trunk, appearing nonchalant. But she hadn't fooled Logan, because he could see the emotions in her eyes, part hurt, part annoyance, part understanding.

Mel hadn't told her.

The jumper's features were indecipherable as she replied, "I've spoken with Saleem a few times. A couple of times in a dream and then in an astral projection. The first time I visited him, I could see that he'd been tortured. And he was confined to his quarters. We didn't have time for him to detail exactly what had happened that ended in him being in chains in his own home, but what he did say was we needed a team, and he told me when to come. I visited him recently again, and this time I walked in on the torturers—figuratively speaking. They were doing the whole let's-whip-the-bottoms-of-your-feet-until-we-break-you routine, with spiked whips, just FYI. So his feet were a bloody mess, though the rest of him did look in slightly better condition. Not sure how much longer that will be for though.

"Anyway, the most shocking part of the scene was the mage who was attending Saleem. He's a MindMelder named Ward who is apparently supposed to be dead. He's a lowlife piece of shit who seemed to enjoy what he's doing to Saleem. I watched him work on Saleem to change his memories, to make him more compliant."

Logan's gut tightened at the mention of Ward's name. Darcy had told Logan that the MindMelder was dead, but the fact that he was still alive meant there was a chance he could help to remove whatever was left in Sienna's mind that was blocking her memories of her past.

Kai glanced at Darcy who replied, "Ward's powerful, but Saleem is a djinn with royal blood. And the future king. Add to that the fact that he's also a strong-willed, powerful, and passionate guy, and I don't think Ward realizes it's not going to be all that easy to crush Saleem."

Logan's fingers fisted. Not only had this asshole raped his sister's mind, he was now doing the same to Saleem, the best friend Logan had ever had.

"Well, they already have Rizwan under their control," said Mel as she pursed her lips. "Which likely happened a long time ago. He betrayed Saleem and helped capture him, so there's going to be some sibling issues we'll have to work through. But Darcy is right, Saleem's not about to give in easily."

Under the oak, Kai pushed off the trunk, about to ask a question when she paused and shook her head. Her green eyes widened. "There's more?" Kai said, then shook her head. "Right. I'll wait."

"So, apart from the back-from-the-dead MindMelder, I ran

into someone else, whose presence raised a shitload of questions."

Mel stopped speaking for a moment, and something told Logan that he wasn't going to like what she was about to say.

"Agent Blake seems to be running things in Mithras."

The clearing erupted with outraged swearing, though Logan's shock had stilled him into silence.

Blake was alive? And involved with Saleem's captivity.

A wave of unadulterated fury rippled through Logan, and only when the fabric of his black leather jacket reflected light from a new direction, did he calm himself. His eyes would have revealed the DragonFyr, and he had to simmer down before he spoke to anyone.

CHAPTER 37

LOGAN

"So what we are likely looking at is a human-run operation to control the djinn realm, for reasons we have yet to discover. Division 7 is going to be who we need to fight." Mel's voice faded as she came to the end of her monologue.

Silence blanketed the clearing for a long moment as the team looked at each other, sharing sober, worried glances.

Then Kai spoke, shattering the tension. "That guy seems to be everywhere. I'd love to know what interest they have in Mithras and the djinn, but I guess we do need to prepare in terms of weaponry."

The gargoyle shifted as he cleared his throat. "I've commissioned a truckload of weapons and ammo, all capable of bringing down a djinn army, or a gargoyle one if it came to that. And any weapons we have that can fell a supernatural is pretty much deadly to a human."

"Problem is, I'm not entirely certain these humans are going to be vanilla."

"Shit," Drake swore, the guttural quality emphasizing his

surprise. "Still, they'd have to be some superhuman meta not to go down."

Mel was shaking her head as Kai shifted on her feet and paced, hands propped on her hips, a scowl on her face. "We ran into those shadowmen, the ones who were boosted with natural shadowmen powers. They were not easy to take down, that much I can say. Granted, I *was* in the astral plane the first time around, which is what made it harder. My second run-in with them went a little better, but they do pack a huge punch, and if you can't teleport, you're in for a bit of a shock."

A snort echoed across the fire, snapping the tension a fraction, enough to elicit a round of chuckles.

"So now you guys know the basics," said Mel, her face sober. "And we have weapons covered. We just need to map out the process. If we had eyes on the inside, or someone familiar with the realm, it would help. Not as though we can hack into the city archives for palace plans."

"Why not?" Baz asked with a scowl. "If they have even a modicum of modern security systems, we should be able to find a loophole and get in. To be honest, it would be far easier if they didn't do things old school. A security system we can hack but manual security rounds, real eyes on every corner…that's going to be a problem."

"Even then, we don't have a clue unless I go back to see the queen. Probably should have thought about that before I stormed off so angrily into the ether."

Drake shook his head. "Still, unless she'd have had access to city planning, she wouldn't know the kind of details we need, like access tunnels, water pipelines, security routes, and schedules."

"And even if she did know something, how much is likely to have been changed by Omega when they took over?" Kai's scowl made Logan smile.

"Leave it to me," Ivy called out. Her frown said her mind was already focused on how she was going to obtain that info. "Sentinel will have the plans, maps, etc. I'll do a little digging and grab what we need."

"Right," Mel said, letting out a breath. "So once we get the maps and city plans, we'll be left with one big issue."

"Which is?" replied Ivy, one eyebrow curving.

"Transport," Mel said. "Once we get inside the djinn realm, we're going to have to be able to get around fast. We have a couple jumpers, but I'm not sure that's going to cut it if we split up. Someone's not going to be covered."

"We'll have a team comm set up. Maybe we could use that to call for emergency extraction?" said Darcy, the worry in her eyes clear.

Logan's history with the woman made his feelings for her a little conflicted. But now, her expression made it clear she hid a deeper fear.

Mel was about to speak, but Logan had already decided he'd remained silent long enough. "You don't need to worry about transport. I think I can manage that part of the mission."

Heads turned slowly toward Logan, remaining unmoving as he moved toward the firelight.

"Logan!" From the other side of the fire, Lily sprang to her feet and raced toward Logan. He winced as the lynx shifter's elbow slammed into Mel, almost tossing her off her feet—though the tracker only grinned as she steadied herself, eyes filled with amusement.

Lily though, was oblivious as she flung herself at Logan, who barely had time to reach out before her arms closed around his waist.

From beyond Mel, Kai watched, a broad smile on her face, her relief clear, though Logan caught a hint of something else. Did she doubt his return? Was she unsure he'd come to stay?

His stomach twisted with the knowledge that she didn't trust him, but he deserved it, didn't he? Sienna's voice in his mind told him as much.

"Lily, if you're done squeezing Logan to death, we'd like to get a chance to do that too," Mel called out, her eyebrow raised.

Lily chuckled and released Logan at last, and he smiled down at her bright and healthy-looking face. The treatments were most definitely working.

"Sorry," Lily said, though she didn't sound at all apologetic. "I'm just so damned glad to see his face. He's all yours now," Lily called out as she scampered back to Baz and Steph.

Mel hurried over to Logan, giving him the same—if a lot less exuberant—treatment. Which Logan returned with equal affection. The djinn's main squeeze was an all-around great gal. He'd told Saleem that he'd given his approval early on in the pair's sort-of relationship.

Saleem had denied anything formal, but formal wasn't needed when emotions came into play.

"Hang in there, Jumper," Logan whispered. "We'll get him back."

One glance down at her tear-filled face had Logan swearing in his mind. Trust him to say something to make Mel, of all people, cry.

Logan gave her a harder squeeze, then turned her around and guided her into the shadows, throwing a glance over at Kai who sat watching from the fireside. Her eyes were filled with understanding, and she sent him a short, almost imperceptible nod, before Logan and Mel were out of sight.

"I thought you weren't going to come," Mel said, even her sniffs managing to sound accusatory.

Logan laughed softly, then said, "I thought I wasn't coming either."

"Did she give you an earful?" Mel asked, eyes wide.

Logan knew who she was referring to and he hid a smile at how right Mel had been about her feisty friend. "That she did. And then some. I deserved it though. It shouldn't have taken me so long to change my mind."

With a shrug of one shoulder, Mel replied, "What difference is a few hours? You're here now, that's what matters."

But Logan wasn't about to allow Mel to let him off that easy.

Sucker for punishment, huh? said Saleem's voice inside Logan's head.

"No. I should have dropped everything the moment Kai told me. I was just…torn. I guess I wasn't sure if leaving Drakys would seem like a betrayal of my duties."

The jumper's response was an inelegant snort. "What did your sister have to say about it?"

Grinning, Logan shook his head and replied, "You know what they say about dragons breathing fire?"

Mel let out a light laugh, her eyes dancing with merriment though they sobered quickly as she said, "I'm glad you're here. The team's large and filled with talents but I'm not a seasoned operative and, to be fair, neither is Kai. We're best working alone or in small teams. With you here, I can breathe a little."

"I'll do whatever is needed, but I won't take point."

"Why the hell not?" snapped Mel, eyes flaring with anger.

Probably good she's not a dragon, or you'd have been toast, came the insolent voice in his head.

Logan paused for a second to study Mel's face, as though that was enough to convince her to retract her expectation. Then he took a breath and said, "You've done everything up to this point. I won't step in now just because I finally deigned to join you."

"You're hilarious, you know that?" Mel replied, her laughter hard and cold. "I'm beginning to wonder if you accidentally fried your brain cells with that new-fangled DragonFyr of yours."

Logan frowned as Mel folded her arms and snapped at him. She'd never been the type to lose her shit, and it hit him hard as he realized that, until this moment, he hadn't really been taking things as seriously as he should have.

Mel took Logan's silence as an opportunity to continue lobbying. "You have years of experience on me, leading missions, taking on military forces. You have the skills in tactical measure and weaponry. Do you think it's smart not to take point when the next best thing is a jumper chasing her tail who barely knows her ass from her elbow when it comes to subversive tactical missions? I'd say you're a little reckless."

"I'd say you're underestimating your abilities and those of your team," Logan replied, his voice even and deliberate. "But this argument would have been moot had I decided not to come," he said, knowing he was wasting his time making that particular point.

"Not a relevant argument," Mel snapped, eyes blazing. "If something goes wrong and I muck things up, you're going to live the rest of your life knowing you didn't do everything in your power to ensure we got Saleem out alive."

The jumper was furious, and Logan tried hard not to smile. "I'm thinking you'll be blaming yourself if the djinn did end up biting the bullet," he said with a smirk.

"No. I'll just be blaming you," was the tracker's reply as she tightened her arms around her torso and stared at the shadows.

CHAPTER 38

LOGAN

Logan felt a rush of affection for Mel. Her passion in bringing Saleem home struck Logan to the core, and he wrapped an arm around her shoulders, then mussed the hair on the top of her head the way he often did with Sienna.

And like Sienna, Mel squeaked her outrage and jabbed an elbow into his ribs. "What was that for?" she demanded, glaring up at him as she fixed her long dark hair.

Logan didn't reply. Instead, he guided the tracker toward the fire and stopped only when they reached Kai's side.

Kai threw Logan a smile that, though sweet, implied trouble—which he deserved. "Did you tell him off?" Kai asked Mel.

"I tried. But he's too much of an idiot," the tracker growled. "I don't think common sense works for him."

Logan watched as Kai struggled with laughter; she had that look she got when she was dying to know something. Mel, though, didn't reply, which gave Logan little choice.

He let out a soft groan. "Fine. I'll take point." A satisfied grin flared on Mel's face, but Logan continued, "But you're still in charge. You don't get off scot-free."

Logan's gaze shifted to meet Kai's intensely green one. "Was she just waiting for me to arrive so she could hand the mission over to me?" Logan grinned as he wrapped an arm around Kai's waist, sending thanks to gods and all matter of immortals that she didn't resist or stiffen against the embrace.

Kai paused a moment then met Mel's gaze before smiling. "She wasn't waiting. We never knew for sure if you'd come. But seeing as you are here, and this is your forte, you may as well get your ass moving."

He swore under his breath then spotted Drake observing the conversation from across the fire. Logan cocked his chin at the gargoyle, saying, "What about Drake? He's Gargoyle military. Surely he's capable." Logan was still keen on finding an out, although he wasn't so sure why when he knew Mel was right. The skills Logan had learned during his time at Omega were exactly what the team needed.

"Hey, dude," the silver-eyed gargoyle called out with a scowl. "I'm the medic in this outfit, okay? I may dabble in weapons but no way you'll get me taking charge, especially with you around."

"See," Mel chirped up, a satisfied gleam in her eye. "Now, I can give you a recap after the meeting's done."

Having heard everything already, Logan should have told her it wasn't necessary, but he remained silent as she turned and made her way closer to the fire.

"Okay," Mel said, loudly, her brisk voice carrying around the fire. "I think we have everything sort-of lined up. We'll text you all the final plans and groupings before we meet tomorrow. So, just before midnight, tomorrow, right here. We meet at my place in the evening first. Please don't be late."

Logan was only paying partial attention as he looked down and held Kai's gaze. Did he really deserve a woman like her?

Just as the meeting began to break up, Ivy's voice drifted toward Logan; she was grumbling, "Fine. Do you want to do this now?" as she shook her head.

Kai's attention shifted to her grandmother and then to Mel.

Then she straightened, moving from Logan's embrace gently enough so he couldn't interpret it as a rejection.

He smiled when Kai scanned the clearing and yelled, "Darcy, Nerina, Cassie. You are summoned."

Logan took that as his cue and hurried after the rest of the team who were trailing Natasha up to the homestead.

He was sure looking forward to extracting the djinn. Then he was going to enjoy the look on the team's faces when he announced their next mission.

CHAPTER 39

LOGAN

Logan had returned to the Odel home with the rest of the clan, remembering too late that it was possible he would be out of a place to sleep. It had taken a few minutes for Ivy to show him to the twins' bedroom where one of the single beds had been made up for him.

The old walker had barely said a word to him, and he'd begun to wonder if he was persona non grata around here for the foreseeable future.

Can you expect anything less with your behavior?

Logan had gritted his teeth and settled into the bed. Kai had been quiet, though not necessarily evasive. In all ways but voice, she'd shown him she wasn't angry, that she wasn't holding his initial decision against him, but Logan wasn't going to accept the option of shoving things under the carpet. As soon as he got the opportunity, he intended to talk a few things through with her.

But as usual, nothing went to plan.

Kai and Logan, for reasons of their own, had ended up passed out until at least three in the afternoon, both receiving stares of curiosity and concern, the former for him, the latter for Kai.

And thus, their concern only exacerbated his own worries.

Outwardly, Kai had appeared fine, but it seemed there was something going on that he wasn't at all aware of. And Logan suspected it had something to do with her sojourn in the lab of hell.

But, as much as he'd wanted to know more, he had neither the time, nor the opportunity to pose those questions. After a shared breakfast of coffee and donuts at four in the afternoon, they'd gathered their things and headed out to Mel's place for pre-mission talks.

That particular requirement on Mel's part spoke volumes for Logan. She was gathering the group around her because she cared, because she knew all too well that nothing was certain when none of them knew what they faced. All they knew was they had to save Saleem, and every single person who'd joined Mel, had done so because they cared, either for her or for the djinn.

And maybe because they cared for you too?

Logan stiffened at the thought, aware that Baz and Lily and Ivy didn't know Mel all that well, and neither did they know Saleem. They were the people Logan had called family. And even if he had said no to joining them because he didn't care about Saleem, the lives of these people on the line…that was enough to have made him change his mind.

And then again, the beauty of hindsight...

~

Later that evening, Logan, Kai, and the team gathered in Mel's kitchen, the last team gathering before they set out to save the djinn's ass. Ivy and Cassie hadn't arrived yet, but Logan knew they weren't likely to be long.

Kai had lingered around the room chatting to the team one at a time, ensuring they were all ready to face whatever may come. She returned to Logan's side where he was studying his tablet, thinking hard about an offensive extraction as opposed to one in which they were all captured.

Nerina and Darcy had paired off again, while the gargoyle and the witch whispered to each other, an unmistakable energy burning between the two. Logan had to wonder how long it would take for the pair to unravel their crossed wires.

Steph, Baz, and Lily were huddled in a corner as usual, when Mel entered the kitchen looking ready for a fight, eyes dark and gleaming.

"And here she is back to the land of the living," said Steph.

Mel glared at the blonde hacker, "Shush. You're way too loud for this early in the morning," she mumbled as she made for the coffee pot.

Mel planted herself at the table and nursed her coffee, glancing up at Logan and Kai who stood at his side, both staring at the jumper who looked like she needed another few hours of sleep.

But they had to prepare. Logan leaned over and tapped on the surface of the kitchen table, and the conversation around them died.

"So, I've sent you all the preliminary plan of attack," Logan said, studying each of the faces that watched him. "We enter using the key, the jumpers make their way to the palace with their passenger, and I'll take those who remain. Everyone's been assigned weapons and ammo—please keep them locked and loaded at all times. I'm thinking it's a little too late to be asking if everyone's familiar with handling firepower."

Laughter echoed within the kitchen and Logan grinned back at the faces of his friends. "Yeah, I get it. Firepower. You guys are so hilarious."

Still smiling, Mel said, "So what do we have to eat. I'm famished, and I will die of hunger if I don't at least have two full meals before we leave."

"Two?" Lily asked wide-eyed.

"One now," Mel said with a quick nod, "and the next one at eleven before we leave. I'm not taking any chances. Who knows how long we'll be in Mithras and even then I have no idea what type of food they have there."

Logan hid a smile. Mel thought of everything, and he wanted to tell her that she'd been through enough to handle the extraction without him, but he was, at last, coming to terms with the truth that they hadn't stood a snowball's chance in hell of success without a fine-tuned strategy and solid battle experience. Something the djinn had known full well.

"Mel, it's the djinn realm not some deep dark corner of Wrythiin or something." Cassie shook her head. "Now that's a realm you need to sample if you want to taste bad food. Whatever those steaks were, they certainly weren't grass-fed, four-legged anything."

What ensued was a round of teasing as everyone questioned her taste in red meat, and the ratio of the number of limbs to the strength of flavor of an animal's meat.

Logan had wracked his brain for details from conversations with Saleem, and had come up with a brief idea of the general layout of the city.

Now, during the meal, he sketched out a route through Kamsin, and prayed that they'd be able to get their hands on a more detailed map before they set foot in Mithras.

"It's a pity you can't project and ask him for details."

"Too risky," Darcy insisted. "Even if she connected with him in a dream the chances of Ward spotting her are high. The dream state is accessible to a MindMelder at any point in time. So when Saleem first contacted you, it was likely that Ward hadn't yet begun his treatments."

Mel nodded, her eyes shadowed. "My hands are tied until the agreed time. I wish I knew what he was planning."

"Are you thinking we're all walking into a trap?" Drake asked. The gargoyle's eyes shimmered as he waited for Mel's response.

"No," Mel rolled her eyes, "but now that you mention it, there is a possibility that we need to take into consideration. Which is why I think we need to make sure that no more than two of us are ever in the same place at the same time."

Logan stiffened then nodded. "Yep. I've paired everyone off, and we're all good to go. Natasha wanted to go over wards and spells and stuff?" He looked at Natasha, and the witch gave a short nod and shifted to pick her satchel up off the floor.

Placing it on the table, she said, "I've prepared a talisman for each of you. It will give you some protection against any kind of magical attack. It also has a semi camouflaging power which will help if you get too close to the enemy."

Natasha slid the bag across the table to Kai who selected a pouch and handed the bag down the line until everyone had their own.

"Now, inside the pouch, you will find a pin. It's not just there for the contribution of the protection of iron. The potion within the talisman needs your blood to be complete and to initiate the protection of your body. Also, please add a strand of your hair to the pouch as well."

Drake's rumbling laugh made Logan smile. "Next you're going to ask for a single drop of tears and a glob of spit."

"Eww," Lily said, picking up her pin and drawing blood from her finger.

"He's not too far off," the white witch said. "We do need some form of a bodily fluid, so tears or spit are fine. I won't recommend you pee into the pouch though. They tend to obliterate the effect of the spell."

"So what you're saying is all I have to do to break the spell is to pee on the hex-bag?" Kai deadpanned, then failed and chuckled.

The witch snorted and gave Kai the kind of look one gave a child who didn't know any better, prompting Logan to again swallow a burst of laughter.

The team performed their rituals, with blood and spit and strands of hair, then with a triple knot, sealed their pouches and hung them from their necks.

Logan grimaced as the bag bumped his upper chest and wondered if the spell would be broken if he rigged up a longer strap.

"Good thing we didn't have to pee on these things," Mel mumbled.

"Yeah," replied Kai dryly. "I don't think I'd have handled a bag of pee so close to my boobs."

This time Logan did laugh. Trust Kai to say the darnedest things.

CHAPTER 40

LOGAN

"Shut up, Kai," seemed to be a joint sentiment as the team burst into laughter.

A relaxed meal had followed, with Logan eating on automatic, out of sheer necessity to maintain the façade that his mind was present rather than hunger.

His mind was on Kai, and on the seemingly vast expanse between them. They'd still not spoken, and with everything going on, it hardly seemed the time to broach personal issues. So he let it lie.

With the meal over, Logan joined Mel, Kai, and Ivy in the study while everyone else found spots to relax in the living room. The elder Odel took a seat in one of Mel's armchairs and let out a tired sigh.

"I've got the plans, but bear in mind, we may encounter changes if any were made in the last two years. I've also done some digging into Mithras and what's been going on there recently. From what we know, they've been huge suppliers of wind energy. They discovered a method to harness energy and store it for a limited time, which is quite a deal-breaker in the Earth-Realm."

"That's an understatement," said Kai softly.

"There does appear to be a clear link between Omega and Division 7, after what you told me about Aisha's captivity and Omega's manipulations and then Agent Blake's presence in Mithras, it was easy enough to parse what was being said between the lines. Sentinel's files were coded above my clearance level, but it didn't take a genius to figure it out. Plus, the details of the investigations into Omega's underhanded dealings over the last decade have uncovered a lot of unsavory transgressions."

Logan's jaw tightened as he replied, "Omega has a lot to be accountable for. The only problem is, I find it hard to see how they can be held to account for any of it. I mean, even if they are found guilty, what justice would any of us see for what they've put us through?"

The smile on Grams' face was filled with sadness. "I know, my dear. But the Immortal Council is well aware that the individuals hurt by Omega—and now Division 7 no doubt—will not likely be compensated. The hope now is that they bring their crimes to a public forum, so the supernatural realms and peoples know what will happen if anyone attempts to emulate or duplicate their efforts."

Kai didn't like it. She crossed her arms tightly over her chest, and Logan hid a smile as she said, "Do you really think this show of justice is going to be making any difference? Omega's been on a totally different track all along. And The Supreme High Council had to accept the blame for their gullibility; they really believed that the members of the Council of Enoch were no longer subverting the laws of the DarkWorld. Pretty naive if you ask me."

Mel nodded firmly. "I'm not really sure how the council was convinced they were towing their line. Depending on how you look at it, we could all hold the Supreme High Council responsible for what happened to us." Then Mel looked over at Logan and Kai at his side. "Logan, Saleem, and even Kai? Who knows who else has been affected. I'm only surprised I wasn't either."

"And how do you know you weren't?" asked Ivy, her eyes glittered as she met Mel's gaze.

"What's that supposed to mean?" asked Mel with a dark scowl. "I'm not the one who's had my mind violated, who's had my memories and my reality stolen, who's almost been killed more than just a few times by random people including Division 7?"

Grams was no longer smiling.

Mel fell silent, eyes on Ivy. "Do you know something? Does it have to do with Ari?" Mel asked softly.

"Well, not exactly."

Grams pulled a stack of photos from her purse and spread them on the desk. Mel took a glance and gasped, her spine going taut. Logan shared a concerned glance with Kai before they also scanned the images.

Crime scene photographs of the murder of a detective from the CPD.

Saleem had told Logan about the asshole who had not only persecuted Mel but had also shown distinct signs of racism toward Saleem.

Mel was shaking her head slowly. "I haven't even given him a moment's thought since I found him."

Logan was speaking even before he realized he'd intended to. "You don't owe the man a thing. He stalked and persecuted you for almost half your life."

Mel glanced up at Logan. "Don't mean I get to be happy he's dead."

Logan's brow furrowed, and his question would have been why she would bother to be so kind, but he swallowed the words, already aware of the answer.

Mel had a heart of gold.

Then, Ivy changed the subject slightly. "While I was reading through the investigative notes, I came across some communications between an agent from Division 7 and Fulbright. He'd been encouraging the detective to keep hounding you, implying that one day you will break."

Mel shook her head. "Are you saying that whatever he's done to me in the past was because some agent was twisting his mind?"

"No, the guy's not that lucky." Grams let the files drop onto the desk. "His passion and ongoing tenacity in remaining on your case must have flagged him. The Division 7 agent approached him a couple of years ago, just keeping himself in the loop, promising to put in a good word for Fulbright, dangling a carrot too...nice cushy agent office job."

"Bulldust," was Mel's most appropriate response.

"Of course." Grams smirked. "But Fulbright did keep him in the loop, so even you've had someone surveilling you for at least the last couple years."

Logan gritted his teeth. Omega seemed to have had their hooks in everyone.

"I feel so blessed at having been included." Mel's tone simmered with amusement as she looked over at Kai.

Ivy clapped her hands to dispel the tense silence within the room. "Shall we get this show on the road? I ain't getting any younger."

Logan shook his head, well aware of where Kai got some of her sass.

"You heard the woman," said Mel.

Logan was only too happy to get the mission underway.

CHAPTER 41

LOGAN

Mel walked over to the embankment and glanced over her shoulder, giving the team a once-over. Logan too scanned the tense expressions on the faces of the group, making sure he knew where they all were.

Just in case.

With a firm nod, Mel faced the water and tossed the portal key into the air where it rose then drew to a stop to levitate over the surface of the pond.

As the key began to spin, the tension within the team rose, and Logan squeezed Kai's hand. Her entire body was rigid, and even Ivy looked tense as grandmother and granddaughter shared a look of support and encouragement.

A column of light flashed and enabled the key's magic, Mel taking it as her cue. The tracker jumped for the portal, hit the white column, and disappeared into the brightness.

And a split second later, the column exploded, throwing Mel out of its center. The force of the blast hit the gathered team head-on, so strong that it threw Mel more than twelve feet until she hit the trunk of an oak broadside.

The rest of the team were also tossed into the air, bodies

flying away from the force of the blast. Kai and Logan fell together in a heap of arms and legs, but though he was aware that she was fine, his peripheral vision told a different story for Grams.

Kai moaned, holding her head as she tried to rise. "Wait a second. Don't move for a bit." Logan shifted to his feet. "I'll be right back. I have to check if everyone else is ok."

At that moment, he didn't want to make Kai aware of Ivy's condition until he was certain.

He crouched before Ivy's unmoving body as he stared at the branch which had impaled the walker through her side. Her breathing was shallow, but Logan would take it. He didn't know how he would have dealt with the reality of Ivy's death.

Natasha approached silently and crouched down at Logan's side, her face white with horror. Without a word she studied the bodies around them as the team began to regain consciousness. Nerina's head rose too, and she scanned the embankment and caught the witch's eye, her expression stunned. Then, the Death-Talker blinked away and was at Logan's side almost instantly.

"Let's take her inside. To my storeroom. There's a bed in there." Nerina nodded and was bending to take ahold of Ivy when Kai rushed toward them.

She sank to her knees beside Logan. "Grams?" Kai's voice broke as she faced the full extent of Ivy's injuries. "No. No, no. Please." Tears filled Kai's eyes, and she looked over at Logan.

He wanted to hold her and comfort her, but something told him that if he only touched her, she'd fall apart. Instead, he gave a slow sober nod, keeping his features expressionless.

He'd be her rock.

Kai gulped down a ragged sob, then slowed her breathing. "Sorry, Nerina. I'll meet you inside?"

Nerina smiled and reached out. The moment Kai took her hand, the DeathTalker blinked away, taking the two walkers with her.

CHAPTER 42

KAI

Nerina solidified inside Natasha's storeroom, Grams' weight pulling the two of us forward as physical solidity brought with it the effect of gravity. I tightened my hold around my grandmother's waist and scanned the room.

Natasha's storeroom wasn't exactly a room to store stuff in. Rather it was more of a library, and from the look of the table littered with bottles and the collections of mortars and pestles, it looked very much like what it was—a lab.

And a library, of course.

Along the left wall was a daybed, something halfway between a chaise-longue and an actual bed, a thick blanket thrown carelessly along one arm. Nerina and I guided Grams onto the bed and then unbuttoned her blood-soaked shirt.

I managed to suppress my gasp, and so did Nerina, but Grams must have sensed our horror as she opened her eyes and smiled.

"Don't worry young ones. I'll be fine. Just give me a few minutes to get myself back together."

I quirked an eyebrow. "Grams, you have a 2-inch splinter of wood impaling you in what appears to be your *heart*. I'm not sure anyone can manage getting back together in a few minutes with that kind of damage."

Grams blinked and then looked down at her bared torso.

"Oh," she said, sounding faint.

I grunted. "You bet your sweet patootie, *Oh*," I said, my tone a little hard.

Grams sighed. "Okay, ladies. I need to make a phone call."

Nerina nodded and took a step away. "I'll leave you—"

"No, no. I need you here. I just have to check on the availability of a friend of mine, and I'd appreciate if you could fetch him for me."

Nerina took a surprised breath and nodded, then looked at me. I merely shrugged in response. Grams was already on her call, talking to someone who appeared to be responding positively to Grams' inquiries of "if you don't mind, I'm in need of your help," and, "I'm so sorry to bother you, but I'd be so grateful for your time." Soon she closed her cell phone and settled back, eyes on Nerina. "My dear, if you wouldn't mind, I'd like you to go to the location that has been texted to your phone. A friend of mine is there, and needs to be transported here. Sadly, he's not able to jump himself, a mystery I'm yet to uncover. Anyway, he's happy to help, but he needs a ride."

"Absolutely, Grams. I'm leaving now." With a brief look at her phone, Nerina was gone, leaving me smiling at my grandmother.

"What are you smiling at, girl. I'm an old woman, injured and near death, and you smile at me?" Grams scowled, but her attempt at bad-tempered old woman failed miserably.

"You just got yourself another grandchild."

Grams merely grinned, though the expression was weak. Whatever I was about to respond with disappeared as soon as Nerina arrived, bringing with her a man who looked suspiciously like Darian.

Grams didn't give us time to ask questions, merely waving us away with a promise to call if she needed us. We had little choice but to obey, and after sharing a glance of concern, we left her alone with this man-who-looked-suspiciously-like-Darian. Only he wasn't Darian.

But he *was* an Ancient.

CHAPTER 43

LOGAN

Logan glanced up at the house, then at the disaster around him. Thankfully, everyone other than Ivy seemed to be okay, with Natasha and Drake checking them one at a time.

Mel's groan echoed from the tree where she'd fallen, followed by a cry of pain.

"Stay where you are until I check you out," yelled Natasha from beside Steph, who had just come to, a hint of fear in the witch's voice as she beckoned Logan to take over before scrambling across the clearing to Mel and dropped to her knees.

"What the hell happened?" Mel's voice drifted to Logan, filled with confusion and pain.

"Something went wrong with the portal key," Natasha replied as she inspected Mel's injuries. "Whatever it was, the blast hit everyone head-on."

Logan checked Steph over, glad to find she was mostly uninjured.

"Was everyone jumping? Were you hurt? Is Nerina okay?"

The witch ignored Mel's questions and said, "We'll need you in the house to sort this out." Natasha boosted to her feet and waved at Logan, her eyes filled with fear. He wasted no time in sprinting over, and Natasha's voice was emotionless as she asked, "Can you get her to the house for me? Be careful with her though."

"Can someone please tell me what's wrong?" Mel snapped, staring daggers at Natasha. "And where's Nerina?"

Logan studied Mel's injuries and frowned, aware now of why Natasha was attempting to avoid stressing the tracker out. He bent and gently lifted her off the ground. "You have a branch embedded in your back. It looks a little too close to your ribs for comfort, so I'd be careful with any movement you make. We don't know how close it is to your lungs."

Mel's mouth was open, but Logan didn't give her a chance to say anything more. He faced the house and boosted into the air, shifting from human to dragon in mid-jump. Mel's shriek confirmed she'd registered either the flight, or the dragon.

Or both.

At Natasha's homestead, Logan landed and shifted smoothly, feet hitting the ground as he strode inside the house and down the hall toward the bedroom. Kai and Ivy were nowhere to be seen—likely in the storeroom the witch had mentioned.

Logan reached the door and nudged it open with his foot, but as he approached the bed and was about to lay the tracker on it, she opened her eyes and squawked like an injured bird.

At first, Logan thought he'd hurt her somehow, but then she lifted a finger, aiming a dark glare at his face as she said, "Wait. Not on that."

"Huh?" Logan replied, eyes narrowed. He looked at the bed, and then at Mel, wondering what the woman was on about. Maybe she hit her head harder than he'd thought?

"That's satin," Mel replied, dead serious as she rolled her eyes. "And probably expensive knowing Natasha. We need a blanket or something…to cover the beautiful fabric."

Logan couldn't help smirking. Mel was amusing with her face

deadly serious even while her muscles clenched with pain. He also knew he couldn't be standing around wasting time. He met Mel's earnest gaze and said, "I think the witch must have some magical laundering skills. She can just as easily make blood stains disappear as she can make people go poof."

"Men," Mel replied with a disgusted shake of her head. "You don't get it, do you?"

"No. Sadly, I don't. Kindly enlighten me."

"It's the principle. You don't intentionally set a bloody body onto expensive fabric. You can accidentally stain it with blood, yes, but on purpose is bad karma."

Logan wasn't sure what to do with that argument. On the one hand, Mel could well be delirious. On the other, what if she was right? Women did tend to be temperamental when it came to things they liked. And he assumed the white witch liked her bedspread a lot.

"What are you doing?" Natasha spoke from behind Logan, and he shifted to look over at her, spotting Kai in the witch's wake. Natasha's eyes were wide as she stared at him, perplexed as he hovered in the middle of the floor with Mel in his arms. "I told you to put her on the bed."

"She wouldn't go," Logan replied, shifting from one foot to the other as he evaded the witch's gaze.

"What?" Logan had to suffocate a groan as the white witch's eyes flared with a silver fire. When she propped her bloodied hands on her hips, Logan's gut told him he was done for.

The big bad dragon king afraid of a little white witch?

Logan blinked, then caught Kai's grin, though the strength of her amusement was decidedly dulled by her pain. He wanted to hold her in his arms and cradle her as she cried. But they didn't have time.

Natasha moved, extending her hand pointing at the bed, one eyebrow curved. "There's the bed. Put her on it."

CHAPTER 44

LOGAN

"What in the name of the sweet mother Crone are you babbling about?" Natasha asked, her tone sharp.

Mel winced then cleared her throat before saying, "Sorry, that was my fault. I didn't want to ruin your bed covers. I asked him to look for a sheet or something to protect it from bloodstains…"

When the witch let out a loud laugh, Logan felt somewhat vindicated that the bedspread wasn't all that big a deal. "Who the fuck cares about stained bedsheets at this point in time?" She looked at Logan, raised an eyebrow, and aimed a finger at the bed.

Logan obeyed the witch, smirking as he made his way to the bed and laid his burden down. "Told you so," he whispered to Mel before stalking back to Kai at the door.

Logan swallowed a chuckle as Natasha said, "You're all just a bunch of idiots, fools, and nincompoops."

He curled his arms around Kai, his heart aching for her as her pain drew a pool of tears to her eyes. He was desperate to provide her with comfort, restricted only by her need for strength and independence.

"What's going on?" asked Mel sharply from the bed where Natasha was turning her over to inspect the wound on her back.

Logan squeezed Kai and then said, "The blast threw everyone back. Some of the team are injured, but everyone will be fine except..."

"Except for?" Mel asked slowly.

"It's Ivy," Logan replied glancing briefly at Kai whose eyes held an inscrutable emotion. "She's hurt real bad. It's going to take a while before she recovers."

Mel's eyes darkened as a dozen emotions flitted across her face. Logan tensed, and so did Kai, and they both shared a look that said they knew exactly what Mel was doing—blaming herself for Ivy's injuries.

"Don't you dare."

Kai moved out of Logan's embrace and hurried over toward the bed, the air around her shimmering with a feline force. Her voice rumbled between a purr and a growl as she spoke.

"She's a strong woman," Kai said, "capable of making her own decisions. Nobody, and I mean nobody, tells that woman what to do. She joined the team because she felt she could contribute. And believe me when I say she was well and truly aware of the possible outcomes. Grams doesn't do anything without being aware of all variables. It could have happened to any one of us, including you." Kai stopped and inhaled slowly, both to calm herself and get some oxygen. "If I know her at all, she'll fight damn hard to recover, so the next thing I think we need to focus on is what in Ailuros' name do we do now that the portal key is fucked."

Mel's smile was weak as she rested back onto the pillow. Then Natasha said, "You need to hold on for a moment. I have to get this branch out of you before the wounds become infected. But it's going to be painful."

Kai's voice quavered as she asked, "Can't we give her something for the pain?"

But Mel was shaking her head. “No time. We need to get it out and go to plan B.”

“Plan B? I wasn’t aware of Plan B.” Kai glanced back at Logan who shrugged.

“I was hoping we wouldn’t need it at all,” Mel replied. “We have to break Aisha out. And I don’t give a damn whether she wants to come or not.”

Beside Mel, Natasha glanced over at Logan, pointing discreetly at the branch in Mel’s back. A silent message that they had to distract the tracker while the witch did her work.

He shook his head at the tracker’s gall, while Kai’s laughter was filled with forced surprise and approval as she said, “You want to abduct a powerful djinn queen from a high-security prison even though she won’t want to go? Pray tell how you’re planning on achieving that?”

Logan tensed as Mel let out a scream, and he knew it took all of Kai’s strength to stay in place—neither Kai nor Mel enjoyed appearing weak.

Even among friends.

Now, almost sobbing, Mel said, “Explain. Beg. If that doesn’t work, then bind her with magic. Plan Z is knocking her out.”

“I’d love to say that such a plan is ridiculously dangerous and impossible, but I won’t,” Kai chuckled. “Instead, I’ll say that such a plan is ridiculously dangerous and possible.”

“You’re hilariously funny,” said Mel before she screamed again.

This time Kai didn’t hold back. She hurried to her friend’s side and took Mel’s hand, then glanced over at Logan. “You think your fire magic can help her at all?”

Logan wasn’t surprised at the question; though he had to admit he hadn’t considered his fire as a possible treatment solution.

A questioning glance at Natasha drew a quick response. “Should work. Let me get this done. I need a few more minutes.

In the meantime, you two get the team in triage in the front room, help Nerina and Drake look after the rest of them. We have to be up and running ASAP."

"Yes. ASAP. 'Cause Saleem gave us a time and the longer we take, the higher the chances are that we will miss the window he gave us. Ugh. You know, I'd trade that pain anytime for a zap or two from a ShadowWraith."

With Mel showing signs of recovery, Logan—suspecting his fire wouldn't be needed after all—left the room with Kai.

"How's Ivy? What did Nerina say?" Logan asked as Kai led him to the witch's storeroom.

Natasha was just behind them when she called out loudly, "Don't you dare sit on my silk. You'll get your blood all over it." Logan blinked at the witch's words and Natasha chuckled. "I'm just messing with her. Let's see what Ivy has in store for us."

Mel's words echoed toward them. "Witch."

"I heard that," the witch yelled back as they stopped on the threshold and stared inside the room.

Logan grunted. "This is not a storeroom, Natasha."

The witch grinned as they stepped into a library-slash-living-room space twice the size of Natasha's bedroom.

Her only response was. "I know."

CHAPTER 45

KAI

My heart stuttered at the sight of a sleeping Grams, pale jeans soaked with dark red blood, white silk shirt torn open and then closed haphazardly so I could see a hint of her lace-edged bra, the color of which was now unrecognizable what with all the blood.

Apparently, she'd not needed either Nerina or me, and now the Ancient was conspicuously absent from the storeroom-library.

I walked quickly over to Grams' side and sank down beside her, reaching hurriedly to rearrange her shirt to preserve her modesty as Logan drew up behind me. I was desperate to know how she was and if the splinter was still embedded inside her chest, but I forced myself to wait.

Grams opened her eyes and chuckled, her chest heaving, "Thank you, dear. Although I believe the young man is familiar with women's undergarments."

I lifted an eyebrow. "I'm pretty sure he is, Grandmother. We'd just rather ensure he isn't familiar with yours."

Logan chuckled and sank beside me, his warmth resting against my knees as the pair of us doted on Grams. Now he smirked and cocked a jaw at me. "See, Ivy. Maybe it's best we don't make her jealous. Already she thinks the sight of your underthings are going to make me fall deeply in love with you."

I made a rude sound while Grams barked a rather unhealthy-sounding laugh. "You are right, young man. I don't think she can handle losing her beau to an older woman."

I sputtered a laugh and reached for her hand. "Grams, really. You were doing so well."

She frowned. "What did I do wrong?" she asked, tone a little confused and a little more put out.

With an inelegant snort, I said, "Nobody but old fogies use the word beau."

Beside me Logan coughed, then out of the side of his mouth he said, "Nobody but old fogies use the word fogies."

I rolled my eyes. "Who do you think I learned the word from?"

"Hey, young people. I'm still here you know."

I grinned, not in the least bit contrite as I said, "We know, Grams. Now can you please update us on your condition?"

Grams smiled gently, looking from my face to Logan's. "Don't you two worry about a thing. This old woman has a few more years left in her yet."

"And then some," I muttered under my breath.

If Grams heard me, she didn't let on. Instead, she waved us off and said, "Go now, and leave me for a bit. I need a few moments to gather my thoughts."

I wanted to say something smart, but I got to my feet and left the room, Logan following in my wake and closing the door softly behind him.

I glanced at him, knowing he wanted to talk, needing to hear what he had to say, but we didn't have the time, and Natasha's hall wasn't the place. And so, neither of us spoke as we headed to the kitchen where the sounds of conversation drifted to us.

CHAPTER 46

LOGAN

Logan and the djinn-queen extraction-team were in the white witch's kitchen checking their weapons in preparation for the mission when she hurried inside, brow creased as she handed three small glass bottles to Mel.

"Be careful. This poison cannot come into contact with anyone else. It's deadly to every other being other than a djinn, and even then it's capable of killing a djinn who isn't all that strong. There's enough in each bottle for a single use. Keep them apart just in case you lose one."

With a nod and a shaky breath, Mel said, "Right, it's do or die. Let's do this."

Kai gave Logan a small smile, and her fingers tightened around her crossbow. She glanced at Mel and said, "You don't sound all that ready. Wanna chicken out?" Kai's eyes were still shadowed—revealing her worries about Ivy's condition—but she was holding it together as best as she could.

Mel only snorted and glanced at Nerina—who was checking her weapons inside her gray DeathTalker cloak—before speaking to Natasha. "So can we at least establish what happened to the portal key? I have a feeling the problem was at Mithras, but I want to be sure." Natasha nodded, and the DeathTalker glanced up as Mel said, "Darcy was on the right track, only she didn't realize how spot on she was."

"Was she?" The subject of Mel's announcement limped in with Cassandra into the kitchen. For some reason, Natasha's kitchen had become the meeting hub for their missions, and Logan almost felt sorry for the witch.

Natasha gave a quick nod. "What was the extent of your understanding of the kind of wards that would have been erected around Mithras?"

Darcy thought for a minute, squinting at the ceiling as though the whitewashed wood bore the answer. "Dark magic for one thing. Definitely blood magic. Nothing a MindMelder like Ward could create. Creating a ward around an entire realm is not possible, is it?"

"Only the access points in the Veil can be warded," Natasha replied. "Or I should say, they can't be warded by less powerful beings. Realm wards are under the skill arena of Ancients and the greater immortal Fae, and perhaps one or two level X-demons."

"Level-X?" Kai asked raising a questioning finger.

Logan stilled, thinking of Baa'ruk, and wondering if the demon was available to help out. He didn't say anything yet though.

"Yes," said the white witch, face full of mock seriousness. "Demons with excessively powerful magical abilities, usually ones either born with such powers or those who received those abilities through learning."

Mel arched an eyebrow. "And by learning, I assume you mean death, darkness, and blood?"

"You forgot pain," Nerina said with an innocent smile.

Logan suppressed a grin when Kai let out a snort-grunt before asking, "Where's a Level-X demon when you need one?"

Taking that as his cue, Logan cleared his throat and said, "Well...if we need one, I can certainly check my little black book."

All eyes turned to him, and he smiled. "Well, I do happen to know one Level-X. He's currently a Demon Overlord in the Boston area."

Kai shifted her head to look at Logan, her eyes a little concerned as she said, "Demon Overlording sounds like not a very good thing. You telling me you trust this powerful demon?"

Shaking his head, Logan let out a soft laugh. "He's definitely not a bad guy. And Overlording only entails ensuring the under-lords do as they are told and don't go wild." Logan paused, and the silence in the room only grew. He sighed and gave in. "Fine, if you must know, I saved the guy's ass once."

"You sure you don't really mean *he* saved *your* ass?" Kai smirked, glancing deliberately at Logan's butt, and eliciting a low ripple of laughter from the team.

With a shrug, Logan added, "Okay, okay. I was young and green, and I ran into a situation without assessing it and got myself neck deep in trouble. Literally. He turned out to be the right demon at the right time to come upon my sorry ass, and he helped me out, no questions asked."

"Sounds like a nice enough guy," said Mel.

"He is." Logan thought of the albino demon's constant obstacles, which the guy had overcome. "Possibly has a little bit of perspective considering his...affliction."

"Please clarify...and do it quickly." Mel waved a hand.

Her tone said hurry it up, so Logan cleared his throat and said, "His name is Baa'ruk, goes by the name Lacroix. Also happens to be probably the only dreadlocked albino demon in existence."

"What?" Kai asked, eyes flashing with surprise, as though she knew who Logan was talking about.

"Yep. What's with the surprise? You know Lacroix?" Logan asked.

Though Kai immediately gave a denying shake of her head,

she did pause. "Not really. I did see him though, in O'Hagan's a few days ago. About the time I ran into the reporter."

Brow furrowing, Logan said, "Right. Odd for him to be in the area—" Then Logan fell silent, aware that he hadn't exactly been accessible in the last few days. He let out an annoyed grunt. "Guess if I'd been in this realm, he would have contacted me."

"Check your messages maybe?" said Mel.

Logan ignored Kai's snort even as she swallowed it down and coughed it away. He retrieved his phone from his jeans pocket and scanned his messages, only to find that the demon had sent him a text on arrival in Chicago with a request to catch up if Logan was available.

"He did reach out. I'll message him back. What exactly am I asking him?" Logan asked Natasha.

Mel replied, "Has he heard any chatter? Was he the one who threw up the ward? If not, does he know who is capable of that level of magic?"

Logan obeyed and put the questions into a text, then sent it off, mentally crossing his fingers that Lacroix would reply ASAP. The longer Logan remained out of Drakys, the more dangerous things got for Sienna, and for their reign.

Mel straightened. "We'd better get on with it."

As the members of the team paired off, Kai gave the tracker a comforting squeeze of the shoulders. "Don't worry. It's a clean plan. Get in, get the djinn MIL, get out."

Mel only smiled as Nerina added, "Besides, she likes you. She'll get over it eventually."

"So why does it feel like I'm about to walk into the gaping jaws of a deadly fire-breathing dragon?" Mel asked with a nervous sigh.

Logan shook his head, and as the team began to disappear from the kitchen, he called out in mock outrage, "Hey, you talking about me?"

CHAPTER 47

LOGAN

The team arrived in a small clearing near a fence that surrounded Omega's safehouse. Logan still couldn't believe the lengths Omega had gone to in order to gain control of Mithras.

"Aisha is in a small suite at the rear of the building," Mel said. "Second floor, looking out on the lawn. She's able to detect astral movement, so she'll know I'm there. So, that's the last thing I'll be doing. First, we disable the watch, and remove any obstacles."

"You're working on the assumption that she may yell for help?" asked Kai.

"She has been adamant that she agreed to not leave her prison." Mel shook her head sharply. "There is a very real chance that the fallout from this may be something we cannot recover from. So, I'm asking you all to remain silent, and if it comes to it, claim ignorance. If she wants to wreak havoc on those responsible, I'm the only target."

Logan frowned, not keen on letting Mel take the fall. And from the looks on the faces of the team, they felt the same.

Mel's eyes narrowed as she stared at them, meeting Logan's

gaze briefly. "Am I making myself clear?" she asked, her tone cool.

Kai glanced at Logan, eyes flashing with anger, but she merely nodded. So did Logan, though he didn't like it.

Then, Mel continued as if she hadn't seen the anger in her friends' eyes. "Teams go in, from the west and the east corners. Eliminate the guards, keep the noise to a minimum. And the death nonexistent. Darcy, you're going with Nerina, Kai's with the gargoyle and Logan stays here. He's our savior in case the shit hits the fan."

"Yeah, he can come in and light that shit on fire," Drake grumbled, glancing over at the mansion beyond the wall.

Then the teams paired off and disappeared, leaving Mel and Logan alone to await their confirmations.

Kai was first. "East watch is non-existent."

Then Darcy who said, "West watch unattended."

"That's odd. And not a good sign," said Logan, scowling at the darkened mansion. "Think they've taken her someplace else? Mithras maybe?"

With a confident jerk of her head, Mel replied, "She's there. I can sense her life-thread on the astral plane. It was the first thing I did when we got here." Mel paused, frowning as she too stared at the mansion. "Stand down and retreat. Give me a few minutes to recon."

The teams all responded, confirming their retreat, though Logan didn't like it at all. His gut was screaming that something wasn't right.

"Watch me," Mel said, meeting Logan's eyes for a brief moment. "I won't be long."

Then, Mel sank to the ground, propped herself up against a tree trunk and fell silent for a few moments. Then she opened her eyes, shaking her head, her expression now reflecting Logan's own unease. She tapped her comms. "Return to base. The place is empty."

When the team returned to the clearing, Drake asked, "Think the queen killed them all?"

"No," Mel replied firmly. "If there were corpses, I would have still sensed the threads. Right now, the place is a tomb. Except for the prisoner."

"So what do they have holding her here? Security must be insane," Nerina said, glancing over at the mansion.

Mel let out a mirthless laugh. "That's where it gets unbelievable. She gave them her word."

"Oh yeah, that," Nerina replied dryly.

"Okay, I'm going in." Mel touched her hip, as if assuring herself that she was prepared to cross the line. "If I'm not back in five minutes, come get us," she said before jumping out.

A few minutes passed before Mel's voice crackled on the comms. "I need a sweep of the building. Look for incendiaries."

Drake let out a growl as Logan shook his head and said, "I knew something was up. Omega doesn't just abandon a safehouse."

The team disappeared in pairs, and Logan shifted and surged into the air to do a wider perimeter sweep, and then be available in case anything exploded.

Only a few minutes passed when Kai's voice sounded on Logan's comms. "I've got a device at the southern corner. It's on a timer set to blow in ten minutes."

Then the gargoyle added, "Confirming incendiary at the western corner. Timer for ten minutes."

Logan shook his head, then swooped around to Kai's side of the building, the minutes counting down too slowly for his liking.

Then, Drake called out over the comms, "Thirty seconds."

Logan swooped down low, eyes cast out at the clearing, waiting to see if the team had gathered there, waiting for Mel.

"Ten seconds," said Drake as Logan swooped in and shifted

into his human form. The gargoyle didn't even blink as he said, "We're leaving, Mel. You're a go."

The team shimmered away, and just as they faded from the clearing, Logan felt a pulsing of the detonation as the bombs exploded.

CHAPTER 48

LOGAN

Logan and the team were waiting in Natasha's bedroom as Mel materialized, jumping the queen of the djinn realm to the witch's bed.

Though relieved, the group remained tense but silent.

Except for Drake.

"Shit, Mel," the gargoyle's eyes flashed. "You sure know how to give a guy a heart attack."

"Stop being dramatic, gargoyle," Mel replied and dropped to her knees beside the bed. "You should thank me for making sure your heart's working. Consider it a drill," the tracker said with a smirk as she sank against the wall behind her.

The team laughed, though Logan wasn't sure if the amusement was more to lower their own tension or to diffuse some of Drake's.

"You cut it way too close, Mel. You're getting reckless," Drake said sharply.

"I know. But I had to time it carefully." Mel didn't sound at all sorry.

"You keep it up, and you'll time yourself dead," Drake said, tone dripping with ice as he folded his arms tight across his chest. When the gargoyle's glamor dropped, silvery tattoos shimmering on blue-black skin, Logan couldn't blame him.

But Mel wasn't being reckless. Or Logan would have stopped her and told her so.

Still, Nerina's gasp of shock, and the fear in her eyes as she stared at the gargoyle in his true form, managed to grasp the attention of the entire room. Even after Drake regained control and returned to his normal form, the tension was enough to slice through with a knife.

Until Mel boosted to her feet and went over to Nerina. "Okay, DeathTalker. Think you can rustle me up some eats. And maybe drizzle a bag of sugar all over it."

"Yuk. You just made me imagine a piece of meat covered in syrup," said Nerina, shaking her head.

"Don't you mean BBQ rib sauce?" Logan added as he followed in their wake.

He glanced at Kai, whose eyes reflected his own concern for Nerina—an issue that hadn't been there until now.

Tensions within the team only made for conflict while on the mission.

And conflict was bad.

As they neared the kitchen, Logan caught Kai's wrist and drew her down to the front room.

Kai sighed as she looked up and met his eyes. "You're worried about Nerina?"

Logan nodded. "That look on her face, that was terror. And if she's afraid of Drake for whatever reason, we'll be left on shaky ground once we arrive in Mithras."

Kai bit her lip and stared down the empty hallway as the team all filtered into the kitchen. "Add that to Darcy and Wade, and that's more than enough rocks in our path. We just need to make sure they are paired off with the right people to avoid making those tensions escalate."

"I'd feel happier to go in without those tensions," muttered

Logan. "But given that we have little choice, let's just keep our eyes and ears open."

Kai nodded. "Maybe you should have a chat with Drake. See if he knows how to smooth things over."

Logan straightened and took a breath. "As soon as I get a chance, I will do just that. Now let's get back to the team before they start wondering if we've snuck off for some sexytimes."

Kai made a rude sound, rolled her eyes, and headed for the kitchen.

CHAPTER 49

LOGAN

Ten minutes later, the djinn queen's scream had the team racing for the bedroom where Logan saw the gleam of fire.

Bad sign.

Mel skidded to a stop inside the door and let out a screech of shock before shouting, "Let her go!"

Logan's jaw dropped as he stared at Saleem's mother who floated above them, fingers wrapped tightly around Natasha's neck. The witch's expression was serene, though her eyebrow rose as she caught sight of the audience, as though saying, "What are you waiting for?"

Aisha turned her head to look at Mel, fire flickering in her eyes, hair floating around her shoulders only adding to her almost-deranged appearance.

Not that Logan blamed the queen.

"You!" Aisha bellowed as her eyes glowed brighter.

"Yeah, me!" Mel shouted. "Let her go. If you need a whipping boy, I'm ready."

Logan glanced at Mel whose mouth had formed a perfect

shocked 'o'. "Mel," Kai whispered, "don't make the nice djinn queen angry."

"Too late," the tracker replied out the side of her mouth. "Been there, done that, got the tee-shirt."

Logan wanted to laugh, and he had to force himself to subdue the urge. Mel was almost comedic in her interactions with the djinn queen, and he had to wonder if perhaps she knew the best way to handle Saleem's extremely powerful mother.

As though to confirm Logan's suspicions, Aisha drifted to the ground and let go of the witch who walked off serenely.

Kai's grin as she glanced at Logan mirrored his own amusement. And from the sight of Aisha's smile, apparently, she too found Mel funny.

But when she spoke, her words were a tad confusing. "I'm a queen of an entire realm, dear. A powerful one to boot," Aisha said as though answering some unspoken question.

Mel just stood there in silence, her back stiff.

Aisha tilted her head and smiled again. "Yes, child. You do need to shut your thoughts off from the astral plane after a jump."

Kai put her hand to her mouth, and Logan knew she was struggling to keep from laughing out loud. A task made harder when Mel backed away from the queen who then said, "Don't worry, I'm not going to burn you to cinders—"

"Stop doing that," Mel bit out.

"Then stop projecting," Aisha replied.

Logan and Kai backed away from the door and stood aside as Saleem's mother walked off regally down the hall to the kitchen.

Mel followed, barely noticing the team's presence as she grumbled under her breath all the way to the kitchen.

When Logan and Kai entered the kitchen, Aisha had a cup of tea before her, and Natasha was saying, "See?" as she raised her hands to display her body. "Still alive and breathing."

"And not roasted," Kai replied, this time unable to hide her amusement.

"I see like attracts like with you and your friends," said Saleem's mother, an elegant eyebrow arching.

Logan almost burst an artery trying not to laugh at the queen's comment. Saleem was going to enjoy this story when Logan finally updated him.

"If you mean I like to hang around with women who speak their mind, then yes," said Mel, arms folded.

"Actually, I meant you are a lot like Saleem when he was a boy. Disobedient, mouthy, little brat."

Mel was at a loss for a reply. She looked at Kai who merely shrugged and said, "She didn't kill you, so I'd consider that a win."

"Yet." Aisha's reply blanketed the kitchen with a deep sense of danger, but Mel only sighed and sat down on the nearest chair.

"Can we please wait until after we save your offspring before you kill me?" asked Mel dryly.

"I believe I can make that happen," replied the queen.

Logan pursed his lips, sharing a wary, though mostly amused glance with Kai and then Drake.

He had a feeling the things were only going to get more fun.

CHAPTER 50

LOGAN

Logan stood on Natasha's porch, staring out into the night. Lacroix had made his entrance, and a sizeable impression on Mel. And it appeared on Kai too. She was currently talking to Lacroix, and Ivy, who had miraculously recovered from near death—there was a story there that Logan meant to uncover or die trying—was keeping the djinn queen company. The atmosphere within the house was one of impatience, what with everyone having been eager to leave for Mithras.

Saleem's window, toward which Mel had been working, had turned out to be a message for the djinn's stubborn mother, a hint at Mithras's economic power in the harnessing of energy. A power it appeared had not been out of reach of Division 7. And it appeared too that Lacroix and Aisha had a bit of a history, something that Cassie and Lacroix also had in common. Logan also had a question for Kai regarding her mysterious benefactor.

Now, with the pressure of getting themselves moving fast in order to save Saleem before his mind is transformed into a mush courtesy of the dead-not-dead MindMelder Ward relieved, the team could gather more forces for a stronger strike on the people holding the djinn realm hostage.

Finish what you need to, Logan, said Sienna in Logan's mind.

Don't you need me at home? he asked.

Sienna chuckled. *Whatever is going on here is not going to stop. The problems we are facing will be here when you get back, trust me on that.*

Logan frowned. He wasn't comfortable with Sienna having to deal with things on her own, but she was right. It made no sense for him to flit back and forth between EarthWorld and Drakys. His presence for a day wouldn't make a difference in the greater scheme of things.

Fine. We should be leaving in the next day or so. I'll keep you updated.

You'd better keep me updated. You don't want me siccing that panther walker on you. Sienna laughed and faded from Logan's mind.

He shook his head as he gripped the balustrade in front of him.

The djinn was waiting for them, and from Mel's description of Saleem's condition, they really didn't have time to waste. Still, as impatient as Logan was, they were better off with a larger, more powerful force when they helped take Mithras back.

Hang in there, Saleem. We're coming.

~ To Be Continued ~

The SkinWalker Series continues with Oath Bound.

ACKNOWLEDGMENTS

A special thanks to my JIT readers who helped make Grave Debt even better: Bryan Ellis and Cindy Jeffers. And thank you to the rest of the JIT and ARC readers who took the time to read and review Grave Debt. Thank you for all of your support!

JOIN MY NEWSLETTER

Join Tee's Newsletter to be the first to know about new releases, giveaways, and bonus content!

http://tgayer.com/subscribe/

ABOUT THE AUTHOR

I have been a writer from the time I was old enough to recognize that reading was a doorway into my imagination. Poetry was my first foray into the art of the written word. Books were my best friends, my escape, my haven. I am essentially a recluse but this part of my personality is impossible to practice given I have two teenage daughters, who are actually my friends, my tea-makers, my confidantes… I am blessed with a husband who has left me for golf. It's a fair trade as I have left him for writing. We are both passionate supporters of each other's loves – it works wonderfully…

My heart is currently broken in two. One half resides in South Africa where my old roots still remain, and my heart still longs for the endless beaches and the smell of moist soil after a summer downpour. My love for Ma Afrika will never fade. The other half of me has been transplanted to the Land of the Long White Cloud. The land of the Taniwha, beautiful Maraes, and volcanoes. The land of green, pure beauty that truly inspires. And because I am so torn between these two lands – I shall forever remain cross-eyed.

Stalk Tee here:

www.tgayer.com

tee@tgayer.com

facebook.com/TGAyerAuthor

twitter.com/TGAyerAuthor

amazon.com/author/tgayer

bookbub.com/profile/t-g-ayer

instagram.com/tee.g.ayer

goodreads.com/TGAyer

www.ingramcontent.com/pod-product-compliance
Lightning Source LLC
Chambersburg PA
CBHW020947120726
47905CB00008B/2706
* 9 7 8 0 9 9 5 1 1 2 5 8 2 *